BEWARE THE DARKNESS

He caught sight of the warm flush that crawled beneath her skin. His fingers strayed down to press against the pulse that hammered at the base of her throat. "Do you know what I think?"

The scent of passion fruit swirled through the air. "What?"

Tarak's fangs lengthened, his body reacting to her sweet scent. His gaze lowered to the soft curve of her lips.

"I think you enjoyed feeding me," he murmured in soft tones.

She shivered, but this time Tarak suspected that it wasn't from the chill. "I suspected you were arrogant. Now I know for sure."

He chuckled, momentarily forgetting his relentless thirst for revenge. Right now, he was engrossed in the feel of this female.

"I'm a vampire."

Her eyes darkened, her lips parting as she released her breath on a soft sigh. "I'm aware of that."

Tarak's fangs throbbed, hunger thundering through him. He'd ached for Waverly since the night she'd entered his prison, but he'd never been so close to losing his tight restraint...

Books by Alexandra Ivy

Guardians of Eternity
WHEN DARKNESS COMES
EMBRACE THE DARNKESS
DARKNESS EVERLASTING
DARKNESS REVEALED
DARKNESS UNLEASHED
BEYOND THE DARKNESS
DEVOURED BY DARKNESS
BOUND BY DARKNESS
FEAR THE DARKNESS
DARKNESS AVENGED
HUNT THE DARKNESS
WHEN DARKNESS ENDS
DARKNESS RETURNS
BEWARE THE DARKNESS

The Immortal Rogues
MY LORD VAMPIRE
MY LORD ETERNITY
MY LORD IMMORTALITY

The Sentinels
BORN IN BLOOD
BLOOD ASSASSIN
BLOOD LUST

Ares Security
KILL WITHOUT MERCY
KILL WITHOUT SHAME

Historical Romance
SOME LIKE IT WICKED
SOME LIKE IT SINFUL
SOME LIKE IT BRAZEN

Romantic Suspense

PRETEND YOU'RE SAFE
WHAT ARE YOU AFRAID OF?
YOU WILL SUFFER

And don't miss these Guardians of Eternity novellas

TAKEN BY DARKNESS in YOURS FOR ETERNITY
DARKNESS ETERNAL in SUPERNATURAL
WHERE DARKNESS LIVES in THE REAL WEREWIVES OF
VAMPIRE COUNTY
LEVET (ebook only)
A VERY LEVET CHRISTMAS (ebook only)

And don't miss these Sentinel novellas

OUT OF CONTROL
ON THE HUNT

Published by Kensington Publishing Corporation

Beware the Darkness

Alexandra Ivy

LYRICAL PRESS
Kensington Publishing Corp.
www.kensingtonbooks.com

LYRICAL PRESS BOOKS are published by

Kensington Publishing Corp.
119 West 40th Street
New York, NY 10018

All Kensington titles, imprints, and distributed lines are available at special quantity discounts for bulk purchases for sales promotion, premiums, fund-raising, educational, or institutional use.

Special book excerpts or customized printings can also be created to fit specific needs. For details, write or phone the office of the Kensington Sales Manager: Kensington Publishing Corp., 119 West 40th Street, New York, NY 10018. Attn. Sales Department. Phone: 1-800-221-2647.

First Electronic Edition: August 2019
ISBN-13: 978-1-5161-0843-5   (ebook)
ISBN-10: 1-5161-0843-4 (ebook)

First Print Edition: August 2019
ISBN-13: 978-1-5161-0846-6
ISBN-10: 1-5161-0846-9

Printed in the United States of America

Prologue

Asia, 1500s

The massive castle sprawled along the remote cliffs of the Himalayan Range, offering a tangible symbol of the power that had been acquired by the King of Vampires. The thick stones and soaring turrets provided an impregnable fortress, as if the dozens of powerful vampires weren't enough to frighten away any potential intruder. Plus, there were layers of fey magic that hid it from the eyes of humans.

The Anasso, however, hadn't been satisfied. He'd insisted on digging a honeycomb of tunnels beneath the castle that led into the mountain, providing easy escape if they were ever attacked.

At the time, Tarak had applauded his master's paranoia. Since gathering the vampires beneath his rule, the Anasso had been forced to defend himself against countless assassins. After all, not every vampire was happy to be hauled out of the dark ages and into a unified species that worked together. For centuries, the clans had warred for dominance; it wasn't easy to become allies.

Plus, the thought of a vampire nation was enough to scare the shit out of every other demon. Many of them were anxious to get rid of the Anasso in the hopes that the vampires would fracture and retreat to their barbaric habit of killing each other. Trolls, orcs, goblins, and other fey creatures had all tried to eliminate the Anasso.

It would make anyone jumpy.

Now, however, Tarak wished he'd paid more attention to his instincts, which had wondered if the Anasso's retreat from his enemies was excessive. Or at least he should have listened to the warnings offered by Chiron.

Hadn't the young male proven to be a devoted servant? His loyalty had been unwavering since Tarak had found him hidden in a cave.

Of course, his own loyalty had been equally unwavering.

Tarak had brought his clan to the Anasso because he fiercely believed in what the male was trying to accomplish. How could they survive in the ever-changing world if they didn't organize into a cohesive force? Squabbling over petty insults or constant power grabs only weakened them.

He didn't want to accept that the male he'd willingly chosen as his master was addicted to feeding on prey with opium and alcohol in their system. Every vampire knew that tainted blood would eventually drive them mad, right? The Anasso would never risk everything by indulging in such a dangerous habit.

So he'd ignored the pleas from Chiron. And even his own unease when his master had started to reveal hints of instability. Then Chiron had challenged Tarak to enter the deepest tunnels and see the truth for himself. He'd refused. He wasn't going to betray the trust the Anasso had placed in him.

But tonight had changed everything.

During the evening feast, he'd witnessed the master slipping out a side door, then returning with a hectic glitter in his eyes and an unsteadiness in his steps that had made Tarak's gut twist with dread.

Waiting for his clansmen to seek out their beds as dawn crested the horizon, Tarak silently moved through the dining hall. There'd been a tense few seconds when a lovely imp had suddenly appeared from the shadows. She'd been most insistent that he share the day in her bed. Not an unusual occurrence. Although Tarak didn't possess the outrageous vanity of most vampires, he knew females found his strong barbarian features, with his smoldering, faintly slanted dark eyes and long ebony hair, a source of fascination. Now, however, he found the female's attention more a source of annoyance than pleasure.

Firmly sending her on her way, Tarak waited until he was alone before he stepped through the hidden door that had been used by the Anasso.

Now his heavy boots crunched on the packed dirt as he followed the passage that headed down at a sharp angle. He'd assumed that he'd been in most of the tunnels that ran like a maze beneath the castle, but he quickly realized he was headed in an opposite direction from the public catacombs. This passage was leading him toward the nearby village, not the mountain.

His sense of dread only intensified. A part of him wanted to turn around. He could seek his bed like his brothers and continue to exist in blissful ignorance. Why not? They were on the cusp of peace for the first time in history.

His feet, however refused to listen to the urging of his heart. *Crunch, crunch, crunch.* They continued forward, even when the pungent stench of unwashed humans and demons polluted the air. Tarak gagged. The odor was laced with putrid illness that seemed to seep into his very skin.

How was it possible that the smell hadn't permeated the entire lair? It would surely take magic to contain the stench to this area.

The question was driven from his mind as he rounded a corner. Skidding to a halt, he instinctively bared his fangs in revulsion. On one side, the stone wall had a gaping opening that revealed the pit below.

Tarak gagged again, but he forced himself to move toward the edge of the floor and peer down. He could easily see through the gloom, making out the groups of captives, a dozen humans who were huddled in a mass of misery in one corner. In another corner, there was an iron cage filled with naked fairies. And on the far side of the cramped chamber there were four pureblooded Weres chained to the wall with silver shackles.

The sight hit Tarak like a punch to the gut. His faithful clansman, Chiron, had been right. The Anasso was addicted to tainted blood.

It was only a matter of time before he went completely insane.

He started forward, only to halt. There was nothing he could do to help the pathetic prisoners until after he'd confronted his master. Pivoting on his heel, Tarak hurried back up the passageway. The sooner he could expose the Anasso, the sooner they could choose a new leader and continue with their plans for the future.

Lost in his grim thoughts, Tarak was impervious to the chill that crawled through the air. The lair was filled with vampires. There were always chills. Sometimes the walls would be coated with ice. No doubt that explained why so many vampires preferred to have their own lairs.

It wasn't until he felt the tremors beneath his feet that he recognized who'd entered the passage. He stopped, his spine stiffening as he watched a shadowed form stroll toward him.

The Anasso.

The king was a large male with bluntly carved features and piercing eyes. He also had legendary vampire powers that had allowed him to claim the throne. Tarak had never encountered another demon who could equal him in raw dominance. Well, maybe Styx. The younger male continued to acquire power with every passing year. But Styx was as devoted to the Anasso as Tarak.

The poor bastard was going to be devastated when he learned the nasty secret their master had been hiding.

The Anasso halted, blocking the passage with his large body. An intentional attempt at intimidation?

"Tarak." The male's voice echoed down the tunnel. "It's late. You should be in your quarters."

Tarak felt a treacherous urge to turn and walk away. Just leave the lair and start over.

It would be the easiest solution.

And the most cowardly, a voice warned in the back of his mind.

The vampires who were depending on the Anasso to lead them into a new future deserved to know the truth. No matter how much it might hurt.

"I had a mission that could not wait," he admitted.

"A mission? That sounds ominous." The older male's tone was mocking, but Tarak didn't miss the fact his words were slurred.

"Yes," he agreed.

The Anasso's brows snapped together as he easily sensed Tarak's tension. "This is a private passage."

Tarak met the male's penetrating gaze without flinching. "Why would you need a private passage?"

The Anasso shrugged. "There are occasions a clan chief prefers to speak with me without revealing his presence. I need to assure him that the negotiations will remain confidential."

The smooth explanation made sense. There had been many chiefs who'd accepted the rule of the Anasso but were reluctant to bend the knee in public. The one thing all vampires had in common was their arrogance.

None of them wanted to appear weak.

But Tarak had already seen the real reason for the tunnel. And he was done pretending this male could continue his reign as king.

"No more lies," he said in a harsh voice. "We both know what is at the bottom of this tunnel."

There was a tremor beneath Tarak's feet. "Be careful, my friend. We have been together a very long time."

Tarak clenched his hands as pain lanced through his heart. "We have. Which makes this all the more difficult."

"Why?" The Anasso stepped toward Tarak, his power crawling over him with a tangible force. "Nothing has changed."

Was he jesting? If so, it wasn't amusing.

"You have made choices that have put us all in danger," Tarak growled.

The Anasso made a sound of impatience. "Trust me, there is no danger. I can quit whenever I choose."

"You sound like a human who is attempting to excuse his overindulgences."

There was a tense silence as the temperature in the tunnel dropped to a level just above glacial.

"I never thought of you as a prude, Tarak."

"It is not prudish to know you are rotting your mind and putting at risk everything we have struggled to achieve."

"It is a harmless means of easing the burdens I must carry."

Tarak hissed, angered by the older vampire's utter lack of remorse.

"It is a weakness." Tarak flicked a gaze over the Anasso's rumpled robe that was still stained from the earlier feast. Even his long hair was tousled, as if he'd been running his fingers through it. Not at all the flawless warrior who'd conquered thousands of vampires. A deep sadness settled in the center of his heart. "And you were the one to claim that any vulnerability must be destroyed."

"Is that what you intend to do? Destroy me?"

Was it? Tarak grimaced. He supposed that was the inevitable conclusion to this confrontation.

"I intend to lay your sins in front of the clan."

The Anasso stepped forward. "No."

"It is not your decision," Tarak informed his master, his chin tilting to a defiant angle.

The Anasso curled back his lips to reveal his massive fangs. "I cannot allow you to ruin all I have worked to achieve."

Tarak frowned. He suddenly realized just how blind he had been. "Do you not mean all *we* have worked to achieve?"

"Of course." The male waved away Tarak's words with a sharp jerk of his hand. "What do you desire from me?"

"I told you," Tarak snapped. "I intend to reveal your secrets to the clan."

"I asked what you desire." The Anasso stepped close enough that his power washed over Tarak like a tidal wave. "A position within the clan? Perhaps your own throne? I could name you as my prince." His voice lowered to a hypnotic purr. "Or perhaps you prefer riches. I have endless wealth. Just name your price."

Tarak's nose flared with disgust. "Your brain truly is rotted if you believe I can be bribed."

Anger flared through the Anasso's eyes before he was attempting to regain control of his temper.

"There is no one above temptation, my son," he said, tiny quakes running beneath Tarak's feet. "Unless you pretend to be a saint."

If Tarak had been thinking clearly, he would have recognized that the Anasso had just offered him an ultimatum. Accept his offer of wealth and power or suffer the consequences. Tarak, however, was too consumed with his tangled emotions.

Anger. Betrayal. And a gut-deep grief.

"I am no saint," Tarak protested, although he was too focused on his clan to enjoy the same hedonistic pleasures of many demons. His only indulgence was his cellar of fine, aged whiskey. It was for the taste, not to get drunk. A vampire's metabolism was too fast for the alcohol to affect them—unless they drank it straight from the vein of an intoxicated prey. "But my mind is unclouded and capable of seeing what you refuse to admit."

The older male made a sound of disgust. "And what is that?"

"You are sick."

"Sick and weak." Dust filtered from the ceiling as the tremors the Anasso was creating spread through the tunnel. "Such words could be considered treason."

"They are the truth."

The Anasso clicked his tongue, holding out his hand. "I am offering you the opportunity to forget what you have seen and walk away, my son. There is no need for any trouble between us."

Tarak refused to back down. Once upon a time he'd have been honored to be called son by this male. It was a sign of honor. Now it just made him sad.

"You know I cannot."

A fleck of blood dribbled down the Anasso's chin. He was too muddled to realize he'd cut his lip with his own fang.

"A pity." The hand he'd been holding out was suddenly slashing through the air.

Tarak frowned. The Anasso hadn't tried to hit him. It was more like he was giving a signal to some unseen onlooker. "What are you doing?"

"The easiest solution would be to kill you," the Anasso threatened.

Tarak shrugged. "I do not fear death," he said. "I've endured it once before."

Vampires had no memory of their lives before they were turned from human to demon, but Tarak presumed that he'd realized the end was near as his sire had sucked the last of the blood from his body.

An unmistakable madness glowed in the ancient vampire's eyes. "We all fear death. Even immortals. Some contain their dread behind a pretense of bloated courage." He released an ugly laugh. "A few prefer to forget the looming specter of becoming a pile of ash with my little entertainments."

Tarak curled his lips, revealing his fangs. Not as a threat, but as a display of disgust. "Another excuse?"

Fury radiated from the Anasso. "An explanation."

There was the echo of heavy footsteps crunching against the rock floor. Tarak couldn't determine how many demons were approaching, but there were more than one.

"Your guards will never agree to kill me," Tarak assured his companion, feeling more relieved than alarmed by the sound. "Not when I tell them what I have discovered."

The large male appeared indifferent to the threat. Was it because he was teetering on the edge of insanity? Or because he was convinced that he had nothing to fear from Tarak?

"I have a wide variety of servants," he said in mocking tones. "These are a few of my most loyal warriors, and I assure you that they will do exactly what I tell them to."

Tarak felt his first stab of fear as a foul scent suddenly laced the air.

"Trolls?" he rasped, staring at the Anasso in disbelief.

No self-respecting vampire would have dealings with trolls or orcs or goblins. It was an unspoken rule.

The Anasso shrugged, indifferent to Tarak's incredulity. "Mongrels," he clarified. "I've discovered that they come in quite handy on occasion."

Tarak shook his head. Why hadn't he listened to Chiron? The younger vampire had been able to see far more clearly than the rest of them. He'd known that the Anasso had fallen into a darkness so deep there was no hope of salvation.

"Pet trolls. Yet another secret, my king?" he rasped. "Do you use them to kill off those who might threaten your place on the throne? A throne, I might add, that you created for yourself?"

His words touched a nerve. The Anasso gave a low snarl, his hands clenching before he managed to regain command of his composure.

"That was my first intention, I will admit," he drawled. "But I suddenly realize that you have more value alive. At least for now."

Tarak narrowed his gaze. Being torn into pieces by a pack of trolls wasn't the end he'd envisioned for himself, but he was fairly sure that was preferable to whatever the Anasso had planned.

"What do you intend to do with me?"

The Anasso lifted a hand, smoothing it down his robe as if he was completely unaware that it was a stained, rumpled mess.

"Several years ago I became beholden to a stranger," he murmured. "I will not bore you with the details."

"And?"

The Anasso smiled as the first troll appeared around the corner of the tunnel.

"And you, my friend, are about to pay that debt," the Anasso said, gesturing for the lumbering troll to approach.

The creature wasn't as large as a full-bred troll, but he was still over seven feet tall, with a bulky body and skin that was as tough as steel. He also had razor-sharp tusks that jutted from his lower jaw. The Anasso spoke in a low voice to the beast as three more trolls crowded behind Tarak. The stench made him gag, but he forced himself to conjure a pretense of calm indifference. Even when the Anasso sent him a taunting smile.

"First, however, my guards have insisted on having their fun. A pity, Tarak. You should have made a better choice."

The first blow came from behind Tarak. A fist that shattered his ribs. Then a club smashed in the side of his skull.

From then on it was a ferocious avalanche of pain that lasted an eternity.

Chapter 1

The demon hotel in the depths of the Florida Everglades was a sprawling structure with two long wings surrounded by lush gardens. A week ago, it had been hidden behind a thick layer of magic, but the spell had been broken, and the demon guests had been encouraged to leave the premises.

At the time, Chiron's only thought had been to have some time alone with Lilah. After all, when a vampire finally located his true mate, it was a time of celebration. And since Chiron was quite convinced that his beautiful witch, Lilah, was the most special mate since the beginning of mates, the celebration had to be something spectacular.

Unfortunately, the best-laid plans of mice and vampires tended to go to hell. And even as Chiron had shooed away the guests and sent Ulric—his faithful Were guard—to track down his master who'd just escaped his prison, he'd realized that any hope of a private oasis was a fantasy.

And, as if to emphasize the fact that the honeymoon was on hold, the King of the Vampires had arrived a half hour ago, demanding a full account of the unfolding disaster.

Now they stood in the middle of the vast lobby of the hotel. Styx, the current Anasso, the formal title for king, stood well over six feet, with stark Aztec features. His hair was long and as dark as midnight. Currently he had it pulled into a braid that was threaded with turquoise medallions. And as usual, his massive frame was covered from head to toe in leather. Oh, and he had a sword the size of a shovel strapped across his back.

Chiron had dark hair as well, but he kept his neatly trimmed. He also preferred to wear designer suits that were tailored to fit his slender frame. He was a wealthy owner of a chain of hotels, spas, and casinos called

Dreamscape Resorts, which catered to humans. He sold sophistication and luxury, so that was the façade he'd adopted over the years.

Beside him was Lilah, his new mate. She was a foot shorter than Chiron with a lush figure and glorious, untamed curls that fell past her shoulders. She had honey-gold skin and her eyes were a swirl of gold and green. Unlike the two male vampires, she was a human witch who stayed young by bathing in the Fountain of Youth that was conveniently located in the back of the garden in a hidden grotto.

Styx folded his arms over his chest, his expression grim. "Explain to me again what happened."

Chiron swallowed his impatience. He was a Rebel, which meant he didn't consider Styx his king, but the ancient male had the sort of power that could flatten the hotel and potentially destroy the fountain that kept Lilah alive. Chiron couldn't risk that.

"I discovered that the former Anasso captured Tarak and handed him over to the King of the Mer-folk," Chiron said in clipped tones.

Styx already knew that his predecessor had locked away Chiron's master, Tarak. That was why he'd given Chiron the scroll that had led to this hotel, and eventually to the key that had released Tarak from his prison.

What none of them had known was that Tarak had been betrayed by the previous Anasso and given to Riven, the leader of the mer-folk, for some nefarious purpose.

Styx scowled. Did the ancient vampire hope that Chiron's story would change? Probably.

"You're sure?"

Chiron nodded. "Positive."

"Why would a merman imprison a vampire?" he snapped.

It was a question that had plagued Chiron since he'd realized who was holding Tarak captive. As far as he knew, the mer-folk had disappeared from the world centuries ago.

"I have no idea," he admitted. "You'll have to ask Riven."

"Oh, I intend to." The ground shook and the lights flickered as Styx's power thundered through the lobby. "First I have to deal with a crazed vampire whom you released to rampage across Florida."

A burst of anger stiffened Chiron's spine. This male had refused to heed his warnings that the previous Anasso was bat-shit crazy. And that he was using intoxicated humans to fuel his addiction. Then he'd accused Chiron of lying when he'd said he was convinced that his master, Tarak, had been taken prisoner, and had done nothing when Chiron was banished.

"I suppose you would have preferred that I leave Tarak in his prison," he accused the older vampire.

Styx narrowed his gaze. "I wouldn't have brought you the key if that's what I wanted. But I'd hoped you would keep him contained until we could determine if he was a danger to the world."

Chiron bared his fully extended fangs. "He wouldn't have been a danger to the world if you had listened to my warnings about your predecessor."

Styx stepped forward, the marble floor cracking beneath his heavy boots. Suddenly, Lilah was grasping Chiron's arm, giving it a warning squeeze.

"Maybe we should concentrate on what we're going to do now instead of squabbling over the past," she suggested in low tones.

The lights flickered before Styx visibly loosened his tense muscles.

"A wise mate," he told Chiron.

Chiron's unbeating heart warmed. It'd only been a week since they'd completed the mating, which might explain why he was still besieged with a sense of acute wonderment. But he was fairly confident his giddy happiness was a permanent thing.

"Yes," he readily agreed with Styx as he placed an arm around Lilah's shoulders and tugged her tight against his side. "And patient," he continued, glancing down at her lovely face. "We're supposed to be on our honeymoon."

She smiled, lifting a hand to lightly touch his cheek. Sparks darted through him.

"We have an eternity together," she murmured. "Right now we need to find Tarak."

"She's right," Styx said.

Chiron glared at the large man. Centuries ago they'd been brothers, fighting with the first Anasso to end the brutal clan wars between vampires and unite them. But the loyalty he'd felt toward Styx had been destroyed when Tarak had disappeared and he'd been banished.

"Are you offering your help?" he asked the older vampire.

Styx shrugged. "We have to keep Tarak away from the human cities. I have my Ravens spread around the wetlands," he said, referring to his lethal personal guards. "What about you?"

Chiron grimaced. "I had Ulric on his trail," he said.

Styx took a second to place the name. "The Were?"

Chiron nodded. He'd rescued Ulric from the slave-pits beneath the Anasso's lair. Since then the younger male had not only become Chiron's devoted bodyguard, but his closest friend. It didn't matter to him that Ulric was a pureblooded werewolf. Everyone had their faults.

"Yes, I sent him to look for Tarak after he'd escaped from the prison. But when it was obvious that my master was simply crisscrossing the Everglades with no apparent destination, I sent him back to Vegas." Chiron exchanged a rueful glance with Lilah. The Were had returned to the hotel a bedraggled mess. His clothing was torn, and his skin was coated with a goopy mud that took an hour to scrub off. "Ulric is a fine warrior, but his temper was near the snapping point at his belief that Tarak was simply leading him through the bogs to be a jackass."

Styx made a sound of impatience. "You have no idea what Tarak is doing?"

"Actually, Lilah has come up with a theory," Chiron said, watching a blush stain his mate's cheeks.

Long ago Lilah had been a ruthlessly ambitious leader of her coven who'd been willing to sacrifice anyone to save her own skin. But after centuries of being isolated at the hotel with no memory of her past, she'd been stripped of her vanity to become a sweetly vulnerable woman who preferred to remain in the background.

"What theory?" Styx demanded.

Her blush deepened. "I think Tarak is trying to capture Inga."

Styx frowned. "Who?"

"My nanny," Lilah told Styx. Then she grimaced. "Or the female I thought was my nanny."

Styx's confusion cleared. "The ogress?"

"Half ogress and half mermaid," Chiron clarified.

"Does Tarak blame her for imprisoning him?" Styx asked.

Inga had worked with Lilah and her coven of witches to create the barriers that had held Tarak captive.

"It's a possibility," Lilah murmured.

"But you suspect he has another motive?" Styx pressed.

"I think it's possible he is planning to force her to take him to the mermaids," Lilah admitted.

Styx appeared startled by the soft words. Like most demons, the ancient vampire had no doubt assumed the mermaids had disappeared forever.

"She can do that?"

Lilah nodded. "She admitted she'd visited them before."

Styx's jaw tightened. "Damn. He's trying to get to Riven."

"It's only a theory," Lilah hastily reminded the powerful vampire.

Styx turned his attention to Chiron, his expression grim. "We need to find the ogress before Tarak does."

Chiron rolled his eyes. "Good luck with that. She's not only huge and lethal, but she's as cunning as an imp. Plus, she can create illusions that would fool even the most powerful demons."

"Illusions?"

"Yeah, the best I've ever seen."

"Damn." A strangely rueful expression settled on the Anasso's face. "We don't need power."

Chiron stared at him in confusion. "What do we need?"

"Levet," Styx revealed. "He can see through any illusion. "Where is the—" The vampire cut off whatever rude word he was about to utter. "The gargoyle?"

Chiron exchanged another glance with Lilah. He'd hoped that Styx would have forgotten that Levet had traveled with him to Florida.

"Actually..." His words trailed away.

Styx snapped his brows together. "Tell me."

"I left him in charge of guarding the ogress after it was revealed she'd been working with the mermaids. When I went back to check on him I discovered that he'd disappeared along with Inga," Chiron admitted. "We don't know if he helped her escape. Or if he's being held hostage."

The temperature in the lobby dropped below freezing as Styx glared at him with a surprising fury.

"Shit. If something happens to that idiotic creature, my mate is going to chew off my ass," Styx rasped, pointing a finger into Chiron's face. "And since she's a pureblood Were that's not a metaphor." The large male pivoted on his heel, heading toward the door.

Chiron took an instinctive step forward. "Where are you going?" he demanded.

"To find Levet," Styx growled, turning his head to send Chiron a warning glare. "You catch that demented master of yours before I have to destroy him."

The heavy door slammed behind Styx as he stepped out of the hotel. The chandelier rattled overhead, and tiny quakes continued to shake the floor.

Styx not only made a dramatic entrance, but he managed to leave with the same theatrical flair.

"So that's the new Anasso." Lilah finally broke the heavy silence that filled the lobby. "He's very..."

"Arrogant?" Chiron suggested.

"Forceful."

Chiron shook his head in resignation. "And I thought the first Anasso was bad."

* * * *

Tarak left the nest of lily nymphs with a sense of dissatisfaction. Although the lovely creatures had been eager to appease his hunger, he'd found their blood bland and tasteless. Like champagne that had gone flat.

He told himself that it was a result of his obsession with his long overdue revenge. How could he enjoy a meal, no matter how tasty, when his thoughts were focused on finding the ogress so she could lead him to the mermaids? Plus, he'd just escaped from a prison where he'd been trapped for over five centuries. Perhaps his taste buds needed time to adjust.

It certainly had nothing to do with the beautiful female who'd visited during the long years of his imprisonment...

As if on cue, the thick vegetation that surrounded him began to glow with a shimmering light. Then the vision of a familiar slender woman appeared directly in front of him.

A strange excitement buzzed through him. As if he was eager for the opportunity to see her once again.

He released a low growl. What the hell was wrong with him? The female was probably a figment of his crazed imagination. After all, there was a good chance he wasn't entirely stable after being locked away. What demon wouldn't be a little stressed after five hundred years surrounded by a barren cell of stone walls? And if she really was appearing before him...then she was the enemy.

Still, the buzzing continued as he took in the sight of her pale hair that was highlighted with hints of blue that fell as smooth as silk down her back. Her wide eyes were the color of aquamarines and her skin appeared as if it'd been dusted with the luminescent shimmer of a pearl.

As always, she was wearing a gown that flowed to her ankles. It had a plunging neckline and was sheer enough to offer glimpses of her naked body beneath.

She was as lovely as all fey creatures, but vampires had little interest in superficial beauty. They had the ability to see inside the soul of creatures. And this female's essence was a fascinating combination of rare innocence and a fierce spirit that she desperately tried to keep hidden.

Plus, she possessed a scent that intoxicated him. Passion fruit, soft air, and an undertone of salt. Like a summer night on the Caribbean Sea.

He shook his head, trying to clear her vision from his mind.

"Stop haunting me," he rasped.

The female stepped forward, her expression hardening in the moonlight. When she'd first started coming to the prison where Tarak was being held, she was a timid, frightened creature. Probably because Tarak had done his best to terrify her. But over time he'd come to look forward to her visits. And not just because she offered him an opportunity to feed from her veins.

She would linger to keep him company, bringing him books that helped to ease the brutal loneliness of his isolation. And in the last fifty years or so, she'd left a device called a television that allowed him to view the humans' entertainment. It was an invaluable tool that kept him up to date on the world. Plus, she'd been the one to tell him that the old Anasso had died a few years before and that Styx had become the new King of Vampires.

He hadn't fully processed the news. There was a mixture of acute joy that the bastard was dead, combined with fury that he hadn't been the one to cut out his heart. Plus, there was a suspicion that Styx, a male he'd trusted like a brother, had allowed him to rot in the prison while he waited for the opportunity to grab the throne for himself.

He hadn't had the time or the interest to work through the baggage.

Over the centuries, however, the female had never talked about herself, or the bastard who was responsible for him being there, but she'd helped to keep him sane. And in time, she'd developed a confidence to approach him without fear.

Now she glared at him in exasperation. "I'm here to protect you, you stupid vampire."

He scowled. Although he'd never been power-hungry like the Anasso who'd betrayed him, Tarak had been a clan chief who'd earned the respect of his people.

No one questioned his intellect.

"Stupid?" he growled.

"Yes, stupid." She tilted her chin. "I know what you're doing."

He reached out, not surprised when his hand went through the female. She wasn't real.

"You're a hallucination from my mind," he rasped.

"I'm real," she insisted, her voice low and husky. Perfectly tuned to stir a male's passions. "My blood runs through your veins."

Tarak shivered, vividly remembering the taste of her. She'd been sweet and warm and as addictive as nectar. And just the memory was enough to make his cock hard. It was no wonder the poor nymphs hadn't been able to satisfy his hunger.

He pulled back his lips to flash his fangs. It pissed him off that he was reacting to her as if he was a drunken goblin in rutting season.

"I'm not so crazy that I can't tell gold from dross," he drawled.

She flinched, as if his words had wounded her. Then her chin tilted an inch higher.

"It's true I'm not physically there," she admitted. "I have the ability to..." She paused, considering how to explain her talent. "To project my image."

Her words did nothing to ease the toxic stew of frustration that bubbled inside him.

"An illusion," he snapped. "Too damn many illusions."

The scent of salt became more pungent, revealing her own flare of temper.

"I came to you in your prison," she reminded him in sharp tones. "My touch kept you sane."

Tarak glanced around the dark, soggy bogs that were coated in a slimy moss. Right now he could be in a luxurious hotel, enjoying a glass of champagne and a hot bath. Or returning to one of the numerous lairs he'd owned around the world. He'd had them glamoured to keep any creature, including humans, from discovering them.

Instead, he was here.

Hot and wet. And not in a good way. Why wouldn't he be consumed with a burning need to lash out?

"Not so sane," he muttered.

She reached out her hand, her expression pleading. "You're free, Tarak. Return to your family."

"Family." He furrowed his brow. He'd once had a clan. Brothers he'd trusted with his very life. But he'd been betrayed. Now he was alone. "It's been too long."

"Then create a new family," she urged.

He curled his hands into fists. "Not until the bastard who held me prisoner for so long is dead. Only then will I be free."

The female gave a shake of her head, her hair sliding over her shoulders. Tarak battled the urge to reach out and try to touch her again. She looked so real.

"Please listen," the woman pleaded.

"No."

"Riven knows you've escaped your prison. He's searching for you."

"Riven." Tarak tested the name. It echoed through him, setting off explosive jolts of fury. He'd never met his captor, but he had a foggy memory of hearing the mongrel trolls talking about the Anasso being in debt to a strange creature who came out of the sea as Tarak had been carried—broken and bloody—from the fortress. "Merman."

"Yes."

A cold smile curved Tarak's lips as a nearby cypress tree toppled over. Like all vampires, Tarak had a unique power. His happened to be telekinesis. A rare and wonderful talent, but occasionally it caused unexpected damage.

"Good. I'm eager for a face-to-face meeting," he told her. "It's long overdue."

Her lips thinned, the air humming with her impatience despite the fact she wasn't there in the flesh.

"He won't come himself. He'll send his royal guards."

"Royal?"

A strange expression rippled over her delicate features. "He's the King of the Mer-folk."

King? Tarak released an abrupt laugh. Of course the bastard was the king.

"He can send every royal guard he has," Tarak assured his companion. "I'm not afraid of a fish."

She looked like she wanted to slap him. Or maybe stick a trident through his dead heart.

"As I said. Stupid," she hissed.

Tarak studied her. She wasn't a figment of his imagination, he abruptly acknowledged. If he was imagining her, she wouldn't be spitting fury at him. No. She would be warm and inviting and, if his fantasy was really good, she would be removing her gown to reveal the slender curves beneath.

Still, he wasn't about to trust her.

He didn't trust anyone. Not anymore. He might be out of his prison, but he could still feel a strange drain on his powers. The same drain he'd felt since he'd first been captured. He wasn't completely free even if he was no longer trapped in his barren cell.

"Who are you?" he demanded.

Despite the fact that he intimately knew her smell, her taste, and the feel of her flesh as he'd drunk from her neck, she'd never shared the most basic facts about herself.

She hesitated, no doubt trying to decide whether or not to share such an intimate detail. There were many demons who could use a name as a weapon. Then, perhaps reminding herself that a vampire didn't possess magic she answered his question.

"Waverly."

Waverly. The name lapped over him like a warm wave of water. "You're a mermaid."

The words were a statement not a question, but Waverly gave a small nod. "Yes."

"Then why are you helping me?"

"I can't bear to see you suffer any further."

His lips twisted into a humorless smile. "Try again."

She glanced around, as if searching for someone. Tarak frowned. Could she see him and the bogs? Or was she looking at something closer to her?

At last she spoke in a low voice. "I want you to tell the vampires what Riven is doing. This can't continue."

"What is he doing?" Tarak demanded.

Her eyes suddenly widened, her head turning to the side. "I must go."

Tarak felt an odd jolt of unease. Was someone coming? Was she in danger? "Waverly."

She glanced back at him, her expression tight with frustration. "Return to your people."

Tarak took an instinctive step forward even as her image vanished as swiftly as it'd appeared.

"Madness," he whispered.

Chapter 2

Inga wasn't a delicate sort of female.

Standing well over six feet, she had a square, muscular body and feet that were large enough to squash a full-grown kobold. If that wasn't intimidating enough, she'd been told by more than one demon that she possessed the sort of face that could send entire armies fleeing in terror.

She couldn't argue. Her reddish hair grew in tufts on top of her head, and her features were roughly chiseled. Her eyes were blue, but they flashed red when she was annoyed, and her teeth were pointed. She was never going to win a beauty contest. But while she looked like she should be comfortable stomping through mud and sleeping in holes in the ground, she was desperate for a hot dinner and a change of clothes.

She ruefully glanced down at the brilliant purple muumuu with yellow orchids that was now covered in gunk. It was one of her favorite dresses, even if Lilah had grimaced every time she caught sight of it.

Inga quickly shoved away the thought of the human witch whom she'd treated as her own daughter for five hundred years. Eventually she would earn Lilah's forgiveness. But first she had to shake off the damned vampire who'd been hunting her for the past seven days.

Who could have suspected that Tarak would be so determined to hunt her down after he'd escaped from his prison? It wasn't like she'd been the one to betray him. All she'd done was help to cast the spell that held him captive. The idiotic leech needed to man up and move on.

Giving a shake of her head, Inga headed toward the seedy demon club hidden in a thick grove of trees. She would have preferred to stay at one of the finer hotels that catered to demons. Perhaps one in Miami Beach, or Key West. She was in desperate need of a spa day and a fruity drink with an umbrella in it.

Unfortunately, she couldn't risk exposing herself. She had to choose a place that was heavily wrapped in illusions, and off-limits to vampires.

And this was the only place she knew of in the state of Florida.

Pressing open the door, she stepped into small lobby that had a low, open-beam ceiling and warped wooden floorboards. She wrinkled her nose at the stench of stale grog and a mass of unwashed demon bodies. The fighting pits had to be just below them.

She paused to glance down at the tiny demon standing next to her. A sharp regret sliced through her.

Levet was a stunted gargoyle who stood barely three feet tall, with large fairy wings that glistened with exquisite jewel tones. He'd arrived at the hotel with the vampire Chiron. She'd known as soon as the two had shown up that they were going to be trouble, but during their stay, she'd become oddly attached to the gargoyle.

He was rude, aggravating, and completely self-absorbed, but he could also be charming, funny, and kind-hearted. A rare combination among demons. Most importantly, he was the first male to see beyond her less-than-perfect façade.

She didn't know how, but he'd been able to sense her wounded soul and had lured her into revealing the truth of her past. Not only the years that she'd been held as a slave, but the painful discovery that her mother's people, the mer-folk, considered her a blight on her family. And he'd reached out to try and make a connection.

In return for his compassion, she'd stripped away his memories of being at the hotel and convinced him that he was her devoted guard who was there to rescue her.

What choice had she had? Once Lilah had discovered that she'd been tricking her for centuries, the powerful witch had wrapped her in threads of magic. The only way to escape and give Lilah the opportunity to calm down and listen to reason was to force Levet to help her.

Now he was traveling through the swamps with her, his memories scrambled, and a furious vampire on their trail.

It was all a mess.

Swallowing a sigh, Inga crossed the floor to stand in front of the wooden counter. A few seconds later a short male with a bald head and stooped shoulders stepped out of a hidden door. Inga sniffed the air. A mongrel, like her. She could detect some goblin blood as well as imp and a hint of brownie.

He shuffled to stand behind the counter, studying her with a speculative expression.

"I assume you're here to fight?"

"No." She gave a firm shake of her head. "I want a room and something to eat."

The male scowled, leaning forward to take in her ragged dress that was stained with mud.

"Show me your money."

Inga clenched her teeth. She could twist the mongrel into a pretzel, but she didn't want to get tossed out before she'd had her bath.

Lifting her hand, she reached beneath the neckline of her gown and pulled out a small but perfect pearl and laid it on the counter. "There."

The male snatched the pearl off the counter, tucking it into the front pocket of his leather pants. Greed touched his round face as he glanced toward Levet.

"Pets are extra."

"Pets?" Levet puffed out his chest, his tail twitching. "I am not a pet. I am the world renown—"

"Not now," Inga interrupted.

Levet sent her an offended glare. "I do not wish to stay at this hotel," he informed her, his French accent more pronounced than usual. He wrinkled his snout. "It smells like doo-doo."

"Hey," the mongrel snapped.

Inga held out her hand, wanting to get out of the lobby before Levet managed to create a scene. "Give me the key."

The male hesitated, no doubt considering whether he could kick them out without returning the valuable pearl. Then, seeing Inga's expression, he paled and reached beneath the counter to pull out a heavy, old-fashioned key. Handing it to Inga, he pointed a shaky hand toward Levet.

"Keep him locked up or I'll toss him in the pit."

Levet flapped his wings, taking a step toward the counter. "You may try to throw me in the pit. I will—"

Inga reached down to grab the gargoyle by the stunted horn, dragging him toward an opening at the back of the room. "Come on."

She waited until they were in the narrow corridor before she released her hold on her companion.

Levet clicked his tongue, sending her a wounded glare. "Why would you not allow me to finish my threat? It was going to be quite spectacular and involved nasty boils on his derrière plus a curse on his mother."

Inga heaved a sigh, her gaze skimming over the wooden doors with rough numbers scratched into them that lined the hallway. Below her feet she could feel the booming chants from the crowds watching the fights.

"I just want a hot bath and some food," she told her companion.

The gargoyle was instantly distracted. He smacked his lips in anticipation. "Food would be lovely. I'm starving."

Inga made a sound of disbelief. "You just ate an entire alligator."

Levet grimaced, patting his belly. "*Oui*, and it has given me terrible indigestion. Now I need a nice bowl of stew and an apple pie to settle my belly."

Inga shook her head. She didn't know whether to be disgusted or impressed.

"You eat more than I do," she said. "Where do you put it?"

"I might be small in stature, but I am *très grand* in power," Levet said in lofty tones. "I need my energy."

"Hmm." Inga came to an abrupt halt in front of a door marked with the number six. "This is it," she said, inserting her key into a metal lock. The door swung inward, revealing a cramped room with a painfully low ceiling and a bed that was barely large enough for a dew fairy. "Why do they always make the beds so small?" she groused, entering the room and waiting for Levet to join her before closing the door.

Levet gave a flap of his wings, landing on the mattress that was no doubt as old as the pyramids.

"Not all demons possess your remarkable size," he pointed out.

Inga stiffened. "Are you calling me fat?"

The gargoyle looked genuinely confused. "Did you wish me to call you fat?"

"No. I…" Inga heaved a sigh at her rare burst of vanity. What did she care if the gargoyle thought she was too large? She was being an idiot. "Never mind."

"You are a very contrary female," Levet complained, lifting his hand to touch a claw to the side of his head. It was something he was doing more and more. An indication that he could sense the memories she had scrubbed. "Explain again how I became your Knight in Shining Armor."

Inga glanced away, the guilt nagging at her. "I told you. I was captured by the witch and you released me."

"And now we are running from a vampire?"

"Yes."

Levet clicked his tongue. "I do not comprehend why you do not allow me to contact my FBI Styx."

Inga was momentarily baffled. The tiny gargoyle could speak perfect English, but he often garbled it beyond recognition.

"FBI?"

"Best friend forever."

"You mean BFF?"

The gargoyle ignored her question, bouncing on the mattress to make the springs squeak.

"He is the Anasso. He could make your vampire disappear like that." Levet snapped his fingers.

"I don't want to cause trouble," Inga said, wincing at the *squeak, squeak, squeak*. "He'll eventually give up the hunt."

"And then what?"

Inga shrugged, not about to admit that she intended to return to the hotel to beg for Lilah's forgiveness. That just sounded... pathetic.

"Then you can return to visit the wood sprites," she instead said. "That's what you want, isn't it?"

Levet furrowed his heavy brow, abruptly hopping off the bed. Thank goodness.

"It seems like that is what I should want." He looked oddly confused. "Wood sprites are always quite welcoming."

"And pretty." The words were wrenched from her lips before she could halt them.

"Oui."

Annoyed at the sensation that felt perilously close to jealousy, Inga released the bag she'd hung over her shoulder and headed toward the connecting door.

"I'm going to take a bath," she muttered. "You stay in the room."

Levet made a sound of protest. "But I want to see the fights."

"Later."

"But—"

"You don't want to leave me unprotected, do you?" Inga demanded, this time not feeling any guilt at using her trump card.

Levet wouldn't last ten minutes among the motley crowd that were no doubt gathered around the pits. A considerable amount of money was exchanged during the fights, and the demons' limited sense of humor became nonexistent.

Levet's wings dropped as he glanced longingly at the door. *"Non.* I do not want that."

* * * *

Tarak paced the edge of the cypress trees, growling low in his throat. Where the hell were they?

He could smell the ogress, although her scent was muted. There was also the tang of granite in the air. A gargoyle? But one who didn't leave the sort of destruction he would have expected from such a large demon.

So why couldn't he find them?

Tarak grimaced. There could only be one explanation. Illusions.

He released another growl. He hated magic. Almost as much as he hated mermaids. And that was a lot.

There had to be a hidden lair. Maybe even a hotel or demon club that was shrouded in illusion. And without a specific beacon built within the spell that would direct a vampire through the magic, he had no way of finding the opening. Like a ship trying to navigate the fog with no lighthouse.

Pacing around the grove, Tarak considered his options. The ogress had been smart enough to remain unpredictable. She would travel during the day and sleep at night. Then she would flip-flop and travel at night.

Her journey through the bogs had been just as erratic. She had no obvious destination. Instead she zigged and zagged like a drunken troll. It made it impossible to anticipate where she was going.

He assumed it was deliberate, since she had to know he was on her trail, but at some point she had to stop running in circles, didn't she?

The scent of lemons teased at Tarak's senses. He came to a sharp halt. Ah. A male imp. Was the creature headed through the illusion?

Tarak shrugged. It didn't matter if that was his intended destination or not. He was going there now.

Tarak weaved a silent path over the spongy ground, watching the demon from the shadows.

The imp was tall and slender with long red hair and delicate features. He was wearing black leather pants and a motorcycle jacket left open to reveal his bare chest. Tarak grimaced. He wasn't a fan of some the current fashion he'd seen on the television. Thankfully, he'd managed to steal a pair of jeans and heavy boots as well as a plain t-shirt from a human house on the edge of the swamp. They were comfortable enough and didn't make him feel like an idiot when he pulled them on.

Giving a shake of his head at his ridiculous thoughts, Tarak concentrated on the male who was about to walk between two towering cypresses. Once the creature reached the barrier of illusion, he would disappear from view.

Moving with a blinding speed, Tarak was standing directly in front of the imp. He reached out to grasp the demon by the throat.

"Going somewhere?" he demanded, careful to use the modern language, including the slang he'd learned from the strange shows that humans seemed to enjoy.

He didn't want to reveal that he'd been imprisoned for centuries. It would give any opponent an advantage. Besides, he was determined to fit into this new world. It was how vampires had managed to thrive since the beginning of time.

The imp widened his green eyes. "Vampire," he rasped in shock. "You aren't supposed to be here."

"Is this your private grove?"

"Not mine. But—"

Tarak narrowed his eyes as the male snapped his lips together. Obviously he didn't want to admit there was something hidden behind illusion nearby.

"Yes?" he prompted.

The imp tried to swallow. "What do you want?"

"I'm glad you asked." Tarak glanced toward the nearby trees. "I want you to take me inside."

"Inside?" The imp tried to appear confused. "Inside where?"

Tarak tightened his fingers. "I'm tired and muddy and in the mood to kill something. Do you want that something to be you?"

The imp made a strangled sound. "No."

"Then take me inside."

"I can't."

Tarak resisted the urge to break the imp's neck. He didn't have time for the male to recover. He needed to get through the illusion before the ogress could take off again.

"Why not?" he snapped.

No doubt sensing the violence that pulsed around Tarak, the imp paled.

"Vampires are off-limits," he said.

Tarak allowed his icy power to swirl through the air. Nearby a branch cracked and fell onto the mossy ground. "That's not very nice, is it?"

"I don't make the rules."

"Then who does?"

Despite the icy chill in the air, a layer of sweat covered the imp's face. "A…a friend," he stammered.

Tarak studied the male he held by the throat. The fey creature's fear tainted the air with scorched lemons, but his expression was set in stubborn lines. He was clearly reluctant to reveal whatever was behind the illusion.

Tarak leaned closer. "What's your name?"

The imp blinked. "Excuse me?"

"Your name," Tarak repeated.

"Puck," the creature finally muttered.

Tarak tightened his grip on the male's neck, lifting him an inch off the ground.

"What's behind the illusion, Puck?"

The green eyes flared with panic. Could he see his own death flashing before them?

"Fighting pits," he gasped.

Tarak frowned. He hadn't been expecting that. "Anything else?"

Puck started to shake his head, only to halt as if he was struck by a sudden thought. "I think there's a few rooms for the patrons who want privacy."

"Where are they?"

The male struggled to breathe. "What?"

Tarak made a sound of impatience. "The rooms."

"I don't know." Puck released a choked squeal as Tarak gave a sharp shake. "Arg. Look, I've never stayed here. I just come for the fighting."

Tarak struggled to contain his temper. "Describe the building," he demanded.

"Old." Puck shrugged. "Wood."

Tarak growled. Had the imp been in the pits too many times? Was his brain damaged?

"Tell me the layout of the inside, you idiot."

"Oh." Puck lifted his hands to grab Tarak's wrist, but he didn't bother to struggle. He was no match for a vampire's strength. "There's a lobby with a door that leads down to the pits."

"What else?" Tarak demanded.

"I don't—" Puck bit off his words, probably realizing just how close he was to having his heart ripped out. "Um…there's a counter with a mongrel who takes the entrance fee." He finally managed to recall. "I think there might be a hallway on that side of the lobby. That must be where the rooms are."

Tarak offered a cold smile. "You've been very helpful."

Acute relief rippled over the male's face. "Yes, well. If you'll release my neck, I'll be on my way."

Tarak kept the imp lifted off the ground, pulling him close enough that they were nose to nose.

"*We'll* be on our way," he said.

Puck trembled. "I don't understand."

"I need to get through the illusion and you're going to help me," Tarak reminded the male.

Something that looked like panic flared through the green eyes. "I told you. Vampires aren't allowed in the pits."

Tarak curled his lips in disgust. Centuries ago the vampires had been infamous for capturing lesser demons and forcing them to fight for the entertainment of the clan chiefs. Other demons, like trolls and orcs, fought for the sheer pleasure of killing. Tarak found the pits a waste of manpower. Why throw away a potential soldier to amuse a bunch of drunken fools?

"I'm not going to fight," he rasped. "At least not in the pits."

Sweat dripped down the imp's face. "I'll be banned for eternity if I help you."

"You'll be dead if you don't."

The imp's gaze lowered to Tarak's fangs that were no doubt gleaming in the moonlight.

"There's no need for violence," Puck croaked.

Tarak abruptly released his grip on the male's neck. "Then let's go."

"Shit." The imp stumbled, nearly falling to his knees as he rubbed his bruised throat. "Can't we talk about this?"

Tarak reached out his hand in a threatening motion, and with a shrill sound of fear, Puck was scurrying toward the trees.

Following close behind him, Tarak resisted the urge to grab the back of the man's jacket. The imp couldn't outrun him. And if he tried...

Tarak's thoughts were driven away as he suddenly imagined he could feel a nasty brush of something over his skin. Magic. Logically he knew that he couldn't detect the illusion, but that didn't stop him from shivering.

They continued forward, at last breaking through the edge of the illusion. Tarak grimaced at the sight of the large wooden building that abruptly loomed in the center of the grove. It was unnerving to know the structure had been there and he couldn't see it.

Giving a shake of his head, he followed the imp toward the front door, his gaze flicking around the opening. He couldn't sense any demons lurking in the shadows, but if they were inside the illusion, he might not be able to detect them.

Together they climbed the steps that sagged in the middle, and across the narrow porch. Then, pulling open the door, the imp walked inside and waved a hand toward the far side of the lobby.

"There's the hallway," he said.

Tarak stepped into the long room with an open-beamed ceiling and a pungent stench of sweat and blood. A quick inspection of the lobby revealed an empty space that might once have been filled with tables and chairs, and a nearby opening that led to a set of stairs going down. That had to be the way to the fighting pits. Already he could hear the noise echoing from beneath their feet. He turned his attention to the long counter at the back and the second opening that looked like a hallway leading to the rear of the building.

He shuffled through the overwhelming tidal wave of scents. Ah yes. There it was. A hint of salt and sea air. And granite. His prey was here.

He glanced toward the imp who was trembling at his side. "Where's the manager?"

"There." The imp nodded toward a crack in the wall behind the counter that was beginning to widen. A hidden door.

In no mood to fight his way past whatever demon was about to appear, Tarak glanced up and released a burst of power. There was a sharp crack of wood splintering, then one of the heavy ceiling beams crashed down, blocking the door.

Puck gave a startled screech and Tarak sent him a wry glance.

"You should go now," he commanded.

"Yeah." Puck offered a sickly smile. "I have things to do, demons to see."

Pivoting on his heel, the imp turned and rushed from the building. Obviously the creature had decided to forgo the fights. Tarak shrugged. Probably a good idea.

He headed across the lobby, forgetting the imp as well as the crowd cheering below. Nothing mattered right now but finding the ogress and forcing her to take him to the mermaids.

Chapter 3

Inga managed to slip into a light doze. She was truly exhausted. In mind, body, and spirit. And for once, she had a roof over her head and a mattress beneath her body.

Granted, the mattress was two feet too short, and the roof was leaking. Plus, Levet was grumbling in the corner at being forced to stand guard rather than heading downstairs to enjoy the fights. But she intended to take advantage of their temporary shelter.

Of course, it couldn't last.

She'd known at an early age that she'd been born beneath an evil star. Her mermaid mother had been raped by an ogre and she'd been bartered off to slave traders as soon as she'd been born. It was fate for her to be plagued with bad luck.

Just an hour into her snooze, there was a blast of frigid air that made her shiver. She clutched the thin blanket around her shoulders, refusing to open her eyes. It couldn't be a vampire. They had no way of getting through the illusion.

There was another blast quickly followed by the sound of Levet's claws scraping against the floor planks.

"Um, Inga," he whispered.

She squeezed her eyes tighter. "I'm sleeping."

"*Oui*, I know. You have been snoring like my great Aunt Bertha," he assured her. "But you did say we were avoiding vampires. A most wise decision. I possess an intense allergy to the bloodsuckers."

Releasing a frustrated sigh, Inga tossed aside the blanket and forced herself to climb out of the bed. Christ, she was tired.

"How did he get in here?" she grumbled, smoothing down the muumuu with large oranges patterned over the silk material. Before fleeing the hotel, she'd taken time to pack a few essentials, including several changes of clothes, thank the goddess.

Levet's tail twitched as he glanced toward the door. "A question we should ponder later."

"Fine." Inga grabbed her bag and slung it over her shoulder like a backpack. She wanted her hands free in case she needed to fight. "Let's go."

Leading the way out of the room, Inga turned toward the lobby. Levet gave a small gasp, reaching out to grab her dress.

"*Non*," he protested. "The vampire is coming from the lobby."

Did the silly gargoyle imagine she couldn't feel the icy power that was thundering down the hallway?

She glared down at him. "There's no other way out."

Levet lifted his arms in a dramatic motion. "I can create an opening."

"No."

He scowled at her sharp refusal. "Are you doubting my powers?"

Inga shuddered, recalling the night before when Levet had attempted to clear a path through the thick vegetation. The fireball he'd created had bounced off the trees, forcing her to dive into a nearby bog to avoid being burned.

"Just the wisdom of releasing it in such cramped quarters." She tried to be diplomatic. A struggle, considering that was a skill she never practiced.

Levet scrunched his snout. "Party crapper."

Inga heaved a sigh. "Pooper. Party pooper."

Levet ignored her. "He's almost here."

Inga futilely glanced around the empty hallway. She was big and strong and capable of beating most demons in a fight, but not a vampire. She had to get out of this building and try to outrun the damned leech.

It was the boom-boom-boom from someone pounding a drum beneath their feet that gave her the perfect solution.

"We have to go down," she announced.

Levet's wings fluttered with excitement. "To the fights?"

"Yes."

"At last." The gargoyle's happiness abruptly disappeared, like a balloon that had been pricked. "But we must go through the vampire to get to the stairs."

"Not necessarily." Inga dropped to her knees, balling her hand into a fist and slamming it against the floorboard.

Levet jumped backward as one wooden plank cracked in two, allowing her fingers to get a firm grip on it. She ripped it aside and grabbed the next floorboard.

"Ah. You are *très magnifique*," Levet breathed. "So strong."

Quickly creating a hole large enough to get through, Inga felt an embarrassed blush touch her cheeks. No other creature had ever seen beyond her ugly features and massive girth. No one but Levet. She didn't know whether to kill him or kiss him.

It was unnerving.

"Being this large should have some benefits," she muttered.

"Fah. Why would you complain about your size? I would give anything to—"

Inga grabbed the gargoyle by the arm and tossed him through the hole.

"Arg!" Levet cried out, giving a flap of his wings as he struggled to avoid the milling crowd below.

Inga didn't have the same luxury. Pushing her legs through the opening, she squeezed through the broken boards and dropped like a stone. With a heavy thud, she landed on top of a cluster of sprites, squashing them onto the hard, stone floor.

Inga grimaced at the pain that radiated up her legs from landing so heavily, but with a grim determination she straightened and cast a quick glance around the space.

It was hot and smoky from the torches shoved into the walls. In the center of the stone floor was a rough, iron cage with two trolls who were currently bashing each other with heavy maces. Around the edges were a mob of screaming demons who were packed in so tightly they could barely move, despite the fact that the space was surprisingly large.

How much magic was being used to create the cavern? There had to be a powerful demon somewhere to keep this underground space not only shrouded in illusion, but completely dry.

Inga gave a shake of her head. She didn't have time to worry about the mystery owner of the place. Not when one of the squashed sprites staggered to his feet and lobbed a silver knife toward her head. Idiot. An ogress had a skull as thick as a brick wall.

Still, it was a natural instinct to duck when someone threw something at her. She heard a whistling sound as the knife flew past, hitting a goblin in the center of his back. The demon roared in outrage, turning to grab the still woozy sprite and toss him across the room.

Instant chaos erupted.

The crowd was already stewing in a noxious atmosphere of violence and passion. It didn't take much to ignite them into a lethal brawl.

Using her superior height and weight, Inga waded through the mass of battling demons. A few she was forced to knock out of her path, and one overly bold goblin tried to take a swing at her. She stomped on the top of his foot, a spot that was far more tender than the dangling bits between his legs.

At last she managed to get to the edge of the crowd where Levet was futilely trying to pull his tail from beneath the foot of a full-blooded troll.

"Come on," she said, shoving the troll hard enough to topple him to the side. Then, as the massive creature turned to fight, she grabbed Levet and plopped him on her broad shoulder. "Hold on."

Levet wrapped his arm around the top of her head, his wings flapping with excitement. "Isn't this wondrous?"

Inga rolled her eyes, starting the arduous task of battling back through the crowd.

"There's something wrong with you," she told the gargoyle.

"*Moi*? Nonsense," Levet chided. "I am perfection."

"You are—" Inga's words cut off as the smothering air was abruptly edged with an icy chill. "Vampire," she hissed.

Halting, she desperately shut out the deafening noise of the brawl and concentrated on the sensation of stone that surrounded her. During her childhood years she'd been owned by a troll who used her to crawl through the mountains of Asia for rubies. During those long, arduous years, she'd developed the ability to smell gaps in the rock.

There was the obvious exit up the stairs on the other side of the cavern, but she could detect another crack in the wall just ahead of her.

Lowering her head to use as a battering ram, Inga charged forward, knocking aside the few demons stupid enough to stand in her path. Then, yanking Levet off her shoulder, she carried him like a human football as she rammed straight into the wall.

There was a dreadful ringing noise in her ears from the crushing impact, and her neck muscles felt as if they'd been turned into rubber, but she'd done it. Opening her eyes, she could see the stone, which had already been weakened, begin to crack and crumble.

A grim smile curved her lips as she used her hands to pull out large boulders. She could already sense the structure above them buckling as brackish water raced through the opening she'd created. Soon the whole place would collapse.

Perfect.

Wading against the greenish muck that was swirling up to her knees, she crawled through the crack and pulled her way up and out of the bog that was now forming around the demon club. Clearly she'd managed to destroy the magic that had kept the building on dry land.

She splashed through the deepening water, locating a mossy pathway that led through the trees. A minor miracle. Lowering the sputtering gargoyle to the ground, she ignored his muttered complaints of being hauled about like a sack of potatoes as she hurried through the trees that formed a ring around the building.

With grim determination she slogged her way through nearly five miles of bog. She was just on the point of congratulating herself for her narrow escape when there was a blur of movement beside her. Inga whirled around, but she was too late. Even as she swung her huge fist toward the zooming figure, she heard a squawk of annoyance.

"Levet," she rasped as she watched the tiny gargoyle being swept off his feet.

She came to a halt, growling toward the vampire who was standing in front of her. He was dangling Levet by one of his stunted horns.

"No more running," the male snapped, giving Levet a shake. "Or he dies."

This had to be Tarak, she knew. She'd never actually seen the vampire when Riven was holding him captive, but she recognized his chilled, almost herbal scent. Besides, what other vampire would be chasing her through the damned bogs?

She glared at him. Like all vampires, he was gorgeous, but Inga was indifferent to the potent male beauty. All that mattered was that he'd been chasing her to exhaustion, and now he was holding Levet hostage. She peeled back her lips, exposing her razor-sharp teeth.

"Let him go."

Tarak held Levet higher, spinning the tiny creature around as he studied him with obvious confusion. "Is he a gargoyle?"

Levet flapped his wings, futilely trying to pry himself free of the vampire's grasp. "Of course I am a gargoyle, you stupid leech."

"You're so small." Tarak pointed out the obvious.

Levet stuck out his tongue, making a rude sound. "I am compact."

Inga stepped forward, well aware that Levet tended to drive most males to violence under the best of circumstance. Right now, he was likely to get them both killed.

"Release him or I'll—"

Tarak pulled a silver knife from a holster at the base of his lower back and held it against Levet's throat. Beheading was one of the few ways to kill a gargoyle.

"Eek!" Levet shrieked.

Tarak kept his dark gaze locked on Inga. "Stay back."

"What do you want from me?" she rasped.

"Take me to the mermaids."

She blinked in shock. She'd assumed he was chasing her because he wanted to punish her for helping to imprison him. The last thing she expected was for him to want to enter the hidden lair of her people.

A vicious pain sliced through Inga. "I can't."

Tarak pressed the knife tighter against Levet's throat. "Now."

Inga held up a hand, her mouth going dry. *No, no, no.* She couldn't let Levet be harmed, but the thought of returning to the castle deep in the ocean made her gut cramp with fear. The mer-folk would kill all of them.

"I just said that I can't," she insisted.

"Then your companion dies," Tarak said, spiking the air with droplets of ice.

"*Non.*" Levet lifted his clawed hands, his ugly little face tight with annoyance. "I shall turn you into a toad, you cold-blooded parasite. A toad with warts."

"Levet," Inga snapped. Did the tiny creature have no sense of fear?

Before she could decide whether to try and negotiate with the leech or simply attack, Inga stiffened in shock. There was no mistaking the sudden tang of salt in the air.

Catching the smell at the same time as Inga, the vampire curled his lips with a wicked anticipation.

"Mermaids." He released a terrifying laugh. "Perfect."

Chapter 4

Tarak continued to laugh. Had the ogress led him into a trap? Were these the royal guards that Waverly had warned him about?

Probably.

Well, let the bastards come.

He intended to destroy each and every one. Eventually Riven, King of the Mer-folk, would be forced to confront him directly.

And then he would die.

He glanced down at the struggling creature he held by the horn. At least he had one mystery cleared up. He'd smelled a gargoyle, and the reason he hadn't seen any trace of him was because he was a miniature version. Odd. With a flick of his wrist, he tossed the stunted demon toward the nearby bog where the creature promptly sank beneath the lily pads.

The ogress released a strange croak, her eyes flashing red. Was she fond of the gargoyle? Tarak assumed that she must be as she prepared to attack. But before she could move, a herd of males stepped into view.

No, wait. Mermen weren't a herd. A guppy? A school? Tarak shrugged. It wouldn't matter what they were called once they were dead.

He backed until he was able to keep an eye on the ogress who was staring at the approaching mermen with what looked like horror. He didn't allow himself to be fooled. He had to assume she was a part of this trap.

Once he was confident that he could keep watch on all his opponents at the same time, he turned his attention to the approaching males.

A casual observer could be forgiven for mistaking them for fey creatures. They had the pale, delicate beauty of a fairy, with the lean muscular body of an imp. It was only when the moonlight peeked through the lacy clouds that covered the sky that the iridescent sheen of their skin and the blue highlights in their long, golden hair became obvious.

They were dressed in a strange silver armor that looked like fish scales. It wasn't metal, since it clearly allowed them to move with a fluid flexibility, but Tarak was willing to bet that it was as hard as steel.

Tarak flashed his fangs. "Ah, I smell sushi," he mocked, secretly proud of his ability to insult the creatures with modern slang.

It wasn't like he'd practiced... Okay, that was a lie. He'd practiced. A lot. What else did he have to do but prepare for this day?

The tallest of the mermen lifted his hand, pointing directly at Tarak.

"That's him," he said, his voice sounding hollow, as if he was speaking beneath water.

Another of the soldiers pointed toward the massive ogress. "And the female ogre."

The first merman smiled, revealing a set of pointed teeth. Natural? No, Waverly's teeth weren't pointed. They had to be filed.

"Ah," the merman's smile widened. "How convenient."

Tarak frowned. Maybe the ogress wasn't working with the mermen. Then he shrugged. It didn't matter. Right now he couldn't afford to be distracted.

"Are you going to fight or show off your pretty costumes?" he taunted.

One of the mermen toward the back of the shoal started to charge forward. "I'll—"

"No." The seeming leader reached out to grab the male's arm and yanked him to a halt. "The king wants him brought back alive."

Tarak hissed. Why would the bastard want him back? Impossible to know.

"How is your leader?" His voiced held an arrogant disdain. When he was outnumbered, he wanted his opponents angry enough to make foolish mistakes. "Still hiding in his lair like a spineless coward?"

The male who was still being held by the larger guard made a gurgling sound. Tarak assumed he was pissed.

"Riven is not spineless."

"Then why didn't he come himself instead of sending his boy band?" Tarak smiled as the males scowled in annoyance. His practice at insults was already paying off.

"We're his royal guard," the same merman snarled.

"Stop talking to him, idiot." The leader released his grip on his fellow soldier's arm and took a step toward Tarak. "We can do this the easy way or the hard way."

Tarak arched his brows. "I've been locked away for five centuries and even I know that's clichéd."

The smell of salt blasted through the air. Clearly he'd hit a nerve.

With a flourish, the leader grabbed the sword out of the scabbard at his side. "Take him," he commanded.

Tarak watched the rest of the males reach for their weapons. Surely they couldn't think they were any match for a vampire?

"You can try." He twirled the knife in his hand, motioning them forward.

"Now," the leader barked.

The males held their swords that suddenly began to glow with a strange power. It was only then that Tarak realized that they weren't swords. Instead they were short tridents that they pointed in his direction.

What the hell? He'd fought a hundred different species of demons, but he'd never seen the mer-folk in battle. He assumed they were a devious, sneaky sort of people who snuck out of the shadows and attacked when their enemies' backs were turned. Just like their king.

Now he felt a rare stab of alarm as he could see threads of silver shoot out of the end of the tridents. *Shit.* The mermen soldiers weren't as useless as he'd assumed.

He'd taken a step backward when the threads began to wrap around him, the silver searing into his skin.

Tarak gave a cry of frustrated agony as the threads formed a net around him, toppling him to the ground. He was trapped.

Trying to ignore the rapidly approaching mermen, Tarak tilted his head back to watch the ogress.

"Release me," he commanded, watching as she lumbered toward him.

Was she actually going to help? He groaned as she stomped past him, seemingly indifferent to his plight. Instead, she lumbered toward the bog where the gargoyle was crawling out of the water.

"Nyles, kill her," the leader commanded. "Noyse, you open a portal to take us home."

Tarak arched his back as agony blistered through him, his gaze locked on the gargoyle who was climbing out of the bog and shaking himself. Like a dog getting rid of the clinging moss.

"Do not fear, my damsel," the strange creature assured his companion. "I am here to protect you."

The ogress released a loud gasp as the gargoyle lifted his hands toward the mermen who had nearly reached Tarak.

"Levet, no!" she cried out.

Barely capable of thinking through his pain, Tarak tried to imagine why the ogress looked so horrified. Before he could reason out an explanation, there was a blinding flash of light. Heat roasted over him, and Tarak instinctively squeezed his eyes shut. At the same time, he sensed the portal opening behind him. Unfortunately, there wasn't a damned thing he could do to avoid being sucked into the darkness.

There was a strange rush of air, and something that sounded like the pounding of waves. But oddly, as he was whisked through the portal, the silver that had been scorching his flesh abruptly disappeared.

Was he being thrown straight back into his prison? Or was there some new hell awaiting him?

A second later he landed against a hard marble floor with a heavy thud. At least one rib cracked, and he saw stars as his skull smacked against the marble wall. Indifferent to his injuries, he forced himself to his feet and prepared to attack.

Except…there was no one to attack.

Puzzled, he slowly turned, his gaze skimming over the vast open space that was dotted with fluted columns. On the walls were painted frescos of mer-folk swimming through the ocean in their primitive forms. They looked so real Tarak was convinced he could smell the salty water and tang of seaweed.

Giving a shake of his throbbing head, he tried to concentrate. It looked like he was in some sort of ballroom. He had no idea how he'd gotten there, or what had happened to the soldiers, but he was fairly certain that he was in Riven's hidden lair.

Another trap?

It didn't matter. He wasn't going to question miracles.

Keeping his knife clutched in his hand, Tarak headed toward the large opening at the end of the room. He was expecting a hallway, or even a staircase leading to another level. Instead he stepped onto a wide balcony.

He hesitated, concentrating on leashing his power. He could already feel the life force of several mer-folk pulsing through the air. Plus, a familiar scent was teasing at his nose.

A low growl rumbled in his throat as he cautiously moved forward, peering over the edge of the balcony. Below him was a massive throne room that was filled with more marble, fluted columns, and walls painted in vibrant colors. At the head of the room was a large dais where Riven sat on a throne with a crown planted on his head.

And standing next to him was Waverly with a matching crown on her head.

Riven's consort.

Chapter 5

Waverly stood at rigid attention next to the throne. Anyone who was watching would see a mermaid princess who was calm, cool and collected. It was a façade she'd practiced in the mirror for centuries. Beneath her arrogant composure, however, was a female who seethed with a maelstrom of emotion. Fear. Hate. And a frustration that gnawed at her like a hungry swarm of piranhas.

She desperately wanted to grab the trident that Riven held loosely in his hand and stab it into his back. Unfortunately, the trident wasn't just any weapon. It was the Tryshu, the mystical symbol of authority for mer-folk since the beginning of time. And no one but the true ruler could touch it.

The memory of her father sitting on the throne, his presence not only commanding but a comfort to his people, formed in her mind. Riven was nothing like him, choosing to lead with fear and intimidation.

Pain sliced through her, but Waverly was careful to keep her expression as tranquil as the sea. After five hundred years she'd perfected the ability to contain her heartbreak, although tonight was more difficult than usual.

She was still aggravated by Tarak's refusal to listen to her urgings to return to the vampires and reveal he'd been held captive by the King of the Mer-folk. She needed Riven distracted by fear of the vampires to continue her desperate search for her sister.

Plus, her nerves weren't soothed by Riven's restless annoyance. The king didn't possess her own ability to mask his emotions, and it was obvious he was infuriated.

Waverly tried to tell herself it was a good sign. If Riven was angry, it meant his guards hadn't located Tarak. Still, his prickly mood was affecting everyone crammed into the throne room. The elegantly attired mer-folk sent covert glances toward one another, clearly baffled why they'd been commanded to watch the king stewing on his throne.

Waverly was confused as well.

At first she'd assumed Tarak had been captured and Riven was in the mood to celebrate.

But now...

Waverly abruptly shivered. Was there a chill in the air? Not unusual. The vast underwater castle was a rambling collection of long rooms and intersecting hallways that created unexpected drafts.

This really wasn't a breeze, though. It was more like a...

Vampire.

The word whispered through the back of her mind even as a tingle of awareness warmed her blood. It wasn't just any vampire. It was *her* vampire.

Tarak.

Panic blasted through her. Had Riven managed to capture Tarak after all? Was he even now being hauled to his prison?

No. With a grim effort, Waverly battled through her irrational fears. There was no way Riven would risk his prisoner being seen by one of the mer-folk. It would spark questions the male couldn't possibly answer.

So how had Tarak gotten into the castle? It wasn't like he could stroll up to the front door. The only way to reach this hidden lair was with fey magic, which meant the royal guard had captured him, but before they could lock him in the prison, he'd somehow managed to escape.

Barely daring to breathe, Waverly cast a covert glance at the male seated on the throne. She couldn't deny that Riven was exquisitely handsome with his lean, perfectly chiseled features and deep, startling blue eyes. His brown hair was kept cut short despite the mermaid tradition of long, flowing locks and he'd chosen to grow a goatee that was neatly trimmed. Waverly assumed he'd taken on the appearance of a human while he'd lived among them, and had simply decided he preferred the look.

He did, however, wear the royal armor. Whatever his preference for human styles, he understood that his people demanded a certain amount of tradition.

At the moment, she wasn't interested in anything beyond his brooding expression.

Did he know that Tarak had escaped his guards? Was that why he'd called for this strange gathering? To ensure that none of the mer-folk accidentally stumbled across a vampire?

She gave a small shake of her head. She would worry about those questions later. Right now, nothing mattered but finding Tarak before he was caught. First, however, she had to find a way to leave the throne room without attracting attention.

She was busy pondering the problem when fate stepped in to provide the perfect solution.

With a faint creak one of the heavy double doors was pushed open to reveal a heavily armored guard. Riven glanced toward the intruder with his brows lifting in a silent question. The guard gave a reluctant shake of his head.

Waverly heard Riven release a gurgling growl before he was shoving himself to his feet. The crowd froze, the faint whisper of their silken gowns the only sound as they waited for their king to speak. Waverly watched them with a sense of regret. From the dais they looked like a reef of brilliant coral, but Waverly could see the brittle unease that had become a part of life for the mer-folk.

Riven was a temperamental, unpredictable leader who could lash out without warning. They all felt like they were walking on broken glass and the tension was starting to take its toll.

Ignoring the expectant crowd, Riven slammed the butt of his trident three times on the dais, indicating that the gathering was at an end. Confused, the mer-folk looked toward Waverly. Her father had been the previous king, which meant she carried the title of a princess, but it didn't give her the birthright to rule. Still, her years of assisting her father to care for their people made them depend on her for unspoken comfort.

Which was precisely why Riven insisted that she stand next to his throne. He was convinced her presence offered him legitimacy as the current ruler.

Plus, he wanted to make sure he could keep a close eye on her.

Maintaining her grim composure, she gave the faintest dip of her head. It was enough to send her people surging toward the exits. Without glancing at Riven, Waverly stepped off the dais and melted into the crowd. She wanted to disappear before Riven could command her to stay. Or worse, to lock her in her rooms. A habit he'd started after Tarak had escaped from his prison.

She remained with the others until they were out of the throne room, then, keeping a slow, steady pace, she peeled away to disappear through an arched opening that led to a flight of stairs.

The chill was coming from above her. Thankfully no one else seemed to realize that the drop in temperature was caused by a vampire. But it was just a matter of time.

Once out of sight, she lifted the hem of her flowing gown to keep it from tangling around her bare feet. Then, racing up the marble steps, she'd just managed to reach the upper balcony when a hand reached out to grab her.

There was no opportunity to struggle—or even to scream—as she was hauled into the ballroom and the door was shut.

Struggling to catch her breath, Waverly discovered her back pressed against one of the fluted columns. In front of her was a tall, gorgeous vampire.

Tarak.

Her heart squeezed and then expanded before racing with breathless anticipation. Just as it had done the first time she'd stepped into the prison to discover the vampire she was supposed to feed. At the time, she'd told herself it was terror. Riven had commanded her to enter the prison without concern that the trapped male might rip out her throat.

Thankfully, Tarak had been wary and infuriated at being held prisoner, but he hadn't taken out his anger on her. In fact, he'd shown nothing but gentle care as he'd taken blood from her throat. And despite the endless years he'd been confined, he'd never touched her with anything but tenderness.

Waverly's fear had slowly eased, but her heart continued to skip and flutter whenever she caught sight of this male. More alarming was the knowledge that she could sense him even when she had returned to the castle. As if they were connected on an intimate level.

Now her gaze swept over his strong features with the bold nose and sensuous lips before meeting the dark gaze that smoldered with fury. And something else. Something that echoed deep inside her.

"Ah. Beautiful, Waverly," he whispered in a low, mesmerizing voice as his slender hands skimmed down the side of her body. "You're very much real this time."

Waverly shivered, staring into the male face that haunted her dreams. "What?"

His hands continued to explore her body, his expression brooding. "You're not an illusion."

With an effort, Waverly managed to avoid becoming lost in the delicious sensations that were vibrating through her. She loved when he touched her.

"How did you get here?" she breathed.

His brows drew together. "I'm not sure. I think the gargoyle did something."

"Gargoyle?" She blinked in confusion. Why would a gargoyle interfere? Then she lifted her hand, preparing to create a portal. "Never mind," she muttered. "You have to get out of here."

A low growl rumbled in Tarak's chest, his spicy male scent swirling through the chilled air.

"Not until I've killed Riven." His gaze lifted to the top of her head. "I assume he was the one wearing the matching crown?"

"My father's crown," she instinctively protested.

"Your father is the king?"

"He was until his death nearly six hundred years ago."

"What happened?"

She battled back the jolt of pain, her hand dropping as she clenched her hands. "It doesn't matter now."

Tarak curled his lips to reveal large fangs that were fully extended. "It's my turn to make the rules," he snapped. "Did Riven kill your father?"

She glared at him in frustration. Riven would have his guards searching the castle, and while those who'd offered their loyalty to the new king weren't the best or the brightest of the mer-folk, they would eventually stumble across this ballroom.

"No, my father died of a broken heart."

"Then how did Riven take the throne?"

She met his gaze that held a blatant suspicion. She sensed that he was determined to distrust everything she said. Understandable. As far as he was concerned, she was as responsible as Riven for his confinement.

"He stole it," she forced herself to admit.

Tarak's suspicion only deepened. "How could he steal it?"

Waverly glanced toward the closed door before glaring at the vampire who appeared remarkably indifferent to the fact they might be discovered at any second.

"We don't have time for this," she reminded him. "I have to get you out of here."

There was another flash of fangs. Waverly trembled, but not from fear. Instead, the memory of those fangs sliding deep into her flesh was sending strange tingles through her body. Like brushing up against an electric eel, only a lot more fun.

Sweet, tingly pleasure.

"I've told you. I'm not leaving until Riven is dead." He narrowed his dark eyes. "Now tell me how he stole the throne."

She swallowed her frustration. There was no way to force the stubborn vampire to enter any portal she created. Clearly she would have to somehow convince him to flee.

"What do you know about the history of the mer-folk?" she demanded.

"More than I ever wanted."

His words hit her like a hammer. Why? She might have allowed her stupid emotions to become entangled over the past five centuries she'd visited this male in his prison, but as far as he was concerned, she was nothing more than the enemy.

She paused, forcing herself to take a deep breath before she continued.

"Once upon a time we traveled freely through the oceans as well as walking on land, but several millennia ago we were caught between two warring dragon clans," she told him. Her voice held a small tremble despite the fact she had no memory of the dreadful dragon battles that'd spread molten fire through the oceans. Entire species of fish had been exterminated as well as the rare coral sprites. "My mother was killed along with thousands of other mermaids before my father created this castle." She halted to clear her throat. "We are free to come and go as we please, but most prefer to spend the majority of our lives within these walls."

His gaze lifted to sweep over the elegant ballroom. "Sounds tedious."

Waverly shrugged. "It can be, but it is also secure. Or at least that was my father's intent when he used his magic to create the castle." She tilted her chin, revealing her pride in her father. He had been utterly devoted to the welfare of his people. Even after the tragic death of his mate. "He was determined to protect me and my older sister, Sabrina, along with our people."

His gaze returned to study her upturned face, his expression grim. "What does this have to do with Riven?"

She hid her grimace. If she'd hoped to soften his attitude toward herself and her people, she was failing. Miserably.

"The mer-folk aren't like many other fey creatures," she said. "My father was the king, and I am a princess by birth, but I don't inherit the throne."

A grudging curiosity appeared to seize Tarak. "Because you're a female?" he demanded.

"No, because I wasn't chosen."

"By whom?"

She ignored the tiny voice in the back of her mind that warned she was revealing mer-folk secrets. What choice did she have? "Not whom. By what," she said.

His hands gripped her hips, not hard enough to bruise, but enough to reveal he was close to snapping.

"Get to the point, princess," he rasped.

"The leader of the mer-folk has always been chosen by the Tryshu."

Tarak arched his brows. "What the hell is that?"

"The trident that Riven is carrying."

"A trident chooses your king?"

"Not any trident," she clarified. "The Tryshu."

His grasp on her hips tightened. "Is this a trick?"

She shook her head. There wasn't time to explain how the first of the mer-folk had been lured from their tropical islands by the call of a potent magic. And that when the trident had appeared from the brilliant coral reef, it had transformed them into fey creatures who could alter their shape to swim freely through the oceans.

It had also chosen their first leader.

A tradition that had remained for endless years.

"From the beginning of time only the true leader could wield the Tryshu." She cut to the important part of the long history.

"What if someone else tried to take it?" Tarak demanded.

She shook her head. When she was very young she could remember a mermaid named Cellas, who'd assumed that her father had been weakened after he'd expended so much magic to create the castle. During a feast night she'd made a mad grab for the trident lying next to her father's chair. The sparks that had danced from the weapon had been blinding and the female's scream had given Waverly nightmares for years. Cellas had survived, but she'd never been the same.

"It would be impossible," she assured Tarak.

Tarak made a sound of impatience. "You just claimed that Riven stole the throne."

The chill in the air thickened and Waverly wished she possessed the physical strength to push him away. It was bad enough to be distracted by her acute awareness of his lean, sculpted body that was just brushing against her. She didn't need to worry about frostbite.

Fiercely she attempted to concentrate on her story. The sooner she was finished, the sooner he would hopefully agree to leave this place.

"In the past, the Tryshu would choose a new leader without warning."

"How?"

"I never witnessed the actual event, but I was told that the current leader would suddenly drop the trident to the ground, as if they had been burned, and another would feel compelled to pick up the weapon." She repeated the words that had been told to her. "It usually happened because the ruler had become weakened, or because the needs of our people had changed. My father remained a king for far longer than most. And even after his death, the Tryshu remained dormant." Her lips twisted into a bitter smile. At the time, she'd thought nothing could be worse than having the throne remain empty. Then Riven had appeared and she'd quickly learned there was at least one thing worse. "We feared that it might have lost its magic with the passing of my father."

His fingers eased their grip on her hips, sliding up to her waist in a soothing caress. Did he sense her grief when she talked about her father? Or had he momentarily forgotten that he hated her?

"What happened?"

"Riven returned. He'd been living among the humans for nearly a century, but one day he appeared at the castle and grabbed the Tryshu." Waverly grimaced. She'd been in shock when she'd watch Riven stride into the throne room and grab the trident. "By the evening he was forcing all of us to bow at his feet."

His lips gave the faintest twitch at the resentment she couldn't hide. She'd never bowed to anyone, let alone gone on her knees for a male she was certain had somehow cheated to earn his place on the throne.

"Which means he's the king," Tarak said.

"I couldn't believe it. Riven has always been..."

"A cowardly bastard?" He offered when her words trailed away.

"Yes," she quickly agreed. Cowardly bastard was the perfect description for Riven. "He has no morals, no decency, and no concern for the mer-folk. When he first left I assumed he would live out his existence among the humans where he could cheat and swindle to his heart's content." She released a short, humorless burst of laughter. "I wish to the goddess he'd stayed up there."

"A king doesn't always have to possess morals." Ice suddenly coated the column behind Waverly as if Tarak was suddenly reminded of the Anasso who'd betrayed him. "Or even to care for his people. Trust me, I learned the hard way."

Waverly resisted the urge to lay her hands against his chest. Tarak didn't want comfort. Not from her.

"I might have eventually accepted his place as king. I could, after all, leave the castle and create a lair far from here. But..." The words died on her lips, the fear that lay over her like a shadow threatening to overwhelm her.

Tarak frowned, studying her face with a searching gaze. "Tell me."

She lowered her voice, barely speaking above a whisper. "Shortly after he returned he came to my private rooms."

"Did he want you as his consort?"

Waverly widened her eyes. She was as startled by the question as she was by his harsh tone.

"Hardly. Riven is too conceited to share his throne with anyone," she told him.

There was a strange emotion that flared through his dark eyes, but it was there and gone so quickly it was impossible to decipher.

"Then why did he seek you out?" Tarak demanded.

"To blackmail me," she whispered.

"What?" Tarak jerked in surprise. Then, slowly, his gaze lowered to her throat. "The bastard forced you to feed me." The words were a statement, not a question.

She gave a small nod. "Yes."

"Why?"

"I don't know." There was another blast of ice and a violent shiver raced through Waverly. "I truly don't," she insisted, wondering if her lips were turning blue. "But I suspect that he's found some sort of magic that allows him to draw power from you."

Tarak's gaze never wavered from her face, but he thankfully dialed back on the ice. She hoped she would be able to feel her toes again.

"Enough power to claim the Tryshu?" he demanded.

"That's my only explanation of why he would hold you captive."

He gave a slow nod, his expression distracted as he considered her explanation. "It makes sense. It would also explain why he sent his guards to capture me, instead of wanting me dead." There was a short pause before he spoke again. "How did he blackmail you?"

Waverly cast a quick glance toward the door, still terrified that Riven might overhear her revealing the secrets he'd forced her to keep.

"He's holding my older sister captive."

"Captive?" He looked surprised by her explanation. "Where?"

Waverly clenched her teeth. She'd spent five hundred years in a futile quest to locate her sister.

"I can't find her. I've searched everywhere," she told him.

"Maybe he took her away from the castle."

Waverly gave an emphatic shake of her head. "No, she's in the castle."

"How can you be sure?" he demanded.

"Her magic protects the nursery," she told him, not revealing that mermaids laid eggs that had to be carefully wrapped in a protective spell that allowed them to incubate in a reservoir filled with warm ocean water. Fewer than two or three children were born in a century, making them utterly precious. They were all relieved that her older sister, Sabrina, had revealed her talent in creating the spells necessary to protect the eggs at an early age, since the previous caretaker had died during the dragon battles. "If she was gone…or dead, the children would start to fade."

Tarak appeared genuinely shocked by her words. "He would destroy children?"

Waverly made a sound of deep disgust. "As I said. He has no morals."

"This castle can't be that large," he abruptly pointed out. "How can he keep your sister hidden?"

"I'm assuming he's wrapped the prison in the same illusion that he used for yours," Waverly said. "And created the entrance somewhere outside the castle."

Tarak frowned, his lips parting to ask more questions. But before he could speak, Waverly was reaching up to press her fingers against his mouth.

"Tarak. The guards are coming," she whispered, catching the metallic scent of the rare armor that was given to the guards. "You have to leave."

Tarak tilted back his head, as if using his powers to determine how much time they had before the guards arrived in the ballroom.

Finally, he glanced down at her. "Where are your rooms?"

"I..." She snapped her lips together at his grim expression. He wasn't going to leave. All she could do was hope they could sneak through the back corridors without getting caught. Pressing him away, Waverly turned to hurry toward the side of the ballroom. Her father had created a secret door for those times he wanted to disappear from a celebration without attracting attention. "This way," she commanded.

Chapter 6

Riven paced the floor of his private suite. He'd claimed the royal chambers as his own, of course. He'd always known that he was destined to become a ruler. In fact, he'd wasted centuries waiting for the Tryshu to choose him. But as year after year had passed and the old, increasingly feeble king had maintained his death grip on the throne, Riven had at last decided that it was time to give fate a push.

Leaving the underwater lair, Riven had traveled the world, searching for a means to take his rightful place as king. It had taken far longer than he'd expected, but at last he'd discovered an amulet that offered the means of claiming Tryshu.

Still, it had taken several more decades before he could convince the Anasso to give him a vampire that he needed. It wasn't like he could use another creature. The amulet only worked on the dead.

Thank the goddess that the service he'd performed for the Anasso had finally paid off. Five centuries ago the ancient vampire had contacted him to say he had a clansman he was willing to sacrifice.

After that, everything had gone as planned.

He'd found the witches necessary to create the prison to hold the vampire, as well as Sabrina, although they had no idea he'd included her in the spell. And as an added benefit, an unexpected creature had quite literally showed up on his doorstep. The mongrel ogress, Inga, had the power to create a key that would open the prison. That stroke of luck meant he could feed the vampire, keeping his strength at a peak level.

But now...

Reaching up, he snatched the crown off his head and launched it across the vast room. It smashed into a delicate mirror with a satisfying crash.

He'd been so eager to put the damned thing on his head. Now if felt as if it weighed a thousand pounds.

And it was all that witch's fault. She'd opened the door to the vampire's prison, somehow avoiding the curse he'd placed on her. He fully intended to punish her for her audacity, but first he had to deal with the colossal disaster that was threatening to destroy him.

Grimly managing to regain command of his composure, Riven smoothed his hands down his elegant satin robes before turning to glare at the guard who was standing next to the double golden doors.

"Let me see if I understand, Rimm," Riven drawled. "I gave you the task of capturing one prisoner."

"A vampire," Rimm said, his tone edged with a disdain that had been increasing evident.

The male had pledged his loyalty to Riven after he'd taken the throne, but while he offered a steadfast loyalty on the surface, Riven sensed he wasn't impressed with his new king.

There was nothing obvious. Rimm was too well-trained as a soldier. Just a vague hint that the male was growing more discontent with every passing day. Whether with the soldiers Riven had chosen to become his royal guard, or with Riven himself, he didn't know.

Whatever it was, Riven wasn't happy about it. Despite the fact that it had been five centuries since he'd proven his destiny by gaining command of the Tryshu, there were too many mer-folk who still mourned the previous king.

"Excuse me?"

The guard's jaw clenched. "Nothing."

Riven took a step forward. "There were four of you. And yet you failed."

"We had him captured."

Riven slammed the butt of the trident on the marble floor. A low thud echoed through the air.

"If that was true, the vampire would be in his prison, wouldn't he?"

Rimm squared his shoulders as if preparing for a blow. Smart male. Riven was ready and eager to kill something.

"As I said, we were interrupted," he insisted.

Riven snorted. "By a magical gargoyle who was with the ogress?"

"Yes."

It'd been sheer impulse for Riven to command his guards to keep an eye out for the ogress while they hunted down the vampire. Inga was supposed to control the witch. Something she'd clearly failed to do. He couldn't allow her to go rogue, running around and potentially revealing his secrets.

She needed to die.

But first…

He had to get his hands on the vampire.

"Was there also a unicorn?" he sneered.

"The gargoyle's spell disrupted the portal," the guard insisted. "There is no way to know where the vampire ended up."

Riven narrowed his gaze. *Idiot.* "Where did you end up?"

"Here."

"And it didn't occur to you the vampire would be here as well?"

Rimm flattened his lips, as if suppressing his urge to share his opinion of being commanded to chase down a vampire with no idea why.

"I suppose it's possible," he finally muttered.

"It's more than possible, you bottom-feeder," Riven snapped. "Gather every guard and search the castle from top to bottom."

A flush stained the guard's face at Riven's insult, but once again his training forced him to remain obedient.

"Yes, my lord." He gave a stiff bow.

Riven waited for him to straighten. "Rimm."

"Yes?"

"Find him or I'll find a new captain of my royal guard."

It might not have been much of a threat if Rimm could simply walk away from his position. But captains didn't retire. They held too many secrets. The only way out was death.

Rimm's expression hardened with determination. "I'll find him."

* * * *

Inga was floating in a sea of peaceful darkness. It was wonderful. In fact, she wanted to stay there. At least for a century or two.

Unfortunately, the peace was destroyed when a sharp blow struck her cheek. Inga tried to ignore the slap. It wasn't truly painful. More of an annoyance. But it kept repeating over and over. Along with an urgent voice that was whispering in her ear.

"Wake up. Wake up."

She wrenched her eyes open and lifted her arm in time to grasp the small hand that was about to deliver another blow.

"Stop."

A familiar, lumpy face hovered over her. "Are you awake?"

She scowled, forcing herself to a sitting position. "My eyes are open, aren't they?"

Levet took a reluctant step back, as if he was considering whether or not she needed another slap.

She didn't.

"*Oui*, but my Aunt Bertha often slept with her eyes open," he told her. "She claimed it gave her a tactical advantage, but I suspect they were glued open because she forgot to scrape the moss from her face."

Inga snorted, beginning to suspect the gargoyle was making up the mythical relative.

"Your Aunt Bertha sounds like a fascinating female," she muttered, managing to shove herself to her feet.

"She is." Levet blinked with an innocence she didn't fully trust. "Indeed, she is the only one in my family that I actually miss. Perhaps one day I shall take you to Paris and introduce you."

Inga gave a shake of her head, then promptly groaned as pain shot through her skull. Right now she didn't have time to waste on Aunt Bertha, or even the stupid pang of regret at the knowledge she would never be traveling to Paris with the tiny demon.

"What happened?" she demanded, her thoughts still fuzzy.

Levet flapped his wings. "I was attempting to save you when that stupid creature opened a portal."

The memory of standing next to the bog as the vampire was surrounded by armored males suddenly seared through Inga. Taking care not to jiggle her aching brain, she glanced around, discovering they were standing in a barren room with stone walls and floor. There was an unmistakable scent of salt, as well as something that might have been seaweed.

"Oh no," she breathed.

"Were they mermen?" Levet demanded.

"Yes."

Levet released a sigh of wonderment. "Are we in the secret mer-lair?"

Inga glanced at him in confusion. "Mer-lair?"

"You know." Levet gave a wave of his hands. "Like a bat-cave."

"Oh. I suppose you could call it that." Inga shrugged, concentrating on creating a portal. "We have to get out of here."

Levet thrust out his lower lip, looking sulky as she lifted her hand. "We just arrived. We should look around before we leave."

Look around? Inga shuddered at the mere thought. The last time she'd been in the castle she'd barely stepped over the threshold before the king had her cornered in his private chambers, telling her that her mother had been the one to sell her to the slave traders. And to make sure there was plenty of salt in the wound, he'd added the fact that she was a ghastly blemish on the mer-folk.

The less time she spent in this awful place, the better.

"Do you want to be skewered by a trident?" she asked her companion.

"*Non*, but—"

Inga interrupted Levet's protest, her brow furrowing in confusion. "I can't open a portal here." Her gaze returned to the barren walls. Last time she'd been here there had been an explosion of fancy-ass decorations everywhere. "Maybe we're in the basement?" she murmured, speaking more to herself.

"Are there kitchens down here?" Levet demanded, patting his round belly. "I could use a snack."

Inga rolled her eyes. "You could always use a snack. And I doubt there is anything down here except the dungeons."

Inga had been joking. She had no idea if there were any dungeons in the castle, but without warning Levet touched a claw to his forehead, his thick brow furrowed.

"Dungeons? That reminds me of something. Hmm. What is it?"

Cursing at her stupidity, Inga pivoted on her heel and marched toward a nearby opening. The gargoyle's mind hadn't been as easy to wipe as most creatures and now her mention of dungeons had clearly touched one of the memories she'd tried to suppress. She had to get them out of there before he managed to completely recall what she'd done to him.

They left the room, moving down a wide hallway in silence. There had to be a staircase somewhere, right?

Intent on her search for an exit, as well as ensuring that there weren't any mer-folk in the area, it took Inga a minute to realize that Levet was no longer behind her. Forcing herself to stop, she turned to discover him standing in the center of the hallway with his head tilted back.

She gave an impatient wave of her hand. "Come on."

"Wait," he whispered, sniffing the air.

"We can eat when we get out of here," Inga chided.

"It's not that," he told her. "I smell something."

Inga was on instant alert. The gargoyle was small, but she'd never encountered another demon with such acute senses.

"What is it?" she asked.

"It's salty," Levet promptly answered.

Inga flexed her large hands. She wasn't going down without a fight. Not this time. "A merman?"

"A mermaid," Levet corrected, sucking in a deep breath. "And the same soft breeze."

Inga was baffled. The air felt stuffy to her. Was there a tunnel hidden behind an illusion nearby?

"Breeze?" she demanded. "You feel a breeze?"

Levet shook his head. "I smell a breeze blowing over the ocean," he said, pointing a claw in her direction. "A scent like yours."

He thought she smelled like an ocean breeze? Melty sensation poured through Inga before she was forcing herself to sniff as if she didn't care. "There's no one like me."

"That is true," Levet agreed, sending her a smile. "You are unique. As I am."

Inga released a sharp crack of laughter. "I suppose that's one way of looking at it."

Levet spread his wings, as if he was offering her an opportunity to admire them.

"It is the only way," he assured her.

A nice thought, but Inga was well aware that anything different, even among demons, was despised by others. She hunched her shoulders at the age-old sorrow that was buried in the center of her chest.

"We need to go," she said in gruff tones.

Levet looked surprised. "Should we not see who is down here?"

"Absolutely not."

"What if they are being held captive?"

"I don't care," Inga snapped. And she didn't. "The mer-folk detest me."

Levet studied her with curiosity. "Why would they detest you?"

She forced back her angry words. Levet wasn't trying to be a jackass. He simply didn't react like other demons. It was both a part of his charm and the reason she occasionally wanted to choke him.

"I'm a reminder of the violence that was inflicted on one of their most vulnerable females," she reminded him.

"You didn't inflict any violence."

"They still blame me," Inga insisted.

Levet scowled, appearing outraged by her words. "Then they are stupid."

A tiny part of her bitterness eased. In the demon world it wasn't unusual to blame the child for the sins of the father. Or the mother. She allowed herself to savor the knowledge that at least one creature didn't assume she was a blight on her people.

"I agree," she said, her hand reaching to grab the gargoyle. She didn't want to drag him down the hallway, but they had to go.

At the same time, however, a soft, lilting voice whispered through the air. "Is there someone there? Can you hear me?"

Levet evaded her hand, moving to lay his palm against the wall. "That's the female I smell," he said in distracted tones.

"All the more reason to get the hell out of here."

"Impossible." Levet folded his arms over his chest. "I'm a KISA."

Inga made a sound of impatience. The tiny demon had an obsession about his supposed role as a Knight in Shining Armor.

"So?"

"So, it is against my code of honor to ignore a damsel in distress."

Inga planted her hands on her hips. "Have you considered the fact that this might be a trap?"

Levet sucked in a shocked breath. "You would not wish me to stain my honor, would you?"

Inga ground her teeth. She could toss the gargoyle over her shoulder and force him to come with her. Or hell, just leave him.

Instead she heaved a harsh sigh of resignation. "Fine, but your stupid damsel in distress better not get us both killed."

Chapter 7

Tarak allowed Waverly to lead him through the castle to a vast suite that was on the top floor.

It was as lavish as he'd expected. Lots of marble on the floor as well as the fluted columns that seemed to sprout everywhere. The walls were covered by vivid paintings of tropical fish and coral reefs, and overhead was a large chandelier that spilled out a soft light. They stopped in what looked like a formal sitting room with puffy couches and chairs that were upholstered with a pale green silk, and exquisite figurines crafted out of gold and studded with precious gems.

His lips twitched. "Nothing but the best for the princess," he muttered.

She halted in the center of the room, her expression defensive. "All the rooms in the castle are…"

"Straight out of Disney?" he supplied when her words faded away. He shrugged when she sent him a startled frown at his pop culture reference. "I've had a lot of time to watch television."

She bit her lower lip, guilt rippling over her expressive face. "I'm sorry."

Tarak stepped forward. He told himself that he wanted to intimidate her. After all, he towered over her by at least six inches. But he couldn't fool himself. It wasn't the desire for a technical advantage that made him halt less than an inch from her warm, delectable body.

It was just plain desire.

"Are you sorry?" he demanded in a husky voice.

Her eyes shimmered like aquamarines as she tilted back her head to gaze up at him. "Of course. I had no wish to hurt you."

The sincerity in her voice flowed through him with a lethal ease. Like a sweet poison that destroyed without warning.

He'd tried so hard to hate this female. Even when he'd held her in his arms and drank deeply from her throat. She was the enemy.

But even now his hand reached out so he could lightly run his fingertips down the curve of her cheek.

"Why didn't you tell me the truth?" he demanded.

"I was afraid of what Riven would do," she insisted. "Our children are rare and precious gifts. I couldn't risk endangering them. And my sister. She's all the family I have left."

He glared down at her. She looked so fragile even as she tilted her chin. Was it a silent threat that she had a stubborn streak beneath that air of delicacy?

If so, he didn't need the warning.

"You should have trusted me," he insisted.

She met him glare for glare. "Do you trust me?"

He flattened his lips. Did she really think they could compare their situations?

"I didn't hold you prisoner for..." He hesitated, fury blasting through him as he realized he didn't even know how long he'd been held captive. "How many years, Waverly?"

She flinched, but she was smart enough to answer the question. "Five hundred."

"Shit." Tarak was vaguely aware that he was coating the room with ice and that he'd toppled over several figurines.

He didn't care. He'd known that it'd been more than a couple centuries since he'd been captured. The changing human technology that Waverly had managed to sneak into his prison had been proof of that. But five?

"I've said that I'm sorry." She shivered, her breath coming out in frigid puffs. "I did what I could to ease your imprisonment."

Tarak leashed his power, allowing the ice to melt, although his anger remained.

"You offered me books and the ability to view a television that offered a glimpse at the human world. Was that supposed to be enough?"

"They kept you sane," she rasped. "And I risked everything by coming to see you far more than I should have."

His fingers skimmed down the obstinate line of her jaw. "What are you talking about?"

"Riven commanded that I feed you once a century to make sure you keep your strength, but I would sneak into your prison as often as possible."

Tarak swallowed his protest. It had felt like endless stretches of time between her visits. That wasn't something he wanted to admit. Not to her.

"Why would you come more than you had to?" he demanded.

"I didn't want you to suffer."

Tarak curled his lips in a humorless smile. Was she hoping to stir his sympathy? Good luck with that. He'd been betrayed and brutalized by his king, and then imprisoned for five centuries. Any sympathy was long gone. Then he caught sight of the warm flush that crawled beneath her skin.

"Hmm." His fingers strayed down to press against the pulse that hammered at the base of her throat. "Do you know what I think?"

The scent of passion fruit swirled through the air. "What?"

Tarak's fangs lengthened, his body reacting to her sweet scent. His gaze lowered to the soft curve of her lips.

"I think you enjoyed feeding me," he murmured in soft tones.

She shivered, but this time Tarak suspected that it wasn't from the chill. "I suspected you were arrogant. Now I know for sure."

He chuckled, momentarily forgetting his relentless thirst for revenge. Right now, he was engrossed in the feel of this female.

"I'm a vampire."

Her eyes darkened, her lips parting as she released her breath on a soft sigh. "I'm aware of that."

Tarak's fangs throbbed, hunger thundering through him. He'd ached for Waverly since the night she'd entered his prison, but he'd never been so close to losing his tight restraint.

"Are you also aware that I can taste your desire as your blood flows through my body?" he demanded, his voice husky as he lowered his head to scrape the tip of one fang along the side of her neck. "And smell it on your skin?" He pressed his lips against her warm, slightly salty skin. "Feel it beneath my fingertips?"

She lifted her hands to press them against his chest. "Tarak."

He nuzzled kisses along the plunging neckline of the elegant gown, the hunger continuing to crash through him. Like a wrecking ball that was destroying his carefully assembled defenses. This wasn't supposed to be happening, but he couldn't stop himself.

"Your heart is racing." His hands gripped the soft swell of her hips, the urge to sink his fangs into the tender flesh almost overwhelming. "Sweet passion fruit."

She grasped his upper arms in a tight grip, as if her knees were threatening to buckle.

"Tarak, we don't have time for this," she breathed.

He barely heard her. He was bombarded by the endless memories of how he'd held her in his arms while her blood filled his senses, and how he'd stored away the feel and scent of her to stave off the madness.

She was right. She had kept him sane.

His hands slid to her lower back, pressing her against his hardening body as he lifted his head to gaze down at her flushed face.

"Do you know how tempted I was to indulge in your unspoken temptation?"

A vulnerable uncertainty flared through her eyes, as if his words had touched something deep inside her.

"Why didn't you?"

"To punish you." He paused before reluctantly confessing the truth. "And myself."

She studied him with a confused expression. "I get wanting to punish me. But why yourself?"

"For not believing Chiron," he said, the bitter regret he'd lived with for five centuries spilling through him like poison.

It took her a second to place the name. "Your clansman?"

Tarak grimaced. He could still recall the night he'd entered the cave to discover Chiron. The younger male had been newly turned into a vampire and was more like a feral animal than a lethal predator, barely surviving on gut instinct. Managing to overpower the male, Tarak had taken him into his clan, teaching him how to blend into the world that was increasingly populated with humans.

Eventually he'd brought him to the Anasso, and they'd worked together in an effort to unite the vampires. He'd had such high hopes for the future. At least until Chiron had come to him with the warning that the Anasso was addicted to tainted blood.

"He was more than a clansman," he said. "He was like my son, although I didn't personally sire him. He was the most loyal male I'd ever met."

"Then why didn't you believe him?"

Tarak flinched. The question felt like a whip slicing through his flesh.

"Because I didn't want to accept that the centuries I'd devoted to the Anasso were nothing but a waste," he said, not adding that he'd taken personal glory in his position as the Anasso's most trusted clansman. What male wanted to admit it was his own pride that had led to his downfall? "It was easier to pretend I couldn't see the hints that warned me of the inevitable destruction of the male I had so deeply respected."

Sympathy darkened her beautiful eyes. "And then he betrayed you?"

"Along with your king," he reminded her in accusing tones.

Her brows snapped together. "He isn't my king. He's a traitor who stole the throne."

Tarak's fingers skimmed over her hips, his head slowly lowering. He told himself he was simply manipulating her. Why not use her desire to convince her to help him? Far easier than trying to force her.

Of course, that didn't explain why his cock was hard and aching, and why his fangs were eager to sink deep into her flesh.

"Then you'll help me," he murmured, brushing his mouth over her parted lips.

She arched against him. "What?"

He allowed his fangs to press against her lower lip. "After I kill Riven, I'll need a portal to return to my home."

Without warning she was jerking away from him, her breath a loud rasp. "No."

Tarak clenched his hands, hurt by her abrupt retreat. Then angered by the fact he was hurt.

Yeah, she had him spinning in circles.

"That wasn't a request," he snapped.

She recoiled, but she stubbornly refused to back down. "Riven can't die until we've found my sister." She held his gaze. "Besides, you can't kill him."

He stepped forward, grasping her by her upper arms. "Watch me."

"No." She laid her hands against his chest, her expression pleading. "It's impossible. He's protected by impregnable magic."

"No magic is impregnable," he snapped.

She made a sound of exasperation. "The only way to kill him is if the Tryshu rejects him as the leader. That's why we've never had to worry about our leader being overthrown by force. It simply can't happen."

He glared down at her, searching for some hint that she was lying. "I don't believe you."

Without warning, she grabbed his hand and pressed it against the center of her chest.

"I'm telling you the truth," she rasped. "You have to trust me."

The sensations jolting through Tarak had nothing to do with trust and everything to do with raw passion.

Allowing his hand to slide down and cup one soft breast, he claimed her mouth in a kiss of sheer possession.

Mine, a voice whispered. A voice that sounded remarkably like his own.

Chapter 8

Waverly parted her lips, trembling at the feel of Tarak's body pressed tightly against her. His muscles were as hard and smooth as steel. She desperately wanted to strip away his clothes and run her fingers over every chiseled inch of him.

With an effort she managed to avoid the urge to melt beneath the gooey pleasure that flowed through her veins.

Tarak was well aware that she couldn't resist his seduction. She'd spent centuries offering her vein. She'd be an idiot not to realize he was using her need for him as a weapon.

Easily sensing her attempts to remain impervious to his potent touch, Tarak nuzzled his lips over her cheek to whisper in her ear. "I think we already established that I have no reason to trust you."

She pressed her hands against his chest, arching away from his destructive lips. How could any female think clearly when he was brushing soft kisses over her skin?

"I thought vampires had the ability to know whether or not a person was lying," she muttered.

He gazed down at her, his expression brooding. He clearly was annoyed that she simply didn't agree to whatever he wanted.

"It's a skill some of my brothers possess," he told her.

Her curiosity was instantly stirred. "So what is your skill?"

"This."

She wasn't sure what she'd expected, but it wasn't the sensation of being gently lifted off the ground. Tarak wasn't touching her. It was his power alone that was allowing her to float just above the floor.

Her lips parted, wonderment warming her heart.

Not for the first time she marveled why people assumed that vampires didn't have any magic. Tarak had been weaving his bewitchment around her for five hundred years.

"That's amazing," she breathed as he slowly lowered her back to the ground.

His brows snapped together as if he was determined not to appreciate her admiration. Who could blame him? Still she had to find some way to convince him there was no way to destroy Riven. Only then would he leave and...

She winced before she forced herself to complete the thought.

He would return to his people and find his true mate. There. That's what she wanted for him, even if the thought ripped her in two.

Tarak took a step back, his expression hardening with determination.

"Tell me about Riven," he abruptly commanded.

"I did," she reminded him.

He gave a sharp shake of his head. "You told me how he captured the throne. Now I need to understand how and why he's stealing my power."

"Oh." She gave a confused shrug. "I assumed that there was something in the prison that allowed him to use your essence to fuel his magic."

Tarak grimaced. "No, I can still feel him pulling on my energy."

Waverly wrinkled her brow as she considered the various options. In the beginning she'd devoted hours to study in the massive library, researching how it might be possible for Riven to use the vampire's power to control the Tryshu. She'd found nothing of use, and eventually conceded she would never discover the truth. "He used witches to create your prison. It's possible they also gave him the means to draw on your energy. Or maybe it was the ogress."

"Half-ogress," he said in a distracted tone.

"What are you talking about?"

"She's a mongrel. She has ogre blood, along with mermaid."

Waverly felt a stab of surprise. She barely taken notice of the ogress or the young witch when she'd traveled to the opening of the prison. She'd been too focused on her upcoming visits with Tarak.

"How odd." Waverly furrowed her brow, recalling how the large female would scurry into one of the tunnels when she entered the caverns. "I wonder why she was so eager to avoid me?"

Tarak ignored her question, clearly not interested in the ogress. "Does Riven ever leave the castle?"

"Not since he took the throne."

"You're sure?"

"Yes." She gave a firm nod. "There's a…" She paused to come up with a way to describe the strange magic that flowed from the weapon. "Vibration when the Tryshu is in the castle," she finally said. "Like a low-level hum." Tarak narrowed his eyes. "He could have left the weapon behind if he wanted to sneak away without being noticed."

"Riven hasn't released his clutch on the Tryshu since he first picked it up. I'm pretty sure he sleeps with the thing." Her voice was thick with disgust. She couldn't count how many times she'd caught sight of Riven standing in front of one of the numerous mirrors with the castle, admiring himself with his crown on his head and the trident held high. She'd wanted to punch him in his smug face. "Besides, he's obsessed with wallowing in his own glory," she continued. "While he's in this castle he can command his people to worship him. Once he leaves here, he no longer has any control."

Tarak's frustration was palpable in the air. Quite literally. The ice droplets floated around her head even as two of her figurines were whisked off a nearby table to crash into the marble floor. Thankfully, none of them shattered.

"Then the artifact that he's using must be here," he rasped. "Does he wear an amulet?"

She furrowed her brow, trying to recall if she'd ever seen Riven wearing a medallion or pendant.

"I suppose he could have one hidden beneath his armor," she suggested, only to catch her breath as she was struck by a sudden thought. "No. Wait."

"What?"

"I remember when Riven insisted that he be given my father's rooms."

He arched his brows. "Did you expect anything else?"

Her lips twisted into a pained smile. "No. I knew he'd insist on the royal chambers. He's an arrogant jerk," she assured him. "But after he moved into the suite he refused to allow anyone to enter. Not even his own guards."

An odd expression rippled over his barbarian features. "What about his lovers?"

"No one," she insisted.

It had been a dramatic change from the past. Her father had often hosted small gatherings in the royal chambers. It was a treat meant to celebrate matings or births or special holidays.

"Did he say why?" Tarak demanded.

"I asked him shortly after he took the throne and he claimed that he collected rare weapons during his travels and he feared a stray guest might hurt themselves." She rolled her eyes. "Like he ever cared about anyone except himself."

"You never questioned what he was hiding?"

She frowned. Did he think she had nothing else to do? "I was too busy trying to locate my sister. The fate of our children remains at risk as long as Riven holds her captive."

Tarak stilled, as if he actually regretted his sharp words. Then he gave a sharp shake of his head. "We need to get into the royal chambers."

"We can't," she instantly protested.

His hands moved to cup her face, his dark eyes glowing in the candlelight. "You need to stop saying that, princess," he warned.

"It's too dangerous, Tarak. I—" Her words broke off at the distant sound of boots stomping against the marble hallway. Her eyes widened. "Guards."

He glanced toward the door, his lips parting to reveal the long, lethal curve of his fangs. "Is Riven with them?"

She sucked in a deep breath, catching the pungent scent of seaweed. "Yes." The word barely left her lips when Tarak was charging toward the door. "Good."

Waverly cursed as she leaped forward to grab his arm. "Tarak, what are you doing?"

"I'm going to destroy the guards and then—"

"Stop," she interrupted, continuing to tug at his arm. "I won't let you do this."

Without warning he halted, glaring down at her. "Are you choosing sides, Waverly?"

Waverly shivered. His voice was coated in ice.

"Think," she urged.

"I don't want to think. I want to kill."

She met his glare with one of her own. "You can't kill Riven," she reminded him in fierce tones. "Not as long as he's in control of the Tryshu."

Several more figurines flew off a nearby table. "I'm not going back to that prison."

Waverly briefly considered the desperate ploy of creating a portal and pushing the vampire inside. If he wouldn't protect himself, she would. Then she gave a shake of her head. There was no way she could overpower a vampire, let alone a clan chief. Even if he was constantly being drained by Riven.

Time for Plan B.

"Come with me," she commanded, hurrying across the floor to push open a door on the far side of the room.

He grudgingly followed behind her, stepping into the connected room. His brows arched as he glanced around at the explosion of vivid colors.

Bright blues, vibrant yellows and deep reds. It made her feel as if she was sleeping among a coral reef. In the center of the floor was a large bed that had been carved out of obsidian and studded with opals.

His eyes darkened before his lips twisted in a strange smile. "I don't think now is the time to satisfy your desire for me, princess."

She hunched her shoulders, stupidly hurt by his mocking words.

"I should turn you over to Riven," she muttered, moving toward a floor-to-ceiling window that offered a stunning view of the ocean that surrounded them.

"What are you doing?" Tarak demanded as she bent down to touch the floor just below the window.

There was a whispered 'whoosh' as a section of the marble disappeared to reveal a narrow hole that was built beneath the floor.

"When my father created the castle, he provided a secret space for me and Sabrina in case we were ever invaded."

Tarak moved to cautiously peer into the darkness. "Wouldn't Riven know about it?"

She shook her head. "No, Father had died before Riven became king, so he never passed along any secrets, and I certainly never told him."

Tarak turned his head to meet her anxious glance. "You want me to hide?"

"Just until I can get rid of Riven."

He stepped back, folding his arms over his chest. "No. I'm not a roach who scurries into the gutters when my enemy appears."

Frustration along with a swelling fear combusted inside Waverly. Damn the vampire and his pride. It was going to get them both thrown in the dungeons.

She planted her hands on her hips, using the only weapon she possessed to force him to act like a rational demon.

"Do you want to kill Riven or not?" she demanded.

His brows snapped together. "Of course I do."

"Then you have to survive long enough for me to figure out how to get the Tryshu from him, right?"

His hands clenched, his power wrapping around her. "Don't betray me, Waverly."

She held his gaze as he forced himself to drop into the hole. Bending down, she closed the panel with a pang of regret. This was the only way she knew how to protect Tarak. At least as long as he refused to leave the castle. But she abruptly understood that it was more than just his ego that made him reluctant to enter the secret room. He'd been locked in his prison for five hundred years.

The cramped space was no doubt triggering a sense of claustrophobia. With a grimace, she rose to her feet and hurried toward the opening that led to the bathroom. Right now nothing mattered but ensuring that Riven couldn't find Tarak.

Rushing to the large, shallow pool in the center of the mosaic-tiled floor, she turned the faucets on full blast. Then she grabbed a bottle of her favorite bubble bath and dumped it into the swirling water.

The room where Tarak was hidden had been magically enhanced to hide his scent, but she needed to make sure that any lingering hint of his presence in her room was eliminated.

Fast.

The soft aroma of lavender floated through the air just as there was a sharp knock on her door. Waverly paused to steady her racing pulse before she forced herself to walk back through her suite at a slow, leisurely pace.

There were several more knocks on her door before she finally pulled it open to glare with annoyance at the males standing in the hallway.

Riven and his shoal of goons.

They were all wearing their specialized armor and Riven had the Tryshu tightly clutched in his hand. But oddly, his crown was missing.

"What do you want?" she demanded.

Riven leaned forward, sniffing the air. "Are you alone?"

She sent him an outraged frown. "Of course I'm alone. I was just about to enjoy a hot bath."

Riven narrowed his eyes. "It will have to wait."

"Why?" She forced a stiff smile to her lips. "Are you calling yet another gathering?"

Riven gave a wave of his hand, his gaze never wavering from her face. "Leave us."

The warriors didn't hesitate to scurry down the hallway. Waverly suspected they inwardly hated Riven as much as she did, but they were willing to abandon their principles for the opportunity to be promoted to the royal guard.

"Must we do this now?" she demanded. "My bath—"

Riven abruptly shoved his way past her. "Where's the vampire?"

Waverly stiffened, not having to pretend her indignation at his intrusion into her private rooms.

"Excuse me?"

Riven scanned her sitting room, his eyes narrowed as he slowly turned to face her.

"The vampire," he repeated. "Where is he?"

"How would I know?" She conjured an expression of confusion. "You told me he escaped."

"Yes, he did." Riven stepped forward, grabbing her chin in a brutal grip. "And if I suspected for a second you were involved I would kill you."

Waverly's breath hissed through her teeth as pain shot through her. He was close to breaking her jaw. "I wasn't. I swear," she rasped. "I had no idea he wasn't in his prison until you told me."

Her words were all perfectly true, giving them the sincerity she needed to convince Riven she had nothing to do with Tarak's escape.

"And now?" he demanded.

She licked her lips. "Now?"

"Has he tried to contact you?"

Waverly was careful to avoid telling a direct lie. "Why would he?"

Riven hesitated. Was he considering how much to give away about Tarak's escape?

"There's a chance the vampire managed to enter the castle," he finally admitted.

She widened her eyes. "That's impossible. Unless you're claiming that one of our people brought him here?"

He released his hold on her chin, as if satisfied that she had nothing to do with Tarak.

"If he is in the castle, there's every possibility that he will seek you out," Riven said.

Waverly resisted the urge to reach up and touch her bruised chin. She had her own share of pride. She'd be damned if she'd let Riven see how much he'd hurt her.

Instead she continued with her pretense of bafflement. "Why would he seek me out?"

"Ah, sweet Waverly." He reached out again, but this time his fingers merely stroked down her cheek before his hand dropped. "I can smell him on your skin. As if he has been imprinted on you. The two of you have bonded."

She flushed despite her best efforts. He knew that she was besotted with Tarak? That was… embarrassing.

"He hates me," she said, once again speaking the truth. "As far as he's concerned, I'm the enemy."

"An enemy that he can manipulate to help him," Riven drawled. "He'd be an idiot not to realize you've become his devoted slave."

She pressed her lips together, only vaguely aware of the sour note of jealousy in the male's voice.

"I did what you commanded me to do," she muttered.

Riven shrugged. "Perhaps at the first, but it became so much more than that, didn't it?" His gaze slid down her body, lingering in a way that made Waverly's skin crawl. "Or did you think I wasn't aware of all those times you used to sneak away to visit the prison?"

Waverly jerked. He'd known that she was visiting Tarak? So much for thinking she was so clever.

"If you knew, why didn't you say something?"

His gaze returned to her face, a smirk playing around his mouth. "The more times you fed the creature the stronger I became."

Waverly felt a queasiness curl through the pit of her stomach. She'd never bothered to consider whether or not her clandestine visits to the prison might have consequences.

Because I was too selfish to care, a voice whispered through the back of her mind. She'd wanted to be with Tarak and nothing else had mattered.

Grimly thrusting aside her self-disgust, she concentrated on getting rid of her unwelcomed intruder.

"If the vampire is in the castle, he didn't seek me out."

Riven glanced around before abruptly heading toward the connecting door.

"You'll forgive me if I take a look for myself," he told her, stepping into her bedroom.

She hurried to join him, scowling as he made a slow tour of the room before moving to brush his hand over the quilt that she'd stitched with her own hands.

"Do you think I'm hiding him under the bed?" she snapped, feeling violated by his presence in her most private sanctuary.

Riven turned to face her. "I think you would do anything to protect your lover."

"He isn't my lover."

His dark blue eyes glittered with a strange heat. One she'd never seen before.

"You better hope that you speak the truth, Waverly—unless you no longer care what happens to your sister?" He deliberately paused. "Or the children."

She stepped forward, her hands clenched. "If you dare hurt them—"

"So fierce." He interrupted her empty threat, a smug satisfaction settling on his handsome features. "That's why I have chosen you for the greatest honor."

"What are you talking about?"

"Didn't you wonder why I called for the gathering this evening?"

"Not really. You make a habit of coming up with excuses to sit on my father's throne and force our people to admire you."

He chuckled, indifferent to the disdain in her voice. His ego was so swollen not even a whale could dent it. "Why else be a king? On this occasion, however, I had a very specific purpose. One that includes you, my sweet." Waverly stilled. Like a guppy suddenly confronting a piranha. The last time she'd been included in Riven's plans she'd ended up as a walking buffet for an imprisoned vampire. Who knew what he would demand of her now.

"Me?"

"Yes, sweet Waverly." A slow, disturbing smile curved his lips. "I have decided that I need an heir."

Waverly studied the merman in confusion. Did he just say he needed an heir?

"Why?"

"To rule at my side," he told her. "Or rather, a loyal prince to watch my back. Plus, an heir gives me the added security of knowing that if something were to happen to me, my son would take my place." Riven ran a loving hand down the silver handle of the Tryshu. "It makes it much less likely an overly ambitious traitor would attempt to get rid of me."

Waverly gave a slow shake of her head. His words didn't make any sense. "The Tryshu chooses the leader of the mer-folk, not the bloodline."

He managed to look even more smug. Not an easy task. "I'm breaking all the rules, or have you forgotten?"

"I haven't forgotten you somehow cheated to gain the throne," she said in scornful tones.

"Careful, Waverly," he growled. "You have your freedom because of me. Don't doubt that I can take it away." He paused, as if struck by a sudden thought. "In fact, it might be for the best if I keep you locked in the royal chambers. It will offer us plenty of opportunities to create my heir."

"Me?" Ridiculously, she hadn't put his words together. She knew he was babbling about an heir and offering her a great honor. But she hadn't realized the male thought that she would actually have sex with him…

"You're out of your mind."

Annoyance flared through his eyes, almost as if he'd expected her to be pleased by his offer.

"You will give me a child, Waverly."

Her lips parted to tell him to go to the netherworld, only to snap shut at the sudden chill in the air.

Tarak.

Despite the heavy magical barrier that surrounded the hidden space his power was beginning to seep through the air. She had to get rid of Riven before he suspected why the temperature was dropping.

Spinning on her heel, she dramatically stomped out of the bedroom and into the front sitting room.

"Before you worry about an heir, don't you think you should concentrate on retrieving your vampire?" she demanded, relieved when Riven followed her.

"If he is in the castle, there's no way he can escape." His expression appeared unconcerned, but Waverly didn't miss the edge in his voice.

He was more worried than he was willing to reveal.

"And if he's not?" she demanded.

"Then my guards will hunt him down." He shrugged. "Or I will find another vampire."

She narrowed her gaze. They both knew he couldn't risk capturing another vampire. Not without the danger of inciting the fury of the new Anasso.

"I wouldn't be so confident, if I were you," she snapped.

Anger rippled over his face before he managed to paste the smug smile back on his lips.

"But you aren't me," he taunted. "And I know something that you don't."

Her heart missed a beat. "What's that?"

He moved forward, drowning her in the bitter scent of seaweed. "I refuse to fail. No matter what I have to sacrifice."

Relief that he hadn't sensed Tarak crashed through her, along with a soul-deep hatred.

This male had cheated, lied, and manipulated his way to the throne. Now he intended to ensure that his treachery lived on for eternity.

The mere thought made her sick to her stomach. "What have you ever sacrificed?"

He deliberately ran a gaze over her rigid body before strolling toward the door.

"Remain in these rooms until I'm prepared to have you moved to mine," he commanded.

She glared at him as he stepped into the hall and closed the door. Then, clenching her hands, she released the pent-up anger that pounded through her.

"Bastard."

Chapter 9

Tarak ignored the pain that radiated down his arms as he slammed his fists against the magical barrier that kept him trapped.

When Waverly had first lured him into the cramped space he'd felt a stab of panic. The sensation of being locked in the darkness had brought back memories that were all too fresh. But oddly, he'd quickly managed to soothe his raw nerves, as if he possessed an instinctive trust that Waverly was trying to protect him.

Unfortunately, he'd barely been able to gather his composure before he'd overheard the conversation between Riven and Waverly.

It wasn't a shocker that Riven could sense Waverly's attachment to Tarak. The mermaid was a victim of her own emotions. There was no way in hell she could disguise them. It even made sense that Riven had turned a blind eye to Waverly's secret visits to Tarak's prison. The extra bursts of energy would've been a bonus to him.

But when the bastard had started talking about an heir—with Waverly— well, he'd gone...

What was the human word?

Apeshit.

Yeah, that was it.

He didn't know why. Waverly was not supposed to mean anything to him, right? She was a tool to use in his effort to kill Riven. But in this moment, she didn't feel like a tool. Especially when he was forced to consider the thought of her in the arms of Riven. Perhaps growing heavy with his child.

No. Hell no.

The air thickened with ice as he continued to slam his fists against the barrier.

Then without warning there was a faint click as a lock was released and the panel above him started to slide to the side. At the same time the magical barrier disappeared.

With a roar, he was surging out of the hole and wrapping his arms around the startled Waverly.

"Tarak," she squeaked, her eyes wide as she pressed her hands against his chest.

He glared down at her. "No."

She arched back, her lips parted. "I can't breathe."

Tarak instinctively eased his muscles, although he kept her tightly clasped in his arms. As if he feared she might suddenly be snatched away.

"No," he muttered.

"No what?"

"He can't have you."

Her wary expression was abruptly replaced with one of female annoyance.

"No male can *have* me," she informed him in stiff tones. "I will make the decision who is allowed to become my mate."

Tarak allowed his gaze to sweep over her lovely features. The stunning aquamarine eyes that were framed by lush lashes. The soft lips. And the noble thrust of her nose. Still, it wasn't her beauty that was sending waves of possessive hunger crashing through him.

It was that strange tug of destiny that he'd pretended for five hundred years didn't exist.

Something he was still trying to pretend didn't exist even when his fangs were aching with the need to claim her.

"Every inch the princess," he murmured, his hands splayed across her lower back as he tugged her against his thickening erection. "You've decided on me."

A flush stained her cheeks. "No longer."

He flinched, his brows snapping together. "You lie."

"It's no lie." She tilted her chin, her expression defiant. "You will be leaving to find your mate."

Mate? Tarak frowned. What the hell was she talking about? He wasn't interested in seeking out his mate. Not when the female he wanted was...

Nope. He slammed the door on that dangerous thought. He wasn't ready to consider the complicated instincts that were churning inside him.

"I'm not going anywhere until Riven is dead," he assured her.

She arched her brows. "And then?"

"I haven't considered anything beyond my revenge."

Her eyes darkened, as if she was battling back an intense emotion.

"Well I have. You will perish attempting to kill Riven or you will succeed and return to your clan."

Tarak grimaced as the truth sliced through him. She was right. Whether he failed or succeeded, their time together was swiftly coming to an end. He instinctively tugged her tighter against him. "And you?" he asked. "What will you do?"

Genuine fear rippled over her face. "If Riven remains king, I will be trapped in the castle."

She didn't have to add that she would also be trapped in the bastard's bed. That knowledge hung in the air like a toxic cloud.

"And if he dies?" Tarak demanded.

Waverly shrugged. "Someone must care for our people until a new leader is chosen."

Tarak scowled. That wasn't the answer he wanted, although he wasn't sure what he did want to hear. Perhaps that Waverly intended to follow him when he left the castle. And that she was pledged to be at his side no matter where he traveled.

"Riven will be dead," he assured her in icy tones.

She shivered, her face paling. Was she recalling Riven's threat to force her into his bed?

"Dear goddess, I pray you're right," she rasped.

Tarak lowered his head, absorbing her scent. Warm, exotic passion fruit and tropical breezes. It swirled through him, sinking deep into the darkness of his soul.

"He can't have you," he stated in flat tones.

Her jaw tightened, her scent sharpening with a hint of frustration. "What do you care?"

"You belong to me."

"I don't—"

He put an end to her protest by the simple method of pressing his mouth against her parted lips. It was effective, plus it had the added bonus of sending glorious heat flowing through his veins.

His hands slid down the silk of her gown to cup her backside. At the same time, he dipped his tongue into the moist temptation of her mouth.

A groan rattled through his chest. He wasn't sure when he'd become addicted to this female, but it was too late to give her up.

For a glorious minute he felt Waverly melt against him, her lips softening in a silent invitation. Tarak deepened the kiss, allowing his fangs to press against the plush curve of her lower lip.

He was suddenly starving for a taste. As if he was under some compulsion to sink his fangs into her flesh and draw deep of her luscious blood.

Was it possible that Riven was using his powers to urge Tarak to feed so he would have more power? No. This compulsion had nothing to do with the merman. Instead it came from some raw, primitive place in the center of his being.

The realization would have rattled him if he'd been thinking clearly. But at the moment he was too distracted by the feel of Waverly snuggled against him to care.

Hell, the roof could probably collapse and he wouldn't notice.

He'd desired Waverly since he'd first set eyes on her. What male wouldn't? But now each sensation that sizzled through him was sharper, more intense. Had the prison muffled his response to her? It would make sense. Any magic that was powerful enough to hold him captive had to have some sort of damper spell involved. That would inhibit his emotions, perhaps even his natural instincts.

Now...

His dazed thoughts were abruptly interrupted as Waverly turned her head, breaking their kiss.

"Stop," she breathed.

Tarak lifted his head, his hands skimming up the curve of her back. She trembled, as if battling her own desire. "Why?"

She turned her head to meet his narrowed gaze. "We have to figure out how to kill Riven."

Her words felt like cold water being tossed over him. It wasn't that he'd forgotten Riven, or the fact that the King of the Mer-folk was currently searching the castle for him. But for a blessed few seconds he'd been allowed to lose himself in something beyond his dark thirst for revenge.

A dangerous indulgence.

Unless he wanted to end up back in his prison, or dead, he needed to leash his potent desire for this female. Once he'd rid the world of Riven, he could decide what he wanted to do about Waverly.

Dropping his arms, he stepped back and studied her with a narrowed gaze. "You claimed it couldn't be done."

She rubbed her hands up and down her arms, as if she was suddenly cold. Or maybe missing his touch.

The thought pleased him.

"And you claimed that it could," she challenged him.

His lips twisted at her quick response. A male would be a fool to ever think this princess would be a docile, easily controlled female. She possessed quick wits and a spine of steel.

Turning away, he forced himself to concentrate on the only thing that mattered. Killing Riven.

Not that there was much to concentrate on. His choices were limited. He could fight a battle that Waverly claimed he couldn't win, or try to destroy Riven's ability to use Tarak's strength. He had no notion if it would compel the male to give up his hold on the Tryshu, but surely it would weaken the bastard.

"If there is no way to kill him, we have to find the artifact," he said

"You make it sound easy."

"It is." He shrugged, turning back to face her. "You wait here, and I'll search Riven's rooms. Once I find the artifact I'll destroy it."

"And how will you recognize it? I thought vampires couldn't sense magic." She held his gaze. "You need me to come with you."

"Absolutely not."

Her features hardened. "Then neither of us will go."

"If Riven catches us together—"

"He's not going to catch us," she interrupted.

Tarak studied her, sensing a determination that had been missing earlier. "You have a plan?"

"As a matter of fact, I do."

"Tell me," he commanded.

She hesitated. Did she suspect he wasn't going to like her plan? Probably. Unless it included locking herself in these rooms and waiting for him to kill Riven he wasn't going to like it.

"I can use my powers to distract the guards—"

"No."

She released an exasperated sigh. "You are impossible. First you insist I help you and now you're angry that I'm offering my assistance."

He glared down at her. "It's your fault."

"Mine?" She slammed her hands onto her hips. "Now you're just being an ass."

He was, but that was tough luck. He'd been held prisoner for five centuries. And every second of those five centuries had been spent dreaming of destroying his enemies. As painfully as possible. Now, when he was at last within striking distance, he was being distracted by the feel and taste of this female.

If he wanted to be an ass, then dammit, he'd be an ass.

"You're making me…"

"What?" She pressed him to continue.

"Question my sanity."

"I assure you the feeling is mutual." She glared at him with a prickly impatience. "Are you going to listen to my plan or not?"

With an effort, Tarak forced himself to bury his primitive need to keep Waverly locked in her rooms. No one knew this castle or Riven better than this female. He'd be an idiot not to accept her help.

"Tell me."

"I can create an illusion of myself," she reminded him. "It will be simple enough to attract the attention of Riven and his guards. Once they're following my image I can keep them occupied long enough for us to search the royal chambers."

Tarak arched a brow, recalling her appearance in the swamp. It'd been real enough to fool anyone at a distance. And since Riven already suspected that Waverly was helping him, they were sure to follow her. "That might actually work."

"Of course it will." With a soft swish of satin, Waverly was hurrying across the marble floor, her skirts swirling around her legs. Pulling open the door, she glanced over her shoulder. "Come on."

With long strides, Tarak was standing directly in front of her. "Princess."

"What?"

"If we run into trouble, I want your promise that you'll let me handle it."

She sent him an offended glare. "I'm not helpless."

He reached to cup her chin in the palm of his hand. "We're not leaving this room until you promise me that you'll escape from this castle if there's the least hint that we've been discovered."

"My sister—"

"Your promise."

Her lips pressed together, but she was smart enough to know that her agreement was non-negotiable.

"Fine. I promise."

* * * *

Inga stomped her way down the hallway, her hands clenched into massive fists. The tiny gargoyle was darting in front of her, his head tilted to the side as he concentrated on the silence that surrounded them.

It'd been like this for the past half hour. They would follow the voice down one long corridor, only to come to a dead end and have to retrace their steps.

Without warning, Levet came to a halt. He paused, then fell to his knees before he pressed his head against the stone floor. Inga released a low growl. Her strained patience was reaching its snapping point.

"What are you doing?"

"Shh." Blissfully indifferent to Inga's smoldering temper, Levet waved a silencing hand. "There is a madness to my method."

"Doubtful," Inga muttered, more annoyed at herself than her companion. She should be grabbing the creature by his stunted horn and hauling him out the confusing maze of hallways. They had to get to a place in the castle where she could open a portal. Instead, she was trailing behind him like a...

She grimaced. Like a besotted cow. Even worse, there didn't seem to be a damned thing she could do to force herself to take command of the situation.

Not for the first time, she wished she possessed the heart of a pureblooded ogre. She wouldn't have given a crap about anyone but herself. But her mushy mermaid heart continued to get her into hot water.

First with her devotion to Lilah, whom she'd protected for the past five hundred years. And now Levet.

Stupid, stupid Inga.

"Bonjour," Levet called out, clearly focused on his role as the Knight in Shining Armor. "Are you still there?"

"Yes, can you hear me?" The disembodied voice echoed through the air.

"You are fading." Levet's wings flapped, his ugly little face scrunching with concentration. "Where are you?"

"The nursery," the voice answered.

Levet lifted his head. "You are trapped in the nursery?" he demanded in confusion.

"Please, I need your help."

There was the faint scent of an ocean crashing over rocks before it suddenly dissipated. As if whoever was talking to them had vanished.

Levet scrambled to his feet and darted toward the end of the hallway. Inga muttered a curse she'd learned from her goblin slave-master and lumbered after him.

"Levet," she called out, fear curling through her belly as they turned the corner to discover a staircase. Had that been there before? Or was the strange voice leading them into a trap? She was betting on the trap theory.

"Where do you think you're going?"

"To find the nursery," Levet said, giving a squeak when Inga reached out to grasp one of his fairy wings.

"Absolutely not."

He glanced over his shoulder, seemingly baffled by her refusal to dash into an obvious snare. "We must assist the poor female."

Inga ground her pointed teeth. Why was the stupid creature so worried about the unknown female?

"What about me?" she burst out.

He furrowed his brow in confusion. "What about you?"

Inga debated giving the gargoyle a good shaking. It might rattle some sense into his thick skull.

"You heard the guards before we were pulled through the portal. They intend to kill me," she said, contenting herself with a petulant glare. "Is that what you want?"

Levet was instantly outraged. "Of course not. If any guard threatens you, I will blast him with this."

The gargoyle held up his hand, allowing a fireball to form in the center of his palm.

"No." Inga leaped to the side as the fireball sizzled past her.

"See," Levet said with obvious pride. "There is no need to fear."

Inga straightened, glancing down to discover several scorch marks splattered down the side of her muumuu. "You singed my dress."

Levet wrinkled his snout. "Not a great loss."

Inga's head jerked up. What was he talking about? This was her favorite muumuu. "You don't like it?"

"That is not what I meant," Levet quickly protested. "It is very…colorful."

Inga smoothed her hands down the soft material. "Bright things make me happy."

His expression softened, as if sensing he'd hurt her feelings.

"Perhaps when we travel to Paris we will stop by the fashion houses and find you a new gown," he suggested in helpful tones.

She jutted out her lower jaw. Did he think she was stupid? She couldn't squeeze one leg into a fancy gown from Paris. And even if she could find one her size, she would look ridiculous.

Besides, she had spent most of her life as a slave. Now that she was free, she intended to savor the ability to make her own choices.

Including her love for garish clothes.

"First we have to get out of here," she growled.

"After we have rescued the prisoner," Levet insisted, heading up the stairs with a speed that made it impossible for Inga to stop him.

"We are not rescuing that female," Inga called out.

Levet clicked his tongue, not bothering to turn as he reached the top and headed down the upper hallway.

"Do not be absurd. We are heroes. It is what we do."

Stomping her feet with enough force to crumble the stone, Inga climbed the stairs.

"Trust me. I'm no hero," she muttered.

Chapter 10

Tarak forced himself to stand across the room as Waverly closed her eyes to weave her magic. Not only did she need to concentrate, but he could no longer trust himself to be next to her and not give into his overwhelming urge to touch her.

Not long ago he would have been humiliated by the realization he couldn't keep his hands off one of the mer-folk. How could he possibly be so obsessed with his enemy?

Now, however, he accepted that some deep, primitive part of him had determined that this female wasn't his adversary. She was—

His mind screeched to a halt, refusing to take the thought any further.

As if it knew he wasn't prepared to accept what was about to be exposed.

"I found the guards." Waverly's words thankfully interrupted his dark musings. Crossing the room, he watched as her lashes lifted to reveal her unfocused eyes. "Riven is with them."

"Where are they?" he demanded.

"Searching through the servants' quarters," she said. "I'll lead them to the kitchens."

Tarak waited, disliking the tension that vibrated through her slender body. She was expending an enormous amount of energy. "How long can you maintain the illusion?"

She hesitated before admitting the truth. "Not long."

He reached up to touch a drop of perspiration that beaded her forehead. "You should stay here and conserve your strength."

She gave a shake of her head, returning her focus to him. "No."

Tarak felt a pang of frustration. It was a perfectly reasonable request. "Stubborn creature."

Her eyes widened at his muttered words. "You spent five hundred years in a prison, and instead of fleeing you're here trying to kill a male who is indestructible," she pointed out in tart tones. "I don't think you're in a position to call me stubborn."

He didn't argue. He told himself it was because he didn't want her wasting her limited strength. A voice in the back of his head, however, whispered that she was right.

A wise vampire would walk away and savor every moment of his newfound freedom. Why risk everything for revenge?

It was a question that was rooted in his very soul.

There was no way he could find happiness if he didn't put the past behind him. And the only way to do that was to kill the demons responsible for imprisoning him. The Anasso was dead. Riven was next.

Wrapping an arm around Waverly's shoulders, he steered her toward the door.

"Let's go." He paused as they reached the hallway. "Which way?"

Her expression was once again distracted. "Left."

They headed down the wide hallway, Waverly leaning heavily against him.

"Are you okay?" he demanded.

She nodded. "They're following my image. Once I have them in the kitchens I'll release the spell. It will take them a while to realize I'm not hiding in one of the pantries."

They continued forward, Tarak's boots clicking loudly on the marble floor. Dammit. If there were any guards around they would hear him coming a mile away. This was why he hated marble.

Eventually they passed through a series of fluted columns, and then up five shallow steps. In front of them were a set of massive double doors.

"I'm assuming the royal chambers are behind the golden doors?" he demanded.

"Yes." She came to a sharp halt, reaching to grab his hand. "Tarak."

He didn't need Waverly's warning. He'd already sensed a merman rapidly approaching from behind. With care, he pushed her toward one of the pillars.

"Wait here."

Her lips parted as if she intended to argue. Then, catching sight of his fierce expression, she heaved a resigned sigh.

"Okay. I'm waiting."

With Waverly out of the line of fire, Tarak whirled to watch the merman charge forward.

"Leech," the male hissed, attired in the strange armor that Tarak had noticed earlier.

"Squid," Tarak taunted.

Keeping his gaze focused on the trident the guard held in his hand, he leaped forward and then leaped again, this time to the side to avoid the lethal strands that shot from the tip of the trident.

Tarak wasn't stupid. He only needed to be netted once with the silver filaments to remember to duck and roll.

Watching the net wrap around a nearby marble statue, Tarak reminded himself that the guard wasn't helpless as he charged toward the merman. The trident could still penetrate his heart or slice off his head. Plus, Tarak had no way of knowing whether or not the merman had some other nasty weapons hidden beneath his armor.

Thankfully the guard was clearly commanded not to kill him, making him hesitate as Tarak pulled the silver dagger from the holster at his lower back.

They circled one another, both looking for a weakness. The merman was smaller, and slower, but he was wearing an armor that Tarak's knife couldn't penetrate, plus his weapon was longer. On the other hand, Tarak had lethal fangs that could easily rip out the guard's throat.

Darting toward the male, he slashed the dagger at his face. The guard danced back, shooting another blast of silvery filament. Tarak managed to avoid the net, quickly striking again. This time he was able to slice a cut along the male's cheek before the merman was shooting more silver in his direction.

Tarak swallowed a curse as he ducked. The trident clearly had an endless supply of the lethal silver.

"Why don't you put down your toy and offer me a fair fight?" he demanded, twirling his dagger in his hand.

He needed to distract the male long enough to get the trident away from him.

The merman narrowed his eyes, his hands tightening on the trident. "As if a vampire would ever know the meaning of fair. Leeches are the dirtiest fighters in the demon-world."

Tarak shrugged. "I suppose that's true. We do whatever necessary to win."

A smug smiled curved the guard's lips. "But you didn't win, did you? You've been rotting in a prison."

Tarak ignored the taunt, his attention locked on the lethal weapon. The male moved the trident in an elongated figure-eight pattern. Left. Right. Up. Down.

"Do you know why?" Tarak demanded, continuing to twirl his knife. He wanted the guard concentrating on the weapon and not on him.

"You attempted to kill our king, so he took you captive," the merman said.

Tarak released a humorless laugh. "Is that the story he told you?"

"It's the truth," the male insisted, weaving the trident in the same pattern over and over.

A weakness that Tarak intended to exploit.

"If your precious king had tried to capture me, I would have ripped off his head," he told the male, casually moving to the side, as if planning another charge forward. "I was betrayed, and Riven is using my power to maintain his grip on the Tryshu."

The guard hissed, releasing another spray of silver netting. "Lies."

With perfect timing, Tarak tossed his knife at the male's face. Instinctively the guard threw his hands up to protect himself from the painful projectile, allowing Tarak the opportunity to reach out and grab the trident.

Using his superior strength, Tarak yanked the weapon from the male's hand and slammed it against the marble floor. With a satisfying crack the trident snapped in two.

Tossing aside the broken pieces, Tarak bared his fangs, watching with satisfaction as the male stumbled backward.

"Tarak." Waverly's soft voice managed to penetrate the red mist filling his mind. "Don't kill him."

He wanted to ignore her plea. He might not recognize the young guard, but he wore the armor of the royal guard. He was as responsible as Riven for the past five hundred years of hell. And Tarak wanted to taste his blood. He wanted to feel the life drain from the male's body before tossing him away like a piece of trash.

For a second, he remained poised on the edge. Then the soft scent of passion fruit eased the haze from his brain. Like a whisper of sanity.

Trembling from the effort of pulling back from the killing blow, he smashed his fist into the male's terrified face, knocking him unconscious. Then he lifted his head to glare toward Waverly who was standing at the top of the steps.

"A friend of yours?" he rasped.

She shook her head, the blue highlights shimmering in her pale hair. "No, but the guards are only following Riven's commands."

"Yeah, the same commands that will have me locked back in his prison and you in his bed," he growled.

She paled, but stiffening her spine, she waved a hand toward the doors behind her. "We need to hurry."

Muttering a curse, Tarak reached down to grasp the unconscious male by his long hair, dragging him up the stairs. He couldn't leave him behind. Not only would someone spot him and call for more guards, but if he woke up and tried to cause trouble, Tarak intended to finish him off. He'd spared his life once. It wasn't going to happen again.

Reaching the doors, he lifted his leg and slammed his foot against the heavy lock. It shuddered. He kicked again. And again. At last the door flew open and they stepped inside.

"Damn," Tarak muttered, tossing aside the guard as he turned in a slow circle.

The sitting room was twice the size of most vampire lairs, with a high, barrel ceiling inlaid with elaborate medallions and a dozen chandeliers that splashed a soft light over the marble floor inlaid with gold. The walls were painted with bright frescos that revealed the Tryshu being created in a swirl of magic. And the eventual crowning of a king and queen who were in their mer-form as they sat upon massive thrones made from coral.

The furniture was made from wood, but studded with rare jewels that threatened to blind him. And at the far end of the room was another set of double golden doors.

"Your father had a flair for the dramatic," he told his companion.

Waverly released a soft sigh. "I think he created this as a tribute to my mother. She loved to surround herself with beauty."

Tarak studied her wistful expression. Was this the first time she'd been in these rooms since her father's death? Probably.

"And you?" he abruptly asked.

She looked confused. "What?"

"Do you prefer a lavish lair?" He kept his expression unreadable even as he realized that her answer mattered to him.

Why?

That was one of those questions he preferred to ignore. He'd already discovered he had a talent for sticking his head in the sand when he was serving his Anasso. Might as well continue his habit of blissful ignorance.

"Not really," she said. "This castle is my home because it makes me feel closer to my father, but I am happiest when I'm swimming through the ocean. It's the only place I feel truly free."

The ice in the center of Tarak's heart melted just a little more at her soft words. Did she truly understand the beauty of freedom? Perhaps she did. After all, she'd been as much a victim of Riven as he had. Only her prison had been this castle and the terror that the bastard would destroy her sister, along with the innocent children.

"Yes," he agreed, his voice harsh. "Freedom is worth more than any precious jewels or piles of gold."

With a swift motion, Waverly was standing close at his side, her hand lightly resting on his arm.

"I can give that to you," she breathed, her expression pleading. "Just leave, Tarak."

He gazed down at her, not even considering her offer. "I can't." He lightly touched her cheek, about to remind her that he was there for one purpose. To kill Riven.

But even as his fingers lingered on the plush temptation of her mouth, Tarak was stiffening with shock.

"What's wrong?" Waverly demanded.

Tarak crossed the long room, drawn by a scent he hadn't encountered for over five centuries.

"I can smell..."

"What?" Waverly demanded, scurrying toward him.

He closed his eyes, trying to pinpoint the exact location of the scent.

"My former Anasso," he said

"That's impossible."

"It's faint, but I would recognize it anywhere," he insisted.

The sound of Waverly's footsteps trailed behind him as Tarak found himself lured toward the far corner.

"I suppose it's possible that Riven invited the King of Vampires to meet with him in secret," she suggested. "They did plot together to imprison you."

"It's possible," Tarak admitted. "But why would his scent linger?"

"Where?"

"Here." He paused in front of spot on the wall that was painted with a pretty jellyfish.

He frowned, touching the wall in confusion.

"Wait," Waverly commanded. "There's an illusion."

Tarak pulled his hand away with a grimace. "Did your father create it?"

"No." She gave a sharp shake of her head. "This belongs to Riven."

Tarak watched as she furrowed her brow and spoke a low word of magic. There was a faint cracking sound, like glass shattering, and then he realized he was standing in front of a towering wood armoire that was intricately engraved.

He silently cursed magic and his inability to detect it, as a combination of smells flooded the room. No doubt he'd never have caught the hint of the Anasso's scent if he hadn't been so intimately connected to his master. They'd fought and nearly died together, not to mention residing in the same lair for centuries.

Now he could also catch a dull, ancient smell that surprised him.

"Blood," he rasped, grabbing the knob of the armoire and yanking open one of the doors.

He frowned as he reached in to grab a green silk cape that was torn and covered in blood. *What the hell?* He reached in again, this time pulling out a necklace.

Tarak froze, horror jolting through him as he took in the sight of the massive emerald that was set in a golden necklace and surrounded by pale pink diamonds.

Leaning forward, Waverly sucked in a startled breath as she caught sight of what he was holding.

"Why would Riven hide a bloody cape and necklace?"

Tarak grimaced. The last time he'd seen the necklace it had been draped around the slender neck of a beautiful imp with a glorious mane of golden curls and eyes the same deep green as the emerald.

"My guess would be that this was how Riven forced my master into handing me over."

Waverly furrowed her brow. "How?"

Tarak stroked his finger over the necklace. "When I first met the Anasso he possessed a favorite courtesan, Mallia."

Her jaw tightened, as if she was offended. "Courtesan?"

He smiled with a wry humor. "It wasn't sexist. Female vampires are just as likely to keep favorite lovers in their lair until they discover their mates."

She didn't look impressed by his reassurance. "Did you?"

Tarak shook his head. In the past he'd had lovers who'd pleaded to stay in his lair. And his Anasso had offered to share his harem, if Tarak was interested.

He hadn't been.

"During my earliest years I was devoted to creating my clan and protecting them," he said, looking back on that time with a sense of nostalgia. His destiny had seemed so clear-cut when he'd been focused on his people: they were his to protect. Simple. Straightforward. "Then later

I was too occupied with carrying out the Anasso's commands to spend time with a female who might have captured my interest."

She flinched. "And then you were imprisoned."

He gazed into her eyes, easily reading the guilt etched in the aquamarine depths.

"Yes," he murmured, although he suspected he was responding to her beauty, not her words.

She cleared her throat, a sudden flush staining her cheeks. "What does the courtesan have to do with Riven?"

Tarak glanced back at the necklace. "Forty or fifty years before I was betrayed, the Anasso traveled with Mallia to visit the various clans he'd conquered."

"Was she a vampire?"

"No, an imp." A hint of grief was laced through his words. Mallia had been with the Anasso even before Tarak had joined him. The realization that she was most certainly dead was an unexpected blow. "She was lovely."

He felt Waverly stiffen. "Of course she was."

Tarak glanced at her in surprise. Was she jealous? The thought was absurdly satisfying.

"I had no interest in her." He found himself instinctively reassuring her. "But my master was besotted."

A portion of her tension eased. "But she wasn't his mate?"

"No." He paused, recalling his master's possessive attitude toward the pretty imp. Once he'd entered the Anasso's lair, he'd quickly learned not to ever spend more than a few seconds speaking with Mallia. And he never, ever remained in a room alone with her. It was only as he looked back that he accepted that his master hadn't acted like a male devoted to a female, but as a hoarder protecting his favorite treasure. "But he considered her as his property," he finally admitted.

Her lips curled. "You admired your king?"

He should be angered by her unconcealed disgust. She was serving a king who'd stolen the throne by keeping him captive for centuries. How dare she judge him?

Instead, he just felt...sad. And weary.

So much of his life had been wasted. First by his loyalty to a leader who was willing to betray him, and then by the merman who'd locked him away.

"I always accepted that he had his faults, but I allowed my admiration for his dreams to blind me to the cost of pledging my loyalty to him," he admitted.

Easily sensing his shame, Waverly's expression softened, as if she regretted her sharp words.

She was far too tenderhearted for her own good.

"What happened to Mallia?" she asked.

Tarak forced himself to dredge up the memories. He hadn't actually traveled with the Anasso during the fateful trip, but he'd heard all the gory details.

"While they were visiting one of the clans she discovered her true mate. They snuck away while the Anasso was meeting with the chief."

Waverly widened her eyes. "Was her mate a vampire?"

"Yes. The Anasso was furious."

His words were an understatement. When he'd finally seen the Anasso the ancient male had been incandescent with rage. In fact, he'd destroyed half the lair before his guards managed to contain him in his private rooms. Wisely, Tarak had chosen to take an extended vacation until the male had managed to gather command of his emotions.

Waverly glanced toward the priceless necklace Tarak held in his hands. "I thought matings were dictated by instinct?"

"They are."

She hesitated, perhaps trying to make sense of his explanation. "Then how could he be angry?"

"I think he was obsessed with her." His fingers tightened around the necklace. "But more importantly, she'd embarrassed him in front of his people. That was an unforgivable sin."

"What did he do?"

"At first he tried to track down her down. Eventually he was forced to return to his lair and resume his duties," Tarak said, not bothering to add that the male had been in a violent temper for several years. "Eventually, I began to hear rumors that he was offering a reward for any demon who could give him the location of his runaway lover."

Her lips parted, her face pale as she quickly came to the same conclusion as Tarak. "You think Riven found her?"

"Yes." He held up his hand. "I recognize this necklace. My master paid a fortune to buy the emerald from a goblin. He claimed it perfectly matched Mallia's eyes. He later designed the setting for the gem."

"But if Riven did locate Mallia, wouldn't your Anasso have returned her to his lair?" she demanded.

He gave a slow shake of his head. The Anasso had been careful not to mention his determination to track down his courtesan to Tarak. And he certainly hadn't said that he'd found Mallia and destroyed her. The older male had a true talent for understanding the vampires that he'd gathered within his inner circle. He would have known Tarak would have found his behavior reprehensible.

"He didn't want her back." His voice was harsh. "He wanted to punish her."

Waverly shivered as she wrapped her arms around her waist. "You believe he killed her?"

He didn't want to, but at the moment it seemed the most likely explanation.

"I can smell her blood on the cape, along with the Anasso," he said, his acute senses capable of detecting that the King of Vampires had been present when the imp had been bleeding. Their two scents blended together. "Besides, it would explain a great deal. Including his descent into his addiction that must have started about the same time. It is one thing to plot your revenge. It is another to destroy the female who you loved."

She sent him a chiding frown. "If he loved her, he could never have hurt her. Even if he was a demon."

"I agree." Tarak quickly soothed her burst of anger. Almost as if he was worried she might think he approved of the cowardly act. "It was obsession and pride and a weakness at his very core. A weakness that led to his eventual downfall."

She nodded, offering her approval before returning her attention to the items in his hand. "None of this explains why Riven would have the cape and necklace."

Tarak shoved the cape and necklace back into the armoire. Just holding them in his hands made him feel as if he was tainted.

Tarak hazarded a guess. "He probably followed the Anasso to watch him destroy Mallia." He knew without a doubt that the Anasso hadn't given the objects to the merman. The vampire probably assumed he'd hidden them where they would never be found. "Then after my master left, he swooped in to grab the evidence."

"Why?"

There was only one reason Tarak could imagine. "To ensure that he got what he wanted," he said. "Me."

She studied his face, as if wondering whether he knew more than he was sharing. He wished he did. Perhaps it might give him some clue to how Riven was tapping into his powers.

"Would the vampires have cared if they learned your master had killed his courtesan?" she asked, clearly assuming that vampires made a habit of murdering their lovers.

Tarak sent her an annoyed frown. "He broke his own laws. Not only is a vampire forbidden from interfering between a mated pair, but we are supposed to take any grievance to the clan chief, not dole out our own punishment," he informed her in stiff tones. "How could he sit in judgment of others when he was going against everything he was preaching?"

She abruptly turned away, her head bowing as if under a tremendous weight.

"It's all so horrible. Your Anasso who would destroy an innocent female because his pride was hurt. And Riven's willingness to use that awful secret for his own ambition." She released a harsh sigh. "Then together they sacrificed you for their own selfish needs."

Tarak couldn't argue.

It was horrible.

Chapter 11

Styx wasn't sure who he was more annoyed with as he tromped through the nasty bogs along with Chiron. His Raven, who'd come to him with the intel that a female ogress had been chased out of a local hotel by a vampire. Or his companion, who'd been foolish enough to release his former master from his prison. Or the previous Anasso, who'd been the cause of this mess in the first place.

Of course, you could always blame yourself, a voice whispered in the back of his mind. He was the one who'd found the scroll that had revealed that Tarak had been held captive for the past five hundred years. If he'd just burned the damn thing he would be home with his mate, Darcy, cuddled in his arms.

Instead...

His size-sixteen boots squished through the mud, his mood growing more foul with every sloppy step.

At last they pressed their way through a ring of cypress trees to discover a worn wooden structure that was sagging precariously in the marshy ground.

According to Styx's guard, the place had been a demon fight club. At least until the magic surrounding it had been shattered and the surrounding swamp had flooded the underground pits.

Now it looked like it was one stiff breeze away from total collapse.

At his side, Chiron studied the building with a curl of his lips. Styx didn't blame him. He'd recently visited one of Chiron's casinos in Vegas. It had dripped with elegance.

This place...

It just dripped.

"Is it deserted?" Chiron demanded.

Styx took a second to test the air. He caught the scents of a dozen different demons, but all of them were fading. All but one.

"There's someone inside. Smells like…" He paused to concentrate on the scent. It was rich and fruity and astonishingly familiar. "Shit."

With long strides he was stomping through the mud to shove open the front door.

"What's going on?" Chiron demanded, hurrying to catch up.

"I recognize that smell," Styx growled, glancing around the lobby.

It was a small space that had tilted to one side, allowing the ceiling to brush the top of his head. Beneath his feet the wooden floorboards felt dangerously flimsy. As if they were just waiting for an opportunity to splinter.

"Yikes," Chiron breathed as a hidden door was pushed open and a male stepped into the room.

The imp was surprisingly large, with bulging muscles that were blatantly outlined beneath the sheer white shirt that was studded with rhinestones and the black leather pants that looked like they'd been hot-glued onto his legs. His long hair was a brilliant red and pulled into a topknot.

There was something exotic and sensual about the male despite his flamboyant attitude.

"Hello, Troy," Styx said in dry tones.

The male flicked a brow upward as he allowed his green gaze to travel over Styx.

"Well, well. I was just saying the neighborhood was going to hell, and you stroll in," Troy drawled, moving to stand in the center of the lobby. "Point. Proved."

Styx silently cursed. What evil god had dumped this particular fey in such an isolated spot?

"Do I look like I'm in the mood for your sarcasm?" he snapped.

"Hmm." Troy ran his finger over the rhinestones on his chest. "Hard to say. You have the whole tall, dark, and brooding thing going on."

Styx reached over his shoulder, grabbing the hilt of his sword. With one smooth motion he had it out of the sheath and pointed directly at Troy's nose. "Does this help?"

Troy stifled a yawn. "There's no need to wave around that oversized knife." The imp turned his attention to Chiron, unduly confident that Styx wouldn't slice off his head. He took a slow, thorough survey of the younger vampire before returning his attention to Styx. "What are you doing here?"

"I was about to ask you the same thing," Styx countered. "I thought you were working with Sophia?"

Sophia happened to be the mother of Styx's mate, Darcy. The female Were had recently returned to Chicago to be reunited with her four daughters. Oh, and at the same time, she'd decided to open a strip club.

Darcy called her mother a rebel. He called her a pain in the ass. Not out loud, of course.

He preferred to keep peace in his lair whenever possible.

Troy shrugged. "I remain a consultant, but recently my cousin purchased this place. He requested that I come down and assist him."

Styx glanced around the filthy lobby that creaked and groaned in an ominous fashion. Whatever Styx's opinion of his mother-in-law, Sophia's club was an elegant, high-end establishment that pulled in a small fortune every evening. So why would Troy want to come here?

"What sort of assistance?" he demanded.

"He'd grown weary of the clientele he was attracting in his fighting pits. He spent more money repairing the damage they were forever causing than he was taking in."

"What sort of club did he want?"

"A strip club, of course." Troy flashed a wicked smile as he ran his hands down his body. "That's my specialty."

"A strip club?" Styx snorted in disbelief. "Here?"

"That was my reaction as well." Troy gave a resigned shake of his head. "I warned him that he would be better off leaving this place to the alligators and moving to Miami." A spark of anticipation glowed in his green eyes. "Now there is a place I could create a club to die for."

Styx narrowed his gaze. There were a lot of demons who had clubs, but most of them were like this place. Dark, dirty, and nearly destitute. The sort of places that wouldn't attract the attention of Viper, who didn't tolerate direct competition to his own chain of demon clubs.

It was only because Sophia was related to Styx's mate that he hadn't stepped in to shut her down.

"And you might die if Viper discovers you're invading his territory," he warned.

Troy sniffed. "It doesn't matter now. Not after your friend managed to trash the place."

Ah. At last, information that actually mattered.

"What friend?"

"I don't know." Troy curled his lips in disgust. "Some vampire."

Styx lowered his sword. "Describe him."

"Big teeth. Bad attitude," Troy said. Styx bared his fangs. They were much scarier than his sword. No matter how large it might be. Troy hastily lifted a hand. "No need to get your thong in a twist, big boy. I forgot how ill-tempered you are."

Styx scowled. "Don't call me big boy."

"Why not?" Troy blinked with a pretense of innocence. "Are you saying there are some parts of you that aren't as full-sized as you want? Don't worry, I have a magical pill for you."

Next to Styx, Chiron swallowed a laugh. *Damned imp*, Styx fumed. And damn his own rules. In the distant past, vampires simply killed anyone who annoyed them. Now he was trying to set a better example for his people.

Which meant he occasionally had to grin and bear it.

"Describe the vampire," he snapped.

Perhaps sensing he was stomping on Styx's last nerve, the imp gave an airy wave of his hand. "Not as tall as you," he said. "He had dark hair, and the face of an ancient barbarian." He gave a delicate shudder. "Deliciously savage."

"Tarak," Styx muttered. "What was he doing here?"

Troy arched his brows, as if unable to believe that Styx would ask such a stupid question. "Causing destruction, of course," the imp chided. "A typical vampire pastime and the reason your sort has been banned from the club."

"You're claiming that Tarak did all this damage?" Styx demanded.

"No." Troy turned to lead them across the lobby. Then he lifted his arm and pointed down the shadowed hallway. "The massive hole in the floor was caused by an ogress who was traveling with a gargoyle I didn't see, but who I suspect was Levet." Troy turned to face them. "How many three-foot gargoyles are there in the world?"

"One is too many," Styx growled.

Troy sent him a mocking smile. "Your mate finds him quite charming."

Styx refused to rise to the bait. He wasn't here to spar with the imp. "Why did the ogress dig a hole in the floor?"

"My guess is that she was trying to get away from the vampire," Troy said. "She jumped through the hole into the fighting pit. You can imagine the chaos that ensued." Troy grimaced. "During the commotion my cousin was injured and the barriers that kept the swamp out of the lower floors were destroyed. Now the building is all wonky."

Styx didn't need a blow-by-blow recap of the pandemonium caused by the ogress. He'd been in fighting pits before. A battle could break out because a demon looked at another demon wrong. An ogress dropping on their heads would have been...epic.

"What happened to the vampire?"

"All reports said that he chased the ogress and the gargoyle into the swamp," Troy said, clearly indifferent to what had happened to them after they fled the pits.

Styx ground his fangs. He'd known it was too much to hope that Tarak would still be at the club, but he'd assumed there would be tracks to follow. But the deluge of swamp water had mixed the scents of the various demons until it was impossible to pinpoint one specific trail.

"Did you notice any strangers in the area?" he demanded.

Styx's biggest fear was that Tarak would terrorize the locals until they rose up to kill him. His second fear was that the mer-folk who'd held Tarak would discover he'd escaped and come searching for him.

He had to locate the vampire before either of those things happened.

Troy shuddered. "As far as I'm concerned, they're all strange." He gave a startled shriek as Styx reached out to grab the front of his shirt.

"Don't screw with me, imp," Styx rasped.

"It's the truth," Troy insisted. "I've only been here a couple of weeks. I don't recognize the locals yet."

There was a sincerity in his voice that couldn't be faked. Styx released his shirt. "Where is your cousin?"

"Unconscious in his lair," Troy answered without hesitation. "We don't know if he'll wake up or not, so I fired the staff and now I'm trying to decide if I intend to burn this place or let it sink into the muck."

Styx studied the male. "You don't seem particularly upset."

"I said he's my cousin," Troy drawled. "I didn't say he was my favorite cousin."

Styx rolled his eyes. This hadn't been a complete waste of his time. He at least could be confident that Chiron had been right. Tarak was chasing after Inga and Levet. Which should make tracking them down much easier. There weren't many places a full-grown ogress could hide.

"If you see the vampire or ogress again, you contact me immediately," he commanded.

The imp fluttered his lashes. "If you're staying in the area, I have a couple of rooms I'm willing to rent."

Styx turned on his heel to stomp out of the building. "I thought it was the gargoyle who was annoying," he muttered.

* * * *

Waverly nervously glanced around the room that had once been her favorite place in the entire castle. Despite his grief that had never eased at the loss of his mate, her father had continued to host entertainments for his people. He understood that they needed to feel pleasure in their hidden lair, or soon they would turn on him.

Or worse, begin to squabble and fight among themselves.

They had the formal ballroom for large celebrations, but this had been a place where small groups of mer-folk could dance or play games or simply relax and listen to music. Plus they had the opportunity to be near her father's magic.

His gift had been filling a room with a sense of peace. He was like a walking, talking Prozac pill for mer-folk.

Truly magical.

A shame he couldn't enjoy the benefits of his own magic. Inside he'd been tormented with fear that he wouldn't be able to keep his children safe even after he'd created the castle.

And now Riven was in these rooms, corrupting the lingering sense of harmony with his wicked selfishness.

"Can you sense any other illusions?" Tarak demanded, breaking into her bitter thoughts.

With an effort, she cleared her mind and concentrated on their surroundings.

"No." She was on the point of turning to leave when she noticed her companion was headed toward the double doors across the room. "Tarak? Where are you going?"

"The artifact has to be here somewhere," he said, shoving open one of the doors.

"We can't stay," she said, unease curling through the pit of her stomach. When she'd released the image she'd used to lure the guards away, she'd lost the ability to keep track of where they were. Which meant they might very well be racing toward these rooms. "Riven has probably already figured out that I'm not hiding in the kitchens."

Tarak shrugged as he strolled into the inner bedchamber. "Luckily this is the last place he'll look for us."

She scurried behind him, her gut continuing to twist and turn. "I don't like depending on luck."

Without warning he came to an abrupt halt, turning to grasp her upper arms as she nearly crashed into him.

"Then depend on me," he commanded, gazing down at her with an intensity that sent a shiver down her spine.

She searched his harshly carved features, wondering if this was some trick. Did he think he had to manipulate her into helping him?

"You consider me your enemy," she at last breathed, her throat tight with an emotion she couldn't fully decipher. "How can I depend on you?"

He reached to stroke his fingers through her hair. "We both know that I haven't considered you the enemy from the moment I tasted your blood." She stiffened. Did he think she couldn't remember the endless years that she'd visited his prison, wanting to offer so much more than her blood, only to be treated with an icy anger?

"But you—"

"I have my pride," he interrupted, his expression rueful. "How could I allow myself to admit that I was fascinated with my captor?"

His words scraped against her raw sense of guilt. "I was never your captor," she protested.

An odd expression settled on his face. "Ironically, your hold over me might prove to be far more permanent than Riven's."

Her hold over him? "What do you mean?"

His fingers skimmed down the side of her neck, his eyes flaring with a midnight fire. Then, with a muttered curse, he was dropping his hand and stepping away.

"You're right. We don't have time to waste," he said in clipped tones. "Can you sense any magic in the room?"

She sent him a wry glance. "Everywhere."

He planted his hands on his hips, his expression tightening. "Show me the items that didn't belong to your father."

She didn't want to. It was bad enough to enter her father's public rooms. In this private space she could still remember the faint scent of her mother's clothes that her father kept hanging in the wardrobe and the musical box that her mother had created with her own hands. Now she could feel the bleak emptiness that echoed through the room. As if the removal of her parents' personal items had left a gaping emptiness Riven was unable to fill.

Still, the sooner they completed their search, the sooner they could return to her rooms and she could hide Tarak from the searching guards.

Gathering her courage, she forced her feet to carry her around the room. She ran her fingertips over the heavy tapestries that now covered the vividly painted walls.

"These are new," she said. "But there's no magic in them."

"Anything else?" Tarak urged her to continue her search.

She walked past the large bed carved from coral that consumed the center of the marble floor. She couldn't bear to look at it. Not when Riven's threat of forcing her to carry his child hung over her head like a dark cloud.

Instead she kept her gaze locked on the towering shelves that had once held her father's massive collection of books. He'd believed that a king's greatest weapon was knowledge. Now they were gone and in their place was a number of knives, spears, and odd artifacts.

"All of these are new as well," she murmured.

Tarak moved to study the various objects. He reached to touch a stack of odd stick-like objects.

"These are curse wands," he said. "They belong to Jumbee demons." She furrowed her brow. "I don't recognize the species."

"They're a small, extremely remote tribe who live in the Caribbean." She moved along the shelves, giving a sad shake of her head. "I suppose Riven spoke the truth when he claimed he was a collector of rare weapons."

"Weapons he shouldn't possess," Tarak said, following behind her, pointing toward a seemingly innocent silver plume. "A harpy feather. Its poison is potent enough to incapacitate a demon, and is forbidden to be owned by any creature that doesn't happen to be a harpy. If they knew it was here, they wouldn't be happy."

She wasn't surprised Riven would have something forbidden. He possessed a stubborn, childish streak that meant he would take pleasure in doing something against the rules.

Waverly halted as she caught sight of a large silver pendant laid on a satin pillow. It looked old, although it wasn't tarnished, and was shaped like a star. Along the edges were strange hieroglyphs.

She didn't know why, but she felt mysteriously drawn to the object. "What's this?"

He grabbed her arm as she reached to touch the pendant. "Wait," he commanded.

She sent him a startled glance. "Is it poison?"

He leaned forward, as if trying to absorb the essence of the silver.

"I'm not sure," he finally admitted.

She leaned forward as well, her nose wrinkling as she caught the pungent stench that clung to the metal.

"Ew. It smells like it's rotting." She pulled back, her skin crawling with disgust. "Why would Riven keep it?"

"That's the question." Tarak's expression was distracted, his gaze locked on the pendant. "Do you feel any magic?"

"No. Nothing," she told him. Why did she feel such a tug of fascination? "In fact it feels…" She shook her head, struggling to come up with the word to describe the void that seemed to pulse around the pendant.

"Dead." He finished her sentence.

"Yes. Dead. That's exactly how it feels. Her mouth went dry as she glanced toward Tarak. "Do you recognize it?"

There was a long silence before he finally spoke. "I am not certain, but I suspect it might have been created by a wizard."

Waverly shuddered. "Why would it smell so bad?"

He pointed toward the pendant, careful not to touch the silver. "Do you see the engraving at the bottom?"

Holding her breath in an effort to avoid the putrid stench, Waverly forced herself to take a step forward. Then, bending down, she studied the narrow band of hieroglyphs.

"It looks human," she said.

"Yes," Tarak agreed. "It represents an ancient sect of magic-users."

Waverly didn't hide her surprise. She'd encountered hundreds of witches on the few occasions she'd traveled among the humans, but she'd never met a wizard. In fact, she'd never known any mer-folk who had crossed paths with the elusive male magic-users.

She suspected they were either a myth or they'd died out long ago.

"Why would you know anything about wizards?" she asked.

He straightened, arching away from the pendant. Did he realize what he was doing? She didn't think so. It was more of an instinctive reaction to the artifact. "Because this sect had a particular magic that can harm even vampires."

Again Waverly was surprised. There wasn't much that could hurt a vampire.

"What sort of magic?"

"Necromancy." There was a bitter edge to his voice. "They can control the dead."

"Very good, leech," a male voice drawled from the doorway.

Waverly spun around, already knowing that Riven would be standing there. How had he managed to sneak up on them?

Her brain was still in the process of trying to accept they'd been caught when Tarak charged forward in a blur of fury.

But it didn't matter how fast or furious he might be. Riven had already anticipated his reaction and lifting the trident he held at his side, he pointed directly at the attacking vampire.

There was the sizzling sound as the Tryshu released its magic, then a grunt of pain as Tarak was tossed backward. Sailing through the air the vampire smashed into the wall with enough force to shatter the shelves. Then he fell to the hard floor with a crushing thump.

"Tarak." Waverly jerkily moved to kneel at Tarak's side. Her breath felt as if it was being squeezed from her lungs by a gigantic hand as she stared down at his unmoving body. "Please don't be dead."

Chapter 12

Riven strolled forward, staring at the vampire lying unconscious in the center of his private bedchamber.

A complacent satisfaction flared through him, banishing his earlier rage when he'd discovered that Waverly had sent him on a wild goose chase.

She would pay for the way she'd embarrassed him in front of his guards, not to mention the fact that she'd dared to lie to him after he'd offered her the honor of giving birth to his heir. She'd been blessed above all other mermaids and she'd thrown it back in his face.

And for what?

A nasty leech?

Stroking his hand down the smooth staff of his Tryshu, he struggled to contain his emotions.

Behind him the royal guards were crowding into the sitting room, all of them trying to get a peek at what was happening. Belatedly he realized he should have commanded them to remain in the corridor. He'd been so shocked when he'd sensed the magical alarm that he'd placed on the doors to his rooms being triggered, he'd simply reacted.

Storming through the castle, he'd headed directly for the royal chambers, indifferent to the soldiers who'd automatically followed behind him.

Now he realized he had to get rid of them. He didn't know what the vampire and Waverly had managed to discover, but he couldn't risk his secrets being exposed.

Pivoting, he eyed his soldiers with a grim expression. "Wait for me in the hallway."

The captain was predictably bewildered by his command. "But—"

"Now," Riven snapped.

Without warning, he heard the swish of Waverly's satin gown. "Rimm, he's deceiving you," she called out.

The guard's brows raised as he tried to peer over Riven's shoulder. "Princess Waverly?"

"You must listen to me," she urged.

"Go," Riven snapped, pointing the Tryshu at his soldier. "Now."

Rimm scowled, but he wasn't stupid. The trident could kill a merman as easily as it killed other demons.

Reluctantly he lifted his hand over his head and then motioned toward the far door. As one, the guards turned and shuffled out.

Riven waited until they closed the door behind him before pivoting back to see the princess hurrying toward the vampire.

"Stop right there, Waverly," he ordered.

She jerked to a halt, stiffly turning to face him. "What have you done to Tarak?"

Riven tightened his fingers around the hilt of his trident. What was wrong with the bitch? She was nothing more than food for the leech, and yet she'd offered him a loyalty she'd denied him.

It was galling.

"He'll survive," Riven drawled, his gaze flicking toward the vampire who was lying at an awkward angle. As if he had more than one broken bone. Good. He hoped the creature was in excruciating pain. "I need him. Unfortunately."

Waverly clenched her hands, tilting her chin in the air. At this moment she looked every inch the princess.

"Because his powers infuse the necromancy pendant you use to trick the Tryshu into accepting your touch?"

Riven's gaze flicked toward the pendant, his lips curling into a humorless smile. "I was afraid you might have figured it out."

"How did you?"

Riven shrugged, recalling the centuries he spent traveling from one demon species to another. He'd used his potent charm to learn everything possible of their various powers, and when his charisma didn't work, he was willing to lie, intimidate, or simply steal the ancient artifacts.

"Trial and error. I attempted a dozen different magical amulets that had no effect," he admitted. "Each time I reached for the Tryshu it would reject me."

Her lips twisted with disdain. "Because you aren't the chosen leader."

He maintained a grim control on his temper. He refused to reveal that her words had struck a raw nerve. He should have been chosen. The fact that he wasn't only proved that the Tryshu was a stupid way to determine who should be king.

Something he fully intended to change in the future.

"The leader should be a merman who is capable of taking destiny into his hands," he snapped.

"By cheating."

"By whatever means necessary," he insisted with a smirk.

She wrapped her arms around her waist, continuing to eye him as if he was carrying the plague.

"You are a blight on the mer-folk," she hissed.

He slammed the end of the trident against the marble floor. "The blight was your father."

"How dare you?" her eyes shimmered like aquamarines in the light of the chandelier. "He was a glorious leader who was beloved by our people."

His anger ran even hotter. Not only was her luminous beauty making him hard with a wasted desire, but she was right. Her father had been beloved. It didn't matter that he'd trapped his people in this isolated castle. Or that they'd been forgotten by the rest of the world.

He had no vision of a future. He was too busy dreaming of the past.

Not Riven. He had plans. Big plans.

"Your father was a weak king who trapped us in this castle because of his own cowardly fears," he informed his companion.

Waverly's face flushed. She acted sweet and docile when she was in public, but he'd seen her anger. More than once.

It was a fault he intended to beat out of her.

"He protected us," she insisted.

"He stole our place in the world."

Her anger faltered as she studied him in confusion. She was as blind as her father.

"Our place?"

"We should be walking among the other demons, not cowering in the depths of the ocean."

She remained confused. "You're free to walk anywhere you want."

He stepped toward her, flicking a glance over her slender body. The desire remained, throbbing through him with an annoying insistence. A desire that was only intensified by the bed that was only a few feet away.

Why shouldn't he enjoy her while he could? She owed him, after all. She'd rejected him for a nasty leech. It would serve her right to discover precisely what she'd thrown away.

He took a step forward, only to halt as sanity returned.

Right now he didn't have the luxury of indulging his desires. Not when the soldiers were standing just outside the door. Rimm had a tendency to interpret Riven's commands in a way that suited himself. Which meant he might charge back into the room with some flimsy excuse. Or the vampire might wake up. Not that he was scared of the leech, he hastily assured himself. Not as long as he was holding the Tryshu. But he hadn't survived by being an idiot. He wasn't going to risk a direct confrontation with Tarak. He wanted the powerful beast safely tucked in his prison before he woke up.

Which meant there was no time to sate his physical need. Instead he would have to content himself with proving he was destined to be far more brilliant a king than her father.

"Perhaps I should clarify," he said in mocking tones. "We should *rule* the other demons."

She looked shocked at his bold claim. "What are you talking about? Mer-folk have never enslaved other species."

He clicked his tongue. Why were his people so narrow-minded? They needed to start thinking in grand terms. World domination.

"I've decided I'm no longer satisfied with being king of this small castle," he informed her. "Why shouldn't I be ruler of the imps or brownies or even the goblins? Once I have my heirs they can help to expand my empire."

Her eyes widened. "That's why you want a child."

Riven shrugged. Did she think he had some sort of paternal urges? Ha. That was a myth that was perpetrated by females desperate to believe they had a mate who gave a damn about the offspring they were producing.

"It's why any male wants a child," he said.

She took a deliberate step back. "That pendant has obviously rotted your brain."

His breath rasped through the air as his leash on his temper threatened to snap.

"It's given me everything I dreamed of possessing."

She took another step backward. "Where did you get it?"

He narrowed his gaze. Ah. She was playing for time. No doubt she hoped her cold-blooded lover would awaken and rescue her.

Riven didn't mind. He wanted to show off his intelligence before he exacted his final revenge on the ungrateful mermaid. It pleased him to think she would spend the rest of eternity regretting her rejection of him.

"I had lived among the Jumbee demons," he told her. At the time he'd been hoping their earthy magic would give him the power he needed. In the end he'd discovered their magical crystals were worthless, but they'd given him the lead he needed for his ultimate victory. "They spoke of a nearby monastery that had monks who could raise the dead from their graves."

Horror rippled over her face. "An abomination."

"True," he readily agreed. "But I wasn't interested in creating a zombie. I wanted the magic."

"Why?"

"I'd discovered I couldn't mask my essence with spells or portions or amulets," he admitted, his gaze straying toward the heavy silver pendant. "But then I realized that my trouble wasn't altering my essence, but hiding it completely. The Tryshu doesn't reject me, because it doesn't sense me."

She looked more confused than impressed by his cleverness. "But you can still wield its powers?"

"Not at first. I tested in secret and realized that while I could hold it, I couldn't force it to obey my commands." His frustration had nearly gotten the best of him when he'd returned to the castle and grabbed the Tryshu. He'd actually been able to touch it for the first time, but his triumph was short-lived when he realized that it refused to respond to his commands. "I decided I needed more power, something that could allow me to force the Tryshu to obey me," he explained.

She remained confused. "Why a vampire?"

He smiled. It'd been nothing less than a stroke of genius that had given him the answer to his problem.

"The pendant is meant to control the dead." His gaze shifted to the unconscious Tarak. "There's nothing more dead than a vampire, is there?"

Riven should have known better than to expect anything but contempt from Waverly. She'd already proven she had no ambition. Still, it annoyed the hell out of him when she gave a sharp shake of her head.

"Our people will never support your desire to enslave other species," she snapped.

As if he cared whether they supported him or not. "I sit on the throne. They will do what I tell them."

"Not when they discover the truth."

"A good thing they won't ever discover the truth, eh princess?" he taunted.

She faltered, no doubt searching for some clever comeback. At last she hunched her shoulders, pretending she wasn't utterly defeated.

"You can't return Tarak to the prison. It's been opened," she reminded him.

"It's true the witch destroyed the key," Riven agreed, his jaws tightening at the mention of Lilah. He'd given the witch immortality, and in return she'd betrayed him. Obviously when he finally chose the female who was going to give him his heir, he would need to ensure she provided him unwavering loyalty. Or perhaps he would simply lock her in the dungeons once she'd given him the children he needed. That way he wouldn't have to worry about her devotion to him and his aspirations. "Eventually Lilah will pay for her treachery," he assured Waverly. "But while the key is gone, the prison remained. And now that you have betrayed me, I have no need to worry whether there is a way to open a doorway. In fact, I prefer it if there's no means to escape."

The smell of her fear wafted through the air. "What are you saying?"

He smiled with a fierce satisfaction. "You, my princess, will be joining your lover in his prison."

* * * *

Waverly knew better than to fight against Riven as he opened a portal to the caves beneath the hotel where the witch lived. She had a brief moment of hope as she caught the scent of vampires. More than one. But before any could appear and rip off Riven's head, the bastard was tossing Tarak through the prison door and shoving her in behind him.

Tarak landed heavily against the floor and she rushed forward to kneel next to him. A second later his eyes were slowly opening.

Relief blasted through her. Despite Riven's assurances that he hadn't killed Tarak, Waverly had feared the worst. She wouldn't trust Riven's word if he claimed the ocean was wet.

But even as she was rejoicing in the knowledge that Tarak was seemingly unharmed from the magic of the Tryshu, he was lifting himself off the floor with one smooth motion.

"No, don't move." She reached out to grab his arm, but she was too late. With surprising speed considering he'd been out cold just seconds before, he was circling the cramped area.

There wasn't much to see. The space was nothing more than an empty gray room with rough walls and a stone floor. She'd never known if her father had created the prisons, or if they'd been used by mer-folk since the beginning of time.

At last he turned back to face her, his expression unreadable. "What happened?"

She straightened, trying to determine his mood. She'd expected him to be furious when he woke to discover himself returned to his prison.

Instead he seemed…

Distracted.

"Riven used the power of the Tryshu on you," she told him.

His lips twisted in a rueful smile as he lifted his hand to rub his nape. As if he was rubbing away a lingering pain.

Did vampires have headaches?

"You warned me it packed a hell of a punch," he said, his tone wry. "In fact, you warned me about a lot of things. I was just too stupid to listen." Guilt twisted her heart. She couldn't bear the thought of this male once again being trapped. Hadn't he endured enough? And why? Because his king had been a spineless addict who was willing to trade his clansman to keep his secret. And her king, who was obsessed with maintaining his hold on the throne.

"I'm sorry."

In a blur of speed, he was standing in front of her, his hands framing her face.

"This isn't your fault." He flicked a disgusted glance around the bleak prison. "None of this is your fault."

Waverly wanted to agree. It made her sick to think she'd been a culprit in Tarak's misery. But when she truly forced herself consider her actions—no, wait... her *lack* of action, she amended, she had to accept that her cowardice had allowed Tarak to remain trapped in this prison.

"I should have gone to the vampires as soon as I discovered there was a new Anasso," she said, her voice thick with regret. "He might have been able to do something to help you."

He placed a finger over her lips. "You were protecting your sister as well as the mer-children," he said. "My own motives were far more selfish."

She sighed, unable to confess that her motives weren't as noble as he thought. Yes, she wanted to protect her sister and the children. It was her top priority. But there'd also been a small, terrible part of her that hadn't wanted him to escape. As long as she knew she would be given the opportunity to see him, even if it was for all too brief periods of time, she could bear her own despair.

It was a horrible thing to admit to herself, let alone Tarak.

"No one could blame you," she said, lifting her hands to lay them against his chest. "There's no demon who wouldn't be obsessed with revenge after what you've been through."

His dark gaze swept over her face, his thumbs brushing the line of her jaw.

"I was so busy focusing on what my Anasso and Riven had taken away from me that I didn't bother to appreciate what I gained," he told her in soft tones.

She paused, wondering if she'd misheard him. "What you gained?"

He stepped closer, his icy power wrapping around her. When she'd first started to visit this prison, the sensation of chilled prickles crawling over her skin had made her tremble with unease. Now it made her pulse race and her mouth dry with excitement.

"I spent five hundred years telling myself that my eagerness for your arrival in my prison was simply because I wanted to keep up my strength," he murmured.

She flinched, her emotions too raw to easily accept that he genuinely cared. Not after centuries of telling herself that it was never, ever going to happen.

"You would be hungry for anyone who was there to feed you," she said, instinctively bracing for his rejection.

Instead, his fingers threaded through her hair, his gaze moving to linger on her mouth. "My need wasn't for your blood. Or even your body."

Her hands smoothed over his chest, savoring the rigid muscles beneath her palms. It was becoming increasingly difficult to think clearly.

"It wasn't?"

"No, it was you," Tarak assured her. "The sound of your voice when you would read to me. And your scent that would linger in this prison long after you were gone."

The protective layers she built around her heart began to shatter. One after the other.

"I was your only contact with reality," she couldn't resist reminding him.

His fingers combed through her hair before they were tenderly tracing the line of her throat. "Yes, you were my touchstone, but so much more."

She furrowed her brow. "Tarak."

His gaze remained locked on her lips. As if he was aching to taste them. "Mmm?"

"I think the Tryshu has messed with your mind," she warned.

"It made me see the light," he rasped, his hands skimming over her shoulders and down her arms. "In more ways than one."

She shook her head. "I don't understand."

And she didn't. He should be ranting and raving at being forced back into his prison. Perhaps even blaming her for her failure to protect him while he was unconscious.

He shouldn't be…

What was he? Not precisely giddy, but fiercely satisfied. Yes, that was it.

"I've never experienced such pain," he told her. "I truly thought that was going to be the end."

A sharp shudder raced through her. She was one hundred percent certain that the sight of Tarak collapsing was going to feature in her nightmares for a very long time to come. "Don't remind me. It was awful."

"In that moment everything became perfectly clear," he told her, stroking his hands down the sides of her body to grip her hips.

"It did?" she demanded, glad that it was clear to someone.

"I didn't regret that I wouldn't have my revenge, or even the years I spent trapped in this place."

She allowed her gaze to roam over his pale, savage features. The wide brow. The bold nose. And the sensual lips that were parted enough to give a peek at his snowy white fangs.

"What did you regret?" she asked in a husky voice.

"Denying my feelings for you," he said without hesitation. "All those years I could have been exploring our mutual fascination. What a waste."

Chapter 13

"Tarak." Her hands slipped up to grasp his shoulders as a crazy sensation zinged through her body. "You're not thinking clearly."

He gazed down at her with the intensity of a predator eyeing his prey.

"I just told you I'm thinking clearly for the first time in five centuries."

"But…" She struggled to keep hold of the threads of her concentration. "We're trapped here," she finally managed to remind him.

A slow, wicked smile curved his lips. "Together."

She shook her head. Maybe she'd been right. Maybe his brains had been scrambled by the Tryshu.

"But you don't understand—" Her words were interrupted when he suddenly swooped his head down to press lips against her open mouth.

Pleasure blasted through her, but before she could wrap her arms around his neck to deepen the kiss, Tarak was straightening.

"Right now, I don't care," he assured her, his eyes smoldering with satisfaction at the blush she could feel staining her cheeks.

She made another attempt to think clearly. Tarak needed to understand the full truth of their predicament.

"But the key was destroyed when the witch released you," she reminded him. "That means we have no way of getting out of here."

His hands slid slowly up and down her back, his chilled touch setting off sparks of fire. "Is there somewhere you want to go?"

An unexpected fury exploded through her. "I want to return to the castle and kill Riven."

He offered her an approving nod of his head. "Later," he promised. "But first I intend to enjoy our time alone." His head began to lower. "Together."

She tilted back her head, trying to avoid his lips. If he kissed her again she would be lost.

"Didn't you hear me? The key is destroyed."

He shrugged. "I'm sure Riven will be encouraged to create a new one." Her anger continued to pulse through her. "My people have been blinded by Riven," she said in bitter tones. "They have no idea he has imprisoned us."

"No, but the vampires do," he reminded her.

Waverly recalled the second before she'd been forced into the prison. She'd been certain that there had been vampires in the caves. It was possible they were already searching for Tarak.

"I suppose that's true."

Unable to reach her lips, Tarak contented himself with nuzzling his lips down the curve of her neck.

"I was too maddened by the thirst for revenge to allow myself to be distracted by the familiar scent when I first escaped," he whispered against her skin.

Her body arched toward him as warmth cascaded through her. What were they talking about? Oh yeah. A smell when he escaped this prison.

"The witch?" she demanded.

"Chiron," he told her, his voice preoccupied. Was he having as difficult a time as she was trying to keep track of the conversation? "He was there. Which means he knows I was being held by your king. No doubt he was even responsible for my release. And when he can't track me down, he'll start demanding answers from Riven."

Waverly grimaced. She understood his hope that his clansman would confront Riven and rescue them. She even applauded the thought of the King of Mer-folk being torn to tiny, bloody shreds by the vampires.

But she couldn't help but worry about her people. They were innocent victims.

"It could mean a war," she breathed.

"Chiron isn't a fool. He'll attempt diplomacy first," he assured her, allowing the sharp tips of his fangs to press against her skin. "But we both know Riven has to be stopped."

She released a shaky sigh. She hated the thought that the mer-folk might be put in danger, but she couldn't argue with Tarak. Riven had gone mad with power. To the point that he thought he could enslave other species. Narcissistic jerk.

"Yes," she slowly agreed, trembling as his fangs scraped over the pulse pounding at the base of her throat.

"Until then, I intend to concentrate on you," he growled.

Anticipation rippled down her spine, tightening the tips of her nipples and making her toes curl.

She'd been held in Tarak's arms before. And even felt the thrilling sensation of his fangs sliding deep into her flesh. But suddenly she felt a deluge of pleasure washing over her.

"This is…" The words dried on her lips. She simply didn't have the means to express what was swelling inside her.

"Glorious?"

"Yes, but more."

He lifted his head to regard her with a faint smile. Was he amused by her lack of eloquence? Probably. She sounded like a water nymph drunk on fermented seaweed.

"More what?" he demanded

She tilted back her head, becoming lost in the inky darkness of his gaze. "Intense," she breathed.

His expression softened, his body brushing against her in a soft promise.

"It is," he agreed, his voice thick with an emotion that made her breath catch in her throat. "It must have something to do with the witch's spell being broken. There's no magic to dull our senses." He pressed a lingering kiss on a tender spot just below her ear. "But be warned, there is a danger."

She stiffened. Was he joking? It didn't really seem the time or place. "What kind of danger?"

"The eternal sort."

"You're being very cryptic," she complained.

"It should be obvious." He gazed down at her, his lips parted to reveal his fangs fully extended. "Unless mermaids are incapable of mating?"

She blinked, barely daring to believe he'd spoken the magical word.

"Mate?" she whispered. "Are you certain?"

He chuckled at her shock. "Do you need me to prove it?" Lowering his head, he kissed her with all the fierce, forceful hunger she'd longed to experience. "Does that help?"

For five hundred years she'd fantasized about this male. His scent, his touch, the feel of his fangs sliding deep into her flesh. Now she didn't want a soft, tentative seduction. She wanted exactly what he was giving to her. A ruthless demand that sizzled through her.

"It's a start," she assured him.

"Oh, I have more," he assured her.

He claimed her lips in another searing kiss. Waverly moaned as bliss flooded through her, so intense it made her head swim and her knees weak.

Easily sensing she was turning into a melty mess of need, Tarak wrapped his arms around her and jerked her tight against his body. Her lips parted, silently inviting his tongue to plunge into her mouth. Waverly made a sound deep in her throat, her hands lifting to clutch at his arms.

If she'd been in her right mind, she'd be demanding an explanation about his claim. You couldn't just throw around the word 'mate' and not follow up with a long, deeply spiritual conversation.

But she wasn't in her right mind. And any urge to discuss the future, or even the past, was lost in the blaze of heat that seared through her.

Her eyes slid shut as his lips eased and he pressed a line of kisses down her jaw.

"I've discovered I'm addicted to passion fruit," he whispered.

"Passion fruit?"

"And salt." He nibbled a path down the curve of her neck.

She hissed as his tongue touched the pulse hammering at the base of her throat. "All mer-folk have salt on their skin."

"I like it," he interrupted in a soft voice, maneuvering her backward until she was pressed against the wall. "You make all other females taste bland in comparison."

His words stirred a vivid memory of his fangs plunged into her neck, drinking deeply of her blood. Her heart fluttered. Really and truly fluttered. Like a butterfly madly zigzagging in the center of her chest.

Unable to resist temptation, she reached to grasp his t-shirt, jerking it over his head in one smooth motion. The fluttering went into hyper-drive as she caught sight of the smooth, hairless skin of his chest. It was the first time she'd seen his bare torso, which meant she hadn't been expecting the tattoo of a golden dragon with crimson wings that spread over his chest. It was disturbingly realistic as it shimmered with an oddly metallic glitter.

"What is it?" she demanded.

His dark eyes glowed with a barely restrained hunger, but his touch was gentle as he grabbed her hand and pressed it against the dragon.

"It's the mark of CuChulainn."

She furrowed her brow. "The mark of what?"

"The mark of a clan chief," he told. "It's given to those vampires who manage to survive the battles of Durotriges."

"I've never heard of Durotriges."

"Because only a vampire can seek out the ancient demon who presides over the tests," he admitted. "Once he accepts you, he uses his magic to take you to another dimension for the actual battles."

She felt an odd stab of anger. She didn't like the realization that he'd risked his life in some ridiculous contest to become a clan chief. He could have died, and she would never have known him.

An unbearable thought. "I suppose your precious Anasso invented the battles?"

He surprised her by giving a shake of his head. "Actually they've been around since the beginning of time. Even in the dark ages we desired a means of choosing our leaders. Not that they prevented open warfare, or ambitious chiefs from forcibly taking over rival clans."

"If I'd been around back then, I would never have allowed you to enter," she scolded.

His lips twitched as his hands stroked up the side of her body. "You sound like a princess," he teased.

A quivering sigh was wrenched from her throat as his hands cupped her breasts.

"I can't bear the thought of you being hurt," she rasped.

His dark eyes flared with satisfaction. Obviously he was pleased that she was worried about him. Then, before she could speak, he was impatiently pulling the gown over her head.

"We're safe for now," he assured her, his fingers drifting along the slope of her shoulders. His touch was cool, but the light caress sent fire cascading through her. "And alone."

She reached to scrape her nails over the glittering dragon on his chest. "Yes," she whispered. "Alone."

He released a growl, lowering his head to capture a nipple between his teeth, stroking it mercilessly with his tongue.

Waverly gasped at the wave of sensations that crashed over her. No matter how vivid her fantasies, they were nothing compared to reality of his touch.

Continuing to tease her breast, Tarak allowed his hands to skim lower. She shivered as he explored the curve of her hips and then the tender skin of her inner thighs.

He gave her nipple a last nuzzle before his head lifted and he buried his face in her neck.

"Have you considered the risk?" he demanded in a husky voice as his fangs scraped down the vein in her neck. "Once I'm mated to you it's for an eternity."

Mated...

The word whispered through her, stirring emotions that she'd kept buried deep inside her. For so long she'd endured the knowledge that her devotion to this vampire was futile. He would never see her as more than an adversary.

One that he would use as a necessary source of blood, but otherwise keep at a firm distance.

It was overwhelming to contemplate a future where they were forever bound together.

"I don't have to consider," she murmured, her hands lowering to deal with the fastening of his trousers. "I've belonged to you from the first moment I entered this prison."

He growled in pleasure, gently brushing aside her hands so he could finish removing his clothing with far more skill than she was able to. Once he was naked, however, she pressed her hands against his shoulder before he could close the distance between them.

She wanted an opportunity to admire his pale skin stretched over chiseled muscles. And the glorious tattoo. Not to mention the large, growingly thick erection. That was a sight that deserved to be savored.

With a breathless pleasure, she used the tips of her fingers to explore the hard planes of his chest. He had no heartbeat, but she felt him tremble beneath her touch. He liked that.

So did she.

His skin was cold and smooth as silk. An intoxicatingly erotic combination.

She allowed her fingers to drift lower, strumming over the six-pack abs before they were wrapping around his arousal. Tarak grunted, sounding as if he'd just been kicked. Or perhaps it was the sheer power of her touch.

The thought made her glow inside.

Clutching her hand tight around his erection, she pushed her fingers down, thoroughly enjoying the tortured expression that twisted his features. After spending five hundred years at the mercy of her emotions, she liked giving a little payback.

But even as she began to pull her fingers back up his hard length, Tarak pressed himself tight against her. Clearly he was interested in something a little more up close and personal.

A choice that had its benefits, she realized at the sensation of his hard body rubbing against hers, creating a delicious friction. Her lips parted on a sigh. It was all the invitation Tarak needed as he captured them in a rough, demanding kiss.

Her arms instinctively circled his waist, her hands stroking up the curve of his back.

Tarak shuddered. "I'm hungry for you, Waverly," he whispered, his fingers smoothing down her hip and then around to her inner thigh. At last he found the aching spot between her legs. "All of you."

Waverly tilted her head to the side, her gaze watching in fascination as his fangs lengthened. It was a stark reminder that he was a predator who could rip out her throat if he wanted.

Still, it wasn't fear that made her tremble.

No, it was sheer, mind-numbing lust.

As if sensing the swelling need, Tarak allowed his finger to dip into her body. At the same time, his thumb pressed against a perfect, glorious spot. Waverly arched toward him, her heart thundering as his finger stroked in and out, deeper and deeper. It felt like there was a whirlpool about to suck her under.

She released a shaky breath. This was amazing, but she wanted more—his fangs buried deep in her neck, and his erection buried deep inside her...

"Tarak," she moaned softly, threading her fingers through his hair and tugging his face against her neck. "Drink."

* * * *

Tarak released a low groan, pushing away the pang of regret that he'd wasted so many years clinging to bitterness. He wasn't going to spend one more second brooding on the past.

Not when he finally had Waverly exactly where he wanted her.

Forgetting Riven, and the fact they were stuck in a prison, Tarak bared his fangs and with one smooth strike had them buried deep into her neck.

Waverly's breath hissed through her clenched teeth, her nails drawing blood as they pressed into his flesh. Tarak didn't mind. A bit of pain only intensified the pleasure.

Feeling as if he was drowning, Tarak savored the sweet and salty blood as it ran down his throat. It was delicious, but it wasn't enough. With a groan he smoothed his hands down the back of her legs, then, with one smooth motion, lifted her off her feet.

She made a sound of satisfaction, enthusiastically wrapping her legs around his waist.

Tarak pulled his fangs out of her throat before he lifted his head. He wanted to watch her expression as he slowly, steadily angled her onto his erection.

They sighed in unison as her tender flesh parted to allow his penetration. Already Tarak could feel the primitive magic coursing through his body.

This wasn't sex.

This was the mating.

The ground beneath his feet seemed to shift as he relished the sense of Waverly deep in his soul. He felt her pleasure as he began to rock his hips back and forth, plunging his arousal as deep as he could go. And the raw emotions that he'd used as a weapon against her.

He'd sworn the moment he was betrayed that nothing would be more important than his fierce need for revenge.

Now he understood he'd been a fool.

Waverly was all that mattered.

All that would *ever* matter.

Waverly made a tiny sound of pleasure and Tarak's control shattered. Five hundred years of hunger was flooding through his body. It was going to be a few decades before he could take things slow and easy.

Whirling around he placed his own back against the wall. He didn't want to risk scraping her tender skin. Then he slid his fangs back into her neck as his hips thrust in a steady rhythm.

"More," she rasped softly, her head lowering so she could press her teeth against his shoulder.

"Bite," Tarak commanded, shuddering as she obediently pierced his skin.

Tarak lifted his hand to press against the back of her head, urging her to drink the blood to complete the mating ceremony.

As she greedily sucked on the wound, an incandescent bliss exploded through him. This was the only magic a vampire could experience.

And it was magnificent.

Withdrawing his fangs, he licked the last drop of blood from her neck as he felt her climax clench around his erection. The sensation sent him spinning into his own orgasm.

A savage ecstasy engulfed him, nearly sending him to his knees.

He'd spent what felt like an eternity in this prison, desperate to escape. Now he knew he could quite happily spend the rest of his life in this precise spot.

As long as he was here with Waverly.

As the last of the rapturous tremors vanished, Tarak slowly lowered Waverly to the ground. He hated having her lying on the hard stone, but there wasn't any choice. Not now. Putting Waverly's discomfort on the very long list of 'reasons to kill Riven' Tarak stretched out next to her. A smile curved his lips as he watched her lightly trace the crimson tattoo that spread up her inner forearm. It was the mating mark. His gaze moved toward the matching mark on his own arm.

A joy that was laced with a large amount of awe spread through Tarak at the intricate crimson scrolls. He'd devoted himself for so long to creating peace for the vampires. An admirable goal, but hardly one that had offered him personal pleasure.

Now he felt almost overwhelmed by the maelstrom of emotions that churned through him.

It wasn't just the lingering pleasure that made his limbs heavy with sated desire. Or the fierce satisfaction of knowing this female was now his for an eternity.

It was the sheer delight of sensing her nestled deep inside him. As if two halves had joined to become one perfect being.

Before meeting Waverly he would have scoffed at such romantic tripe. Who needed a mate? He was satisfied with his existence without the demands of a female who would be in constant need of attention.

What a spectacular idiot he'd been.

This exhilaration that was filling his soul was magical. As if he'd just been offered a place in paradise. At the same time, he felt an enormous pressure settle around him. It was the knowledge that he now had to care for his precious treasure.

His life's mission was now to ensure she was safe, and happy, and that she possessed everything she might need.

All admirable ambitions. And completely impossible at the moment. How could she be safe or happy or have anything she might need when they were trapped in this damned prison? Frustration bubbled through him, threatening to destroy his euphoria.

Beside him, he could feel Waverly begin to stiffen, easily sensing his darkening mood. With a grim effort, he forced away his anxiety.

Right now all he wanted to think about was his new mate.

He gently brushed the hair from her cheek, cherishing the dewy warmth of her skin. "Tell me about your childhood."

She blinked, clearly caught off guard by his demand. "What do you want to know?"

"Were you happy?"

She paused before giving a slow nod. "There was always a hole in my heart at the loss of my mother, of course, but I was happy," she assured him. "The mer-folk are a very close-knit species. Probably because there are so few of us. I knew I was loved."

"I can believe that." His fingers stroked over the tip of her ear, just now realizing they were faintly pointed. An indicator that mermaids had fey blood. "I assume you were the pampered princess?" he teased.

"No." She gave an emphatic shake of her head. "That was Sabrina."

It took a second for him to recall the name. "Your sister?"

"Yes."

He rolled onto his side, gazing down at her with a genuine curiosity. "Why was she pampered?"

"Because she deserved to be," she answered in a firm tone. "She was always sweet and kind to everyone. The perfect nurturer." A wistful smile touched her lips. "Looking back, I wonder if she felt compelled to take on that role after the death of my mother."

"Why?"

"Before her death, my mother was responsible for the magic that protects the nursery."

Tarak could tangibly feel the sadness that tugged at her heart.

"Your sister inherited the gift after your mother died?"

"I assume it had been dormant inside her since she was born." She pressed her face against his hand, as if seeking his comfort. "And once it was needed, it appeared. She claimed that it was a blessing."

He brushed a gentle kiss over her forehead. "You don't think it was?"

"Perhaps, but it was also a burden that fell on her shoulders at a very early age." Her gaze became distracted, as if she was becoming lost in her memories. "Unlike me, she had to put away her childhood and assume her duties."

His fingers traced the line of her jaw. "Ah. That's the reason you've been so desperate to find her," he murmured. "You feel guilty that she was forced to take on the role of an adult while you could remain a child."

Her brows snapped together. "I was desperate because I love my sister and because I'm terrified that something might happen to the children."

"And?" he prompted.

She heaved a rueful sigh, perhaps just now sorting through the tangle of emotions that'd inundated her after her sister had been taken captive.

"And I suppose there's some guilt," she slowly admitted. "And if I'm forced to be completely honest, a little bit of envy as well."

She managed to catch him off guard. "Envy?"

"She had a purpose in her life. A glorious purpose that ensured she was deeply admired by everyone. While I…" Her words trailed away, her expression suddenly hardening with regret. "While I stood by my father's side and smiled."

Tarak was puzzled by her reaction. "Did you wish you had your sister's magic?"

"No, as I said, she had an instinctive urge to nurture others." She wrinkled her nose. "I didn't."

"What did you want to do?"

She hesitated, a hint of wariness darkening her eyes. "You'll laugh."

His lips twitched. He wasn't going to start off their mating with a lie. Not when she could sense it.

"Perhaps," he admitted. "Tell me."

"I wanted to be a warrior."

He studied her with confusion. He'd expected her to say something silly. Like she wanted to be a jellyfish.

"Why would I laugh?" he asked. "Aren't mermaids allowed to be warriors?"

"Usually, but my father's obsession with protecting me meant he wouldn't even discuss allowing me to become one of his guards." She scowled as she watched his smile widen. "I knew you would find it funny."

He tapped the end of her nose with his finger. "I don't find your dreams funny," he assured her. "I'm smiling at your claim that you didn't become a warrior."

"I didn't."

"You've been battling against Riven since he stole the throne."

Her lashes lowered, no doubt hoping to hide her pain at his words. "I wish that was true," she muttered, her tone bitter. "I've been a coward. My father was right not to allow me to pick up the trident."

He cupped his hand beneath her chin and tilted her head back. "Waverly, look at me."

"Please don't tease about this, Tarak," she implored in a raw voice.

Tarak jerked in astonishment. This wasn't just a false modesty. She truly didn't realize just how amazing she truly had been.

"I'm not teasing. Look at me, Waverly." He waited until her lashes slowly lifted to reveal the beauty of her aquamarine eyes. "If I've learned nothing else, it's that rushing into danger and waving a sword or trident makes you an idiot, not a warrior."

"I did nothing," she protested.

His fingers tightened on her chin. "You obeyed Riven's demands to keep your sister alive and ensured that I had enough strength to escape when the opportunity arrived," he reminded her. "It's not your fault I was too stubborn to listen to your warnings."

She shook her head. "I wanted to do more."

"Trust me, sometimes the bravest thing you can do is wait."

His tone was harsh with his own sense of failure. If he'd simply agreed with the Anasso's bargain when he'd found him in the secret tunnel, he would have been free to walk away. Later he could have spread the truth about the ancient vampire's addiction. But no. He had to be filled with self-righteous anger, refusing to back down.

She brushed a hand over the dragon tattooed on his chest, no doubt sensing his remorse. "I hate feeling helpless."

He'd known this female for five hundred years, but he'd been blind to the fact that she was as much a prisoner as himself. And that she'd been seething with the same desire to destroy Riven.

Blind about so many things.

"Your greatest weapons are here." He lightly touched her forehead, indicating her clever brain. "And here." He touched the center of her chest, feeling the leap of her heart beneath his finger. "Use them wisely."

She looked like she wanted to protest, then she heaved a resigned sigh. "Fine, but I want a trident when we finally get out of here."

He chuckled at her petulant tone. "Did you play with one when you were a little guppy?"

"Maybe."

"I can see you dashing through the castle with a trident twice your size."

"I also had a helmet I stole from the armory. It was way too big, and it kept slipping over my eyes when I made my charge."

Tarak stilled. This female was always beautiful to him, but with the mischievous amusement sparkling in her eyes, she was breathtaking.

At least if he had any breath to take.

"That could be a problem."

"It was." She offered a wise nod. "One day I was attacking a pile of pillows I'd stacked in a corner and I accidentally stabbed my dance instructor who'd come into the room."

He tilted back his head to laugh with a rich enjoyment he hadn't felt in far too long. It was all too easy to imagine a young Waverly wearing an oversized helmet, and with a trident clutched in her hand as she dashed toward the dastardly pile of pillows. She probably even had her own war cry.

"What happened?" he asked.

Her amusement dimmed. "My father took away my weapons and gave me the position of his royal advisor. He assumed that would keep me out of trouble."

He allowed his fingers to drift down her throat. He understood her frustration, but he also sympathized with her father. The male had lost his mate. How could he possibly bear to lose his children?

"Did it keep you out of trouble?"

"No." She suddenly looked smug. "But I never got caught again."

Chapter 14

Waverly swallowed a groan at the sensation of Tarak's fingers lightly brushing over the very spot where he'd sunk his fangs deep into her flesh. There was no pain, but the skin remained acutely sensitive. As if Tarak's bite had created a new erogenous zone.

The thought sent a shiver through her as she traced the edge of the tattoo that was spread across his chest. It was going to take time to accept this glorious creature was truly her mate.

Maybe a few thousand years or so.

"Tell me about your clan before you joined with the Anasso," she urged.

His eyes softened. They always did when he spoke of the vampires he'd gathered during his years as a clan chief. As if they were a special part of his life. Perhaps a part he'd forgotten after he'd pledged himself to his Anasso.

"It was smaller than most," he said. "Chiron used to call us the Band of Misfits."

She arched her brows. Tarak might be stubborn, aggravating, and occasionally a pain in the neck—in more ways than one. But she would never consider him a misfit.

"Why?"

"Because I never sought out the strongest or the most powerful vampires," he explained.

"Who did you want?"

He allowed his fingers to trail over the curve of her bare shoulder as he considered his answer.

"Vampires who were intelligent, as well as visionaries," he finally said.

"They could see into the future?" she asked. She'd heard of demons who were prophets although she'd never met one.

"No, but they weren't afraid of embracing change."

She nodded. She knew that the reason he'd joined with the Anasso was because Tarak understood that survival meant adapting. And she agreed. Eventually the mer-folk would be forced to consider how to embrace the rapidly evolving world. Right now they were protected by her father's magic, but as the humans invaded the oceans, and the toxic pollutants threatened their precious water, they would have to make hard decisions. Something Riven would be incapable of accomplishing.

She jerked her thoughts away from the future. She had quite enough to worry about right now, thank you very much.

"So they had to be smart and visionary," she murmured, returning her thoughts to the man at her side. When she was gazing into his dark eyes she wasn't thinking about Riven, or the fact she was trapped in a prison, or even the hard stone beneath her. Yeah, it was sappy. But true. "Anything else?"

"Loyalty."

"I suppose every leader hopes for that," she agreed.

His jaw hardened. "Not blind loyalty, but one of mutual respect," he clarified. "That's the only certain way to be sure your clansman will have your back when things get messy."

She studied him with a blatant curiosity. "I always thought vampires were..."

He looked more amused than offended as her words trailed away.

"Barbarians?" he suggested.

She snorted. She didn't miss the irony. He'd been a barbarian before becoming a vampire. It was after he'd been turned into a demon that he'd gained his quest for peace.

"Yeah."

His fingers drifted down her arm, sending sparks of desire firing through her.

"The vampires have a brutal past, but not all of us wanted our future to be bathed in blood." A muscle tightened in his jaw. "A damned shame I wasn't more careful with my own loyalty."

She lightly scraped her nails over his chest, anxious to distract him.

"What other skills did you want in your clansman?" she asked.

"Bravery."

She flinched as the word scraped against a raw nerve. "Ah."

His brows snapped together, a genuine annoyance hardening his features. "Waverly, stop it."

"Stop what?"

"You are not—and never have been—a coward."

She turned her head to gaze at the ceiling above them. Tarak didn't understand. How could he? He'd been a human soldier, and then a vampire who'd faced deadly battles to become a clan chief. He'd never been trapped by the love of a father's expectations. Or blackmailed by a bully.

"You have to say that," she muttered.

"Why would I have to?" He sounded genuinely puzzled.

"Because I'm your mate."

"Ah." His smile widened to reveal his fangs. "Which means I'm incapable of lying to you."

"Really?" She searched his face, not sure if he was teasing.

"Concentrate on our bond."

Closing her eyes, she tentatively focused on the strange sensation of Tarak buried deep inside her. She'd known it was there from the moment the taste of his blood had hit her tongue. Just as she'd felt the sizzling heat of the tattoo forming on her inner arm. But it was all... overwhelming. Like standing in the center of a hurricane after years of swimming through calm seas.

At first she couldn't define more than the dazzling explosion of new, and wondrous feelings that swirled through her. But as she focused on the bond that pulsed between them, she realized she could sense his emotions. The adoration that seeped through him as he gazed down at her. The wonderment at their mating. And an underlying fury that they were lying on the cold stone of this prison.

He was right. If he was lying to her, she would know.

"That's amazing," she breathed, then her eyes widened as she realized the bond would work both ways. "And a little scary."

"So you know I'm telling the truth when I say you have more courage than most warriors I've ever known," he said.

She scowled. Clearly he hadn't been listening when she said she'd given into Riven's demands.

"I've done nothing," she insisted.

His hand cupped her cheek as he lowered his head. Almost as if trying to force her to accept the truth of his words.

"You remained in the castle," he reminded her. "After Riven claimed the throne you could easily have fled."

"He held my sister hostage."

He looked unimpressed with her reasoning. "A coward would have walked away regardless of the fact that someone they loved was in danger," he asserted. "That doesn't even include the fact you walked into a prison with a rabid vampire."

Her fingers continued to stroke over the dragon tattoo. Very soon she intended to use her lips and tongue to explore every vibrant color of the clan chief marking. It fascinated her. "You weren't rabid."

"I easily could have been. I was injured, frightened and trapped. The perfect ingredients to send me over the edge. I could have ripped out your throat the second you entered the prison."

His voice was stern, as if he was angered by her decision to risk entering the prison to feed him. Which was a little unfair. Would he have preferred another mermaid had offered her vein? She thrust away the horrifying thought. No one was feeding this male but her.

Period. End. Of. Story.

"I'm glad you didn't," was all she allowed herself to say.

"So am I," he assured her, obviously sensing her tangled emotions. "My point is that you entered with the full knowledge you might be severely injured, if not killed outright."

Put like that, it did make her seem like one of the champions she'd read about in her father's library. Perhaps Stellara, a legendary mermaid who'd fought back an attack by an ambitious tribe of sirens who'd attempted to lure the mermen into a trap with their potent song.

A flush stained her cheeks. "I had no choice."

"Of course you had a choice, but you risked your life to protect your sister, and the children." His eyes darkened as his finger slid over the upper curve of her breast. She didn't need their bond to know he was becoming distracted. "And your father's legacy," he added.

Desire trickled through her. Amazing, considering that minutes ago she'd been sated to the point of exhaustion.

"Just as you sacrificed your freedom to protect your people," she said in soft tones, her hand skimming down the rippling muscles of his stomach.

"Mm." His fangs lengthened, shimmering with a lethal, pearly glow in the muted light that filled the prison. "We are both very heroic."

She sent him a wry glance. "I'm not sure it's very heroic to be trapped in a prison."

His thumb found the tip of her nipple, stroking it to a hard peak.

"A temporary glitch."

Waverly hissed in pleasure. Her brain was threatening to shut down as a delicious heat spread through her body. "A glitch?"

"A *temporary* glitch," he corrected.

He said it with such certainty that Waverly didn't bother to protest. "And after we escape?"

"We kill Riven."

A fierce need to watch Riven being shredded into bloody ribbons blasted through Waverly. It was something that had been in her dreams for centuries. But she pressed her fingers across Tarak's lips, holding his gaze. "First we have to find my sister," she warned.

He kissed the tips of her fingers before gently pulling them away from his mouth. "That won't be necessary once Riven's head is removed from his body."

She glared into his determined expression. As much as she might sympathize with his urgent desire to make Riven pay for what he'd done, there was no way she was going to risk her sister's freedom.

"No, Tarak," she rasped. "If Riven dies, we'll never find the entrance to her prison."

"You're right." His cheerful tone made her consider the pleasure of punching him in the nose. Mate or not, she wasn't going to let him endanger Sabrina. Easily sensing her annoyance, he leaned down to brush a light kiss over her lips. "Because the prison will be gone," he said against her mouth.

She pressed her hands against his chest until he lifted his head. "How can you be so sure?" she demanded.

He waved a hand toward the gray walls that surrounded them. "This place wasn't created by the same magic that was used to build the castle."

She wanted to believe him, but… "I thought vampires couldn't sense magic?"

"I can't," he admitted. "This prison carries the stench of Riven."

So it had been Riven who'd created them. Relief raced through her. She'd hated the thought that her father might have been responsible.

But that did nothing to ease her anxiety. "Which means that when he dies, the ability to open the prison will be lost forever."

His hand cupped her breast, his thumb continuing to tease at her nipple. "This isn't the magic you use to project your image. Or even what your father used to create the castle," he said, his gaze locked on her flushed cheeks. "This is created by human witches, and something else… maybe the ogress." He paused to consider before giving a shake of his head. "But the fuel to keep the prison in place is provided by Riven's life force. That's why I can smell him."

"So his personal talent wasn't being able to create places like my father," she muttered. "It's using his powers to manipulate other people's magic."

A sudden flood of fury poured through her. "Dammit, I should have killed him centuries ago."

His arms abruptly wrapped around her, his hands running a soothing path down the curve of her spine.

"Not much of a talent, if you ask me," he assured her, obviously attempting to distract her from her bitter self-disgust. "It's not nearly as cool as projecting your own image."

Waverly released a slow, shuddering breath. She'd be angry with herself later.

For now...

Her fingers explored downward, a smile curving her lips as she heard the low growl that rumbled in his throat.

"Or making things float," she said.

There was a faint breeze before the air molded around her, almost like a blanket. Then, with amazing ease, she felt herself being lifted off the ground, still wrapped tightly in Tarak's arms.

"Like this?"

Waverly's lips parted in amazement. She'd experienced Tarak lifting her, but she'd never imagined he had the power to hold both of them in midair. And seemingly without effort.

"I feel like I'm surrounded by water," she breathed, looping her arms around his neck as she arched her body tight against him. "Floating on the current."

His hands skimmed down to cup her backside. "Soon you'll be swimming free."

She trembled. Could Tarak sense how much she longed to be in her mermaid form as she soared through the vast ocean? Probably. The need was almost as intense as her desire for this male.

Almost.

"I like the sound of that," she told him, her voice husky.

"Me too." He pressed his lips to her forehead, then stroked them down the length of her nose. "What else do you like?" he demanded. His fingers slid between her legs. "This?"

A moan was jerked from deep inside her as she wrapped her legs around his waist. "Oh yeah."

"And this..."

Together, they slowly began to spin in the air as he pressed his erection into the welcoming heat of her body.

Magic.

* * * *

Inga was a few steps behind Levet when he pushed open the door at the end of the hall. Someone had to keep an eye out for guards. And the gargoyle was blithely indifferent to any danger that might be lurking just out of sight.

Typical.

But then she caught the delicate, fresh scent that suddenly filled the air.

"Wait," she commanded, scurrying to catch up with her companion.

Levet turned his head to send her an impatient frown. "Now what?"

"You can't just go charging into the nursery," she chided the small demon. "Mer-babies are very fragile."

Levet was instantly on alert. "Why?

Inga blinked, trying to recall the rumors she'd heard over the years. None of them had been very specific. After all, the mer-folk had been hidden from the world for centuries. But the one thing she'd heard over and over was that there were very few children that survived. "I'm not sure. I think it has something to do with the magic."

Levet tiptoed into the room, his wings kept closely folded against his back. Like a child walking through a store filled with spun glass.

"I feel it," he murmured in hushed tones. "You are right. It is fragile."

"Yes." She entered the nursery behind him, able to sense the magic that floated around the room. It was as soft as a spider's web, brushing over the ornately carved cribs.

"And it is fading." Levet added, still speaking in a soft voice.

Inga glanced around the room. Unlike the rest of the castle, the nursery looked as if it'd been carved out of the seabed. The floor was as hard as granite and the walls roughly chiseled from a dark stone. And every surface was coated with a thick layer of salt. On each side of the room were deep pools of ocean water with what looked like an egg in each one.

It was as if the babies needed the most primal surroundings to thrive.

But even as she cautiously stepped forward, she understood what Levet was talking about.

The magic that splashed over her was...thin. Like the edge of a wave that barely tickled your toes.

"I don't understand," she said, speaking more to herself than her companion. "Why would the mer-folk allow their magic to fade?"

Levet tilted his head to the side, considering the question. "I believe it has something to do with the female we are seeking."

Inga warily glanced around. The female voice had led them to this place, but why? There was no one here, unless they were invisible.

A thought that did nothing to ease her jangled nerves. "Do you think she's draining the magic?" she asked.

"*Non.*" Levet gave an emphatic shake of his head. "She *is* the magic."

Inga scrunched up her face. She hated mysteries. They always ended badly.

Always.

"Where is she?" she demanded.

"I am not certain." Levet sniffed the air, slowly crossing the floor as if drawn by some unseen force. "The magic is much stronger here," he murmured.

Inga tried to walk softly as she followed the gargoyle. Of course, she still sounded like a rhino on steroids. There was no way a female her size could prance around like a fairy.

Or a mermaid.

A flush stained her cheeks as the stone beneath her feet groaned in protest. It was bad enough her head nearly brushed the ceiling without turning the floor to dust. Then she was thankfully distracted by a shimmer of light that appeared on the wall.

"There's something…" she breathed.

Levet pressed against her leg. "What?"

A tingle of pleasure raced through Inga. Males never touched her. Not unless it was in anger. Or to force her to obey their commands. Now it didn't matter whether or not Levet was unaware of what he was doing. She felt a delicious warmth spread through her.

With an effort, she forced herself to study the magic that was beginning to pulse and spread.

"It feels like an opening," she said.

"*Oui.*" Levet took a step forward, pressing his hands against the chiseled stone. "I sense it. *Bonjour,*" he called out. "Can you hear me?"

"Yes, I'm here," a muffled voice echoed through the wall.

Inga pressed her lips together. Until this moment, she'd been convinced they were being led into an ambush. Why else would the strange voice insist they come to the nursery? But now they were here, she was beginning to think she might have been wrong.

Levet was right. The magic swirling through the room was coming from this precise spot. As if whoever was in charge of caring for the babies was trapped on the other side of the wall.

So did she walk away and save herself, or…

She heaved a resigned sigh. Of course she was wasn't going to walk away. Not if there was any chance the babies were in danger.

Shoving the sleeves of her muumuu up her arms, she stepped forward.

"Stand back," she ordered, pressing her hands against the wall.

Levet readily scuttled away, his wings stirring a soft breeze around Inga. Yet another thing she loved about the tiny demon.

"What are you going to do?" he asked.

"Try to connect our magic," she told him, tapping into the power that bubbled deep inside her.

The magic flowed through her body, as sweet and intoxicating as a siren's song. Inga shivered. She rarely allowed herself the luxury of indulging in her mermaid side. Her life had been too violent, and brute strength was the only way she'd survived. Now she felt almost drunk with the heady power.

Closing her eyes, she concentrated on the magic that was pulsing through the wall. She wasn't sure what the hell she was doing, but she allowed herself to be guided by instinct. There were some things that had to come from the gut.

Her palms warmed, the bubbling magic feeling like it was spilling through the stone and into her body. It wasn't scary. It was thrilling. And oddly familiar. As if she was being reunited with an old friend.

Or family.

The heat spread from her hands into her body, easing the knots of tension in her shoulders. Was the mystery person doing it on purpose? Maybe hoping to lure her into a sense of complacency before they attacked?

The thoughts were still forming when Levet abruptly clapped in delight.

"Ah. Bravo, *ma belle.*"

She opened her eyes to see what was happening. *Oh, crap.* Dropping her hands, Inga stumbled backward. She'd sensed that she'd connected with the other female, but she hadn't known that their magic was carving a hole in the wall.

It wasn't until she looked closer that she realized it wasn't a hole. It was, instead, some sort of spell that was allowing her to see through the barrier.

Not sure what the hell was going on, she studied the female who was illuminated by a strange glow. She was beautiful. Of course. All mermaids were gorgeous. Except for her. The unknown female had dark golden hair that held a hint of blue, and her eyes were a swirl of seafoam. She was also tall and slender and was wearing a gown that was nearly translucent.

"Thank goodness," the female said, seeming to float forward as she offered them a dazzling smile.

Inga scowled, feeling large and clumsy as Levet brushed past her with a flutter of his wings.

"Who are you?" he asked.

"Princess Sabrina," the female answered.

Inga's scowl deepened. Of course she was a stupid princess.

"I am Levet." The gargoyle performed a low bow before straightening and waving his hand toward Inga. "And this—"

"Poyson," the mermaid interrupted, her lips parted with shock.

Inga shook her head. Was the female demented? That could certainly explain why she was locked away. "No. My name is Inga," she said.

The female drifted closer to the magical window, still appearing shocked. "Poyson's baby," she whispered.

Inga gasped. "You know my mother?"

"Of course. She's my aunt." The brilliant smile widened. "Dearest cousin. Welcome home."

Chapter 15

Riven returned directly to the royal chambers after dumping the vampire and Waverly into their prison. He paced through the rooms, checking to see if anything had been broken or disturbed.

Long ago he'd cursed his seeming lack of talent. He couldn't create massive buildings like the king, or paint exquisite works of art like Poyson. He didn't even have the ability to protect the nursery, although that seemed like a lame-ass talent.

Eventually, however, he'd discovered an amazing ability to control the magic of other creatures. It didn't matter if the power came from a demon or a human—he could manipulate it to fulfill his own purpose.

Once he'd realized his astonishing skill, he'd known that nothing could stop him from claiming the throne.

Riven shook his head, returning his attention to the various artifacts and crystals he used to focus his powers. None of them appeared to be missing. Still he continued to pace through the room.

He wanted to wallow in pride at the knowledge that he'd managed to deal with yet another potential disaster. What other merman could have reacted with such swift efficiency? None.

He alone had the skills and cunning to lead the mer-folk into the future.

No matter what Waverly might claim.

Riven's hands clenched. Why had her accusation that the people would never follow him struck a nerve? It wasn't like he cared if the mer-folk approved of his decisions or not. The old king might have inspired a sickening amount of adoration, but Riven had a different management style.

He didn't want his people's love, he wanted their fear.

They would obey or be locked in the dungeons. Simple.

So why couldn't he shake his peevish anger? Maybe he should have spent more time punishing Waverly. Yes. That must be it. Frustrated lust crawled through his body, leaving behind a sour sense of dissatisfaction. If he'd spent time sating his desire for the bitch, he wouldn't be pacing the floor.

Lost in his thoughts, Riven ignored the light tap on the door. It wasn't until a shadow fell across the floor that he realized someone had dared to disturb his privacy.

"Your majesty."

Whirling on his heel, he scowled at Rimm who was standing at attention in the doorway. "What do you want?" he snapped.

The male ignored the overt lack of welcome, his expression stoic. "I assume that you returned the vampire to his prison."

"Of course I did. Is that all?"

Rimm stubbornly refused to be dismissed. "No. I've been unable to locate Princess Waverly."

Riven stilled, careful to keep his expression bland. Somewhere in the back of his brain he'd known he'd have to come up with a convincing story about Waverly's abrupt disappearance. The princess was as annoyingly popular among the mer-folk as her father had been. There was no way they wouldn't notice she was gone.

But he'd assumed he would have time to fabricate a reasonable story. Stupid mistake.

"Why have you been looking for her?" he demanded, playing for time.

"I wished to ensure she was unharmed."

Riven's jaw tightened. What was Rimm's interest in the princess? Did he harbor some futile hope he might someday capture her interest? Probably. Most males in the castle harbored fantasies of bedding Waverly.

"She's fine." Riven forced himself to stroll toward a bowl of fresh fruit that was kept on a table next to the sofa. He sent one of his servants to the land above to acquire a variety of food he'd grown accustomed to during his travels among the humans. It was one of the perks of being king. At the same time, he shuffled through various excuses to explain Waverly's absence. "In fact, she's decided that she wishes to spend some time exploring the world," he said, grabbing an orange from the bowl.

There was a suspicious silence before Rimm took a step forward. "Exploring where?" the guard demanded.

Riven pretended to concentrate on peeling the orange. "Does it matter?"

"It just seems odd."

"What seems odd?"

"Why would she choose to leave now?"

Riven dropped the peeling on the floor, popping one of the orange sections in his mouth as he glanced up.

"I really prefer not to reveal the truth, Rimm," he chided in soft tones.

The guard studied him with a wary expression. "Why not? The people will be asking questions. First Princess Sabrina retreats to her rooms and refuses to speak with even her closest friends, and now Princess Waverly has disappeared."

Riven continued to eat his orange, pretending to consider the male's words. It had been remarkably easy to convince his people not to worry about Sabrina. She'd always preferred to avoid her father's social events. Plus he'd commanded Waverly to convince anyone who asked that her sister was perfectly fine.

They might not believe him, but they were happy to accept Waverly's reassurances.

This wasn't going to be nearly so simple.

He tossed aside the orange and pulled out a lacy handkerchief to wipe the juice from his fingers.

"Perhaps you're right. I wouldn't want my people to worry. The truth is..." He paused, letting the suspense build. Not only to prime his audience, but because he enjoyed the drama. At last he tucked away the handkerchief and delicately cleared his throat. "The truth is that Princess Waverly has revealed herself to be a traitor."

Rimm jerked as if Riven had smacked him in the face. "I don't believe it."

With a low hiss, Riven was striding to grab the Tryshu that he'd propped against the wall.

"What did you say?"

"I would swear on my life that the Princess is loyal," Rimm said, grimly holding his ground despite the lethal weapon pointed at him.

Riven might have admired his courage if the male wasn't being a pain in his ass. Why should he have to explain anything to his servants? Or anyone else for that matter.

He was the king. It was beneath him to be questioned. His word was law. Or at least it should be.

Anger vibrated through him. Obviously the sooner he could create his personal empire, the better. His heirs would be taught at an early age to offer him complete respect.

First, of course, he had to produce his heirs. Something that was easier said than done among the mer-folk.

What he needed was a harem, not a consort, he abruptly decided. The more females he could have in his bed each night, the more likely to produce a child.

Starting tonight.

But first he had to deal with Rimm and the missing Waverly.

"I don't blame her," he drawled, forcing his tension to ease. "She was bewitched by the vampire."

"I thought he was locked away?"

Riven shrugged. "She's been secretly visiting his prison."

Rimm looked confused. "Why would she do that?"

"I had no opportunity to discover the reason. I presume she'd already known the leech before I captured him," he suggested. "Or perhaps he was capable of using his powers of compulsion to force her to come to the prison. Vampires have an uncanny ability to reach the delicate minds of females." He heaved a sigh, as if deeply disappointed in Waverly. "In either case, she was the one who helped him to escape."

Rimm made a sound of shock. "She opened the prison?"

"How else could he have gotten out?" Riven demanded.

Rimm absently ran his fingers along the hilt of his trident, visibly trying to process the thought of the female he'd known for centuries suddenly revealing herself as a traitor.

"And then they returned to the castle?" he demanded, not yet convinced of Waverly's guilt.

"He's determined to kill me."

"I still don't understand why."

Riven seethed at the male's refusal to drop the subject. For a crazed second he considered blasting the male with the Tryshu. He had plenty of guards. Any of them could take over as captain. Right?

No, the voice of common sense whispered in the back of his mind. He had to be patient. There were still those among the mer-folk who resented his place on the throne. Even if he held the Tryshu. If he started randomly killing off those who annoyed him, it might give them ideas of rebellion.

Once he could be certain he had a stranglehold on his power, he would kill whoever he wanted.

"An old grudge," he at last said, his tone warning he wasn't going to discuss the vampire.

Rimm glanced around the room, as if seeking some sign of the missing princess. "And now Princess Waverly has decided to travel around the world?" he asked with a dubious expression.

Riven heaved a loud sigh. "I asked her to leave."

"You banished her?"

"She's a traitor." Riven narrowed his gaze. "Would you prefer that I lock her in the dungeons? Or have her executed?"

The male's face paled with horror. "No."

"Then you agree with my decision?"

Rimm pressed his lips together at the venom that dripped from Riven's words. At last he seemed to comprehend that he was treading in dangerous waters.

"You're the king," he said stiffly.

A mocking smile touched Riven's lips. "It's so nice you finally recalled who is boss."

"Forgive me." Rimm gave a small bow. "I'll return to my duties."

Riven watched the male turn to walk away, before abruptly calling out. "Wait."

Rimm glanced over his shoulder. "Yes?"

"I need you to gather everyone in the throne room," Riven commanded. The male blinked. "Again?"

"Yes, again," Riven snapped. "I have an announcement that's going to change the future of the mer-folk." He allowed another dramatic pause. "Forever."

Chapter 16

Inga flinched. Why hadn't she paid more attention to Levet when he'd said that the scent was similar to her own? She'd assumed he meant she smelled like a mermaid. Not that they were related.

Now she felt herself floundering as she stared at the female with a raw sense of apprehension.

There wasn't much of a family resemblance. No surprise. The mermaid looked like an angel, while Inga...

Well, no one would mistake her for a celestial being.

"Cousin?" she managed to choke out.

"Yes." The female held out her hand, as if trying to reach through the barrier and touch Inga. "I'm so happy to finally have you home. At last."

A dangerous warmth crept through the ice that surrounded Inga's heart. *Home.* It was a place she'd been searching for her entire life.

Was it possible?

No, no, no. With a sense of panic Inga shattered the tiny bud of hope.

What was wrong with her? She didn't doubt the female was her cousin. But her claim that she was happy that Inga was home was nothing more than a desperate ploy.

"Bullshit," Inga growled.

Sabrina slowly lowered her hand. "I don't understand."

"We came here to help you," Inga said, the words flat. "There's no need to pretend you're not horrified by my presence in your castle."

The mermaid pretended to be confused. "Why would I be horrified?"

Inga hunched her shoulders, hating the pain that sliced through her. After all these years, why did the rejection of her family still hurt? "Please don't play this game."

"There is no game, Inga," Sabrina insisted. "I swear."

Scowling, Inga glared at her cousin. "Do you think I've forgotten my last visit to this place? It might have been five hundred years ago, but the words were burnt into my brain."

Sabrina managed to look shocked. "You were at the castle?"

"After I escaped, I had a ridiculous hope that my family would want to know that I survived," Inga confessed, using mocking tones to disguise her distress. "You see, at the time I didn't realize that it was my beloved mother who'd sold me to the slaver."

There was a shocked gasp as Sabrina pressed a hand to her heart. "That's a lie. I don't know why you would believe such a terrible thing."

Inga clenched and unclenched her hands. Did the princess think she could fool her? Probably. Most creatures took a look at her lumpy, ugly face and assumed she must be stupid.

"Because your king told me," she informed the mermaid.

"King?" Sabrina blinked. Then blinked again. "My father?"

Inga gave an impatient shake of her head. "Riven."

Sabrina's lips parted, but it took a few seconds before she could actually speak. "That bastard," she finally rasped.

"Finally, we agree on something."

"He lied to you."

Inga snorted at Sabrina's claim. "Why would he lie?"

A bitter hatred twisted the female's beautiful features. "Because whenever his lips are moving he's lying," she spat out. "And because he enjoys hurting people. And because he was no doubt trying to manipulate you to suit his own purpose."

It was hard to dismiss the fierce sincerity in Sabrina's voice. Inga tried. How could she possibly trust this female? At best, she wanted their help. At worst, she was leading them into a trap.

Then Inga felt the brush of fingers over her tightly clenched fist.

"You should listen to her, *ma belle*," Levet urged in soft tones.

Inga swallowed the lump forming in her throat. Maybe he was right. The goddess knew that no one with a brain in their skull would trust Riven. "My mother didn't sell me to the slavers?" she demanded, remaining wary.

"Never," Sabrina hissed. "Never, never, never."

Okay. That was adamant.

"So what happened?" she asked.

Sabrina paused, casting an anxious glance around the nursery. Was she searching for something?

Or someone?

Eventually she returned her gaze to Inga. "After my father created this lair, he was worried about losing the ability to keep in contact with the outside world," she said.

Inga wrinkled her nose. "I don't know why. The outside world is pretty sucky."

"I agree, but we'd ignored the threat from the dragons until it was too late, and we paid a heavy price." Sabrina's eyes filled with tears. "Including my mother."

"Oh." Inga felt a grudging pang of pity. She understood the pain of living without a mother.

Sabrina cleared her throat, blinking away the tears. "My father understood that our isolation wasn't enough protection," she continued. "We needed to know what was happening among the other species. Especially the humans."

"He sent my mother to be a spy?"

Sabrina shrugged. "Among others."

Inga tried to wrap her brain around her mother sneaking around like a secret agent from a human movie. "Is that when the ogres kidnapped her?"

Sabrina looked surprised by the question. "She wasn't kidnapped."

Inga stiffened, her chest feeling oddly tight. "If she wasn't kidnapped, how did I happen?"

Sabrina gave a lift of her hands. "The way that babies usually happen. Poyson fell in love with the leader of a tribe of ogres."

Love? Inga stumbled back, falling on her butt as her muumuu fluttered around her like a parachute. She barely noticed. The earth was tilting on its axis and it was taking all of her concentration just to force the air in and out of her lungs.

"She loved my father?" It was weirdly difficult to form the words.

"Very much. We were all…." Sabrina floundered as she searched for the right word. "Surprised," she at last landed on. "But love is love. At least as far as we were concerned."

Inga shook her head, trying to clear away the fog. Her father hadn't been a violent rapist. And her mother hadn't given her away to slavers.

Everything she believed was crumbling around her.

In a good way.

Well, in a mostly good way. She hadn't missed the edge in Sabrina's voice.

"Not everyone was happy with their union?"

Even through the barrier, Inga could see the mermaid pale. Was the memory causing her physical pain?

"When it was discovered your mother was about to have a child the ogres went into open rebellion."

"Because she was a mermaid?" Inga asked.

Sabrina muffled her bitter laugh, as if worried about disturbing the sleeping babies. "They claimed it was because your father had been promised the day he was born to mate with a female from a rival tribe. The bride price had already been paid and there was the threat of war."

Inga curled her lips in disgust. It was possible her belief that her father had been an aggressive brute had colored her opinion of ogres. After all, she'd heard plenty of rumors that there were tribes that had managed to become civilized. And if her mother had fallen in love with one, they couldn't be all bad. Still, it was hard to think of them as anything but savages.

"There's always a threat of war with the ogres," she groused.

"True, but the breaking of the oath offered a perfect opportunity for one of your father's overly ambitious lieutenants to kill his leader and take control of the tribe," Sabrina said. "He was the one who led the rebellion."

Inga paused, allowing the words to seep into her heart. She'd never thought about her father. The knowledge of what he'd done to her mother had made her stomach cramp. Now a slow anger burned in the pit of her stomach.

Not only had she lost her father, but she hadn't been allowed to properly mourn his death. Instead she'd been taught he was a monster. "He murdered my father," she rasped.

"Yes," Sabrina said in soft tones. "I'm sorry."

Inga waved off the female's sympathy. She'd deal with her complicated daddy-daughter feelings later. First she had to know what happened to her mother.

"And Poyson?" she asked, the name unfamiliar on her lips. "What did they do to her?"

A salty blast of air managed to penetrate the barrier. "She'd just given birth to you when the soldiers burst into the lair. They..." Sabrina's trembling words faded.

Panic jolted through her. Ten minutes ago she wouldn't have given a crap if her mother was alive or dead. Now she couldn't bear the thought she was gone.

"Please don't tell me she's dead," she pleaded.

Sabrina shook her head. "They thought she was. They stabbed her through the heart and tossed her over a cliff like she was a piece of trash. Thank the goddess she had a devoted servant who snuck her away and nursed her back to health. It took years before she fully recovered."

Inga released a shaky breath. "What about me?"

"It didn't make any sense they would have murdered your parents but left you alive. We all thought you were dead. Everyone except your mother. She swore she could feel you. In her heart."

She heaved a shaky sigh, forcing herself to her feet. "Where is she?"

"Looking for you."

"Truly?"

"Truly." Sabrina's features softened. "She has devoted her life to finding her baby."

A weight that Inga didn't know she was carrying suddenly seemed to lift off her shoulders. Her mother was alive. And she was looking for her.

"I didn't know. I thought—" Her words lodged in her throat.

"You were abandoned?" Sabrina asked softly.

"Yes. All this time I could have been here with my mother. Instead I was torturing myself with the belief that I was a stain on my family." Fury bubbled and then detonated through her. Like an exploding volcano. "I'm going to kill him."

Clearly sensing that Inga was about to rush from the nursery in a crazed rage, Sabrina pressed her hand against the barrier.

"No, Inga," she protested. "You can't."

Inga narrowed her eyes. "Oh yes I can."

"No." There was an unmistakable urgency in the mermaid's voice. "He can't be killed as long as he holds the Tryshu."

"The what?" Inga demanded.

"It's the trident he holds," Sabrina told her. "It contains a powerful magic that makes him impervious to injury. You can't kill him." The bitterness returned to the mermaid's face. "No one can."

Inga scowled. She'd encountered hundreds of powerful demons. Some that were near god-like. But everyone had a weakness.

"There has to be a way."

"Listen to me, Inga, I need your help." Sabrina muttered a curse when Inga continued to dwell on the best means of killing the King of the Merfolk. "The babies need your help," she said, effectively capturing Inga's full attention.

Inga planted her fists on her hips and studied her cousin through the barrier. "Are you on the other side of the wall?"

"Not exactly. I'm locked in a magical prison created by Riven."

"Why?"

The tears returned to Sabrina's eyes. "He was using me as a pawn to force my sister, Waverly, to feed the vampire."

Inga's breath hissed through her teeth. For centuries she'd watched the mermaid who'd appeared in the caves beneath the gardens of the hotel. She'd kept her distance, unwilling to reveal her presence. Now she realized that she could have discovered the truth centuries ago if she'd just talked to the female.

"She was at the hotel," Inga breathed in a harsh voice. "My cousin. And I didn't even know." She shook off her frustration. "Can we bust through the barrier?"

"No. He was forced to leave a window open so my magic can continue to protect the nursery, but there's no way to physically force your way through it." Sabrina abruptly slammed her hand against the barrier. "Believe me, I've tried everything."

Inga glanced around. "So where is the doorway?"

"I'm not sure."

Well that was inconvenient.

"Then how do I reach you?" Inga demanded.

Sabrina lowered her hand and squared her shoulders. As if preparing to pronounce some bad news. "You can't."

Inga felt a flare of annoyance. What was she talking about? "There has to be some way to find the doorway. Riven isn't that smart."

A small smile flickered around Sabrina's lips before it quickly faded.

"Not in time." Her gaze strayed toward the reservoirs filled with water and the precious babies, a profound sadness rippling over her face. "My powers are failing."

Inga glanced toward Levet who gave a small nod. The tiny gargoyle had sensed the fading magic the moment they'd entered the room. She returned her attention to the mermaid. "Then what do you want from me?"

The female answered without hesitation. "You need to kill me."

Inga waited, wondering if this was some sort of test. Did she have to prove her loyalty to her family?

"Kill you?" she at last demanded.

Sabrina nodded as if Inga had asked if she wanted dinner, not to be murdered. "With my death the magic will pass to a new guardian," she explained.

Inga didn't have to consider her answer. Not for a second.

"No."

Sabrina looked desperate. "Please, Inga. I don't fear death. At least not my death." She waved a hand toward the waters. "I will sacrifice anything to save the children."

Inga understood the woman's desperation. The babies were utterly vulnerable. They had to be protected.

But she'd spent her entire life without a family. Now that she finally found a cousin, she wasn't going to kill her.

"I can't."

"Inga, please," Sabrina entreated.

Inga whirled around, managing to smack a hole in the wall with her clenched fist. She grimaced, holding her arms close to her side as she carefully hurried out of the nursery. The last thing she wanted was to further damage the nursery on her way out.

Once she reached the hallway, however, Levet had scurried to stand directly in front of her.

"Where are you going, *ma belle?*"

Inga halted, only then realizing her breath was bellowing in and out of her lungs. She sounded like a steam engine trying to chug up a steep hill.

She took a minute to calm her tangled emotions. "I can't kill my cousin," she said, her stubborn tone warning she wasn't in the mood to argue. "But I can kill the person responsible."

Levet's wings fluttered, his eyes wide. "*Non.* You heard the princess. Riven cannot die."

"Anything can die," Inga growled, stepping to the side.

She fully intended to sweep past the gargoyle to go in search of Riven. The lying, spineless King of the Mer-folk had to be in the castle somewhere.

But glancing down, she felt a sudden pang of guilt as she met Levet's worried gaze. She didn't know what was going to happen when she confronted Riven, but it was quite likely that it wasn't going to be good.

She couldn't put Levet in danger.

It was time to let him go.

Chapter 17

Levet was braced to try and stop his companion. Not the easiest task. She was quite large, and in her current mood, he wasn't sure that a full-grown troll could hold her back. Thankfully, his magic was awesome. And he had just the perfect spell to halt the female in her tracks.

But even as he prepared to dazzle the ogress with his powers, Inga was reaching down to grasp him by one horn.

Levet felt himself being lifted off the ground and then they were charging down the corridor at a teeth-jarring pace.

"Eek!" Levet futilely wiggled to get free of the female's grasp. A wasted effort. He might as well have tried to release himself from the jaws of a Cerberus demon. And he should know. He'd been caught by one of the mangy creatures when he'd tried to sneak into the underworld. Hades was such a party-crapper. "Put me down."

"I'm sorry, but I have to get to a place where I can open a portal."

"There is no need to carry me about like a sack of potatoes."

Inga ignored him, jogging up a staircase with the grace of a drunken goblin. Levet's teeth rattled and his insides felt like they were being bounced into places they shouldn't go.

The things I endure for this ogress. And all because...

His brow furrowed. Because why? The truth was, he wasn't sure. A part was no doubt his natural urge to protect any female. He was a Prince Charming *extraordinaire*, even if his talents were not always appreciated. He could never resist the urge to rush to the aid of a damsel in distress. But this was more. It was almost as if he was being compelled to safeguard the female by a force greater than himself.

Fate? Destiny? An illusion?

He wasn't sure. And bizarrely it didn't bother him nearly as much as it should.

They reached the top of the staircase and Inga turned toward a door that led to a long corridor. This one, however, wasn't chiseled out of ocean bedrock. Instead it was lined with murals that were almost as glorious as the ones Inga painted. At least he seemed to have a vague memory of admiring her artwork. The floors were marble with flecks of real gold. Above their heads he could catch sight of strange globes of light that floated near the curved ceiling.

Levet was fascinated. He'd seen fairy lights, but these were different. The glow had a shimmer that changed colors and pulsed as if it was connected to someone's heartbeat. Mermaid magic. It was beautiful.

Still contemplating the source of power, Levet was astonished when he was abruptly surrounded by darkness. Had he gone blind? He blinked. No. They were moving through a portal.

He breathed a sigh of relief as he caught the scent of stone and moss and the musk of vampires. They were in the caves near Lilah's hotel.

"Thank the goddess," he breathed. "You have come to your senses."

She looked down at him, her expression sad. "Not really. But at least you'll be safe." Without warning, she leaned down to stroke her hand over the top of his wing. A shiver of pleasure raced through Levet. *Mmm.* Her touch was surprisingly gentle. "A shame we never got to visit Paris."

Levet scowled, his relief fading as he caught sight of the steely determination in her eyes. "You're returning to the castle?"

She shrugged. "Someone has to deal with Riven."

Levet stomped his foot. Princess Sabrina had just told them that Riven couldn't be killed. What did she think she could do on her own to hurt the King of Mer-folk?

"It is a suicide missile."

"Mission," she absently corrected him.

He gave another stomp of his foot. Stubborn creature. "Fine. Suicide mission."

Her eyes turned a brilliant red as she bared her pointed teeth. "He lied to me. He made me believe that my mother sold me to slavers. And that I was a blight on the mer-folk," she ground out in fury.

"Oui." Levet held up a hand. "He is a despicable creature, but you cannot fight him without some help." Levet paused, a fuzzy idea beginning to form. "We must ask the vampires to join us."

She glanced at him in surprise, as if caught off guard by his suggestion. Then she slowly shook her head. "No. I have to do this on my own."

There was a haunting sadness in her voice. Levet reached up to grasp her hand, giving her thick fingers a squeeze.

"Never on your own, *ma belle*," he insisted. "Have you forgotten you have a Knight in Shining Armor at your service?"

She smiled, but the sadness lingered. "Not this time."

"What do you mean?"

She gently tugged her fingers out of his grasp. "I want you to stay here."

Levet stiffened. Had the female lost her mind? No one with any sense would deprive themselves of his magnificent magic. Especially when facing a crazed merman who couldn't be killed.

"You doubt my powers?"

She looked shocked by his accusation. "Of course not."

"Then I will stand at your side." He squared his shoulders, his wings spread to reveal their full glory. "Where I belong."

Unexpected tears filled Inga's eyes. "You belong here with your friends."

His friends? Levet didn't know who she was talking about. He possessed thousands of friends, but he had no urge to be with them. Not now.

His place was with Inga. Was it not?

"You cannot keep me from following you," he warned the ogress. "I will find a fey creature to create a portal."

She heaved a deep sigh. "Levet."

"What?"

She bent over, putting her face a mere inch from his own. "Look at me," she commanded.

Levet obediently met her gaze, noting that the crimson had faded to reveal the sea-blue of her eyes. He also noted they were quite pretty. Large and clear and surrounded by a lush frame of lashes. Were they a gift from her mermaid mother?

The ogress was no doubt intending to kiss him goodbye. Females tended to find it difficult to keep their hands off him. It was his fault, of course. He had too much charm to keep contained in his delicate size.

"I realize that I am irresistible, *chéri*," he assured her. "But now is not the time to play smoochy-face." He reached to pat her cheek, hoping to ease the sting of his rejection. "Perhaps later."

Her hand lifted, her fingers touching the center of his forehead. "Remember."

Levet clicked his tongue. It seemed that she didn't intend to kiss him after all. That was…disappointing.

"Remember what?" he asked, distracted by the strange sensation of tingles crawling beneath his skin. It felt like someone was removing a cobweb. Or perhaps the crackle of a spell being broken. "What have you done?" he demanded.

Inga straightened, her expression impossible to read. "I've given you back your freedom."

"I do not…" Levet's words died on his lips as a curtain slowly parted in his mind. Fragments of memory began to form, as if waking from a deep sleep. "Wait," he breathed, gazing at the ogress with a growing sense of outrage. "You worked at the hotel with Lilah."

Inga squared her shoulders, looking like she was preparing for battle. "Yes."

Levet turned his head to glance around the caverns. He hadn't forgotten being down here, but his memories had been…smudged. He had a perfect image of chatting with Inga near the large stone altar in the center of floor. But now he could also recall that the ogress had grabbed him by the horn and hauled him to the nearby dungeons.

Standing as still as a statue—an easy task for a gargoyle—Levet tried to piece together the past.

He'd come to the hotel with Chiron. *Oui.* They'd come to search for the male's missing master.

"And that vampire who was chasing us was Tarak," he said in accusing tones. "You imprisoned him."

Inga hunched her broad shoulders. "Not me. Riven."

Levet snorted. Did she think she could deflect her sins onto the merman? It wasn't Riven who'd held him prisoner. Or wiped his mind of his memories. Or compelled him to assist her on her mad flight from the furious Tarak.

"You were helping him," he stubbornly insisted.

"He tricked me."

"As you tricked *moi.*"

She grudgingly nodded. "Yes. I'm sorry."

He waved aside her apology. "Why?"

"Because I needed your help to escape from Lilah's spell," she admitted. Suddenly Levet recalled that he'd been standing guard over the ogress after Lilah had wrapped her in a magical web. "And because—" The ogress bit off her words, her face flushing.

"Because?" Levet pressed her to finish.

She gazed at him with a strange intensity, as if trying to memorize the lumps and bumps of his face.

"It doesn't matter," she abruptly assured him. "Not anymore."

Levet snapped his wings. Was this a jest? She had befuddled his mind. He deserved answers. "It does to me."

She reached out to brush her fingers lightly over the top of his wing.

"Take care, my Knight in Shining Armor."

She stepped back, disappearing into the portal. Levet gasped as he rushed forward.

"Wait!" he cried.

There was the sound of a snap as the portal closed. Levet skidded to a halt, his tail tangling around his feet.

Sacré bleu.

He had known his share of exasperating females. He preferred a challenge, after all. The more complicated the object of his affection, the more fascinated he became.

But Inga...

He was furious with her. She had abused his trust and manipulated him with magic. He expected such behavior from his family, but not an ogress who claimed to be his friend.

But for all his anger, Levet still felt a driving urge to follow the female.

Was it magic? Perhaps a lingering side effect from her spell? Or even a different one that Inga hadn't bothered to remove?

It didn't feel like that. It was more a response that came from the center of his being. Somewhere between his chest and his gut.

He scrunched up his nose, telling himself it must be gas. Or heartburn. Unfortunately, his stern lecture did nothing to ease the acute fear that something terrible was going to happen.

He had to get to Inga.

Turning to leave the cavern, Levet came to an abrupt halt as he caught a familiar scent. It was cold, and lethal. Like a snake. An angry, ill-tempered snake.

Styx.

The leather-clad vampire stepped into the cavern, his massive sword held in front of him. Clearly he'd sensed that someone was in the caves and had come to check out what was happening.

Levet impatiently watched the male approach, impervious to the scowl on the vampire's face. The Anasso was in his usual mood. Pissy. No doubt it had something to do with being the King of Leeches. Who would want such a nasty job?

"Levet?" Styx growled, his eyes narrowed with suspicion. "What the hell are you doing here?"

Levet sent the male an annoyed frown. He didn't care that Styx could rip him in two with his bare hands.

"I need to open a portal," he told the vampire.

Styx came to a halt, blinking in confusion. "Why?"

Levet glared toward the spot where Inga had disappeared. "That stupid ogress is going to get herself killed."

"Inga?" A cold chill blasted through the cavern. "Where is she?"

Belatedly realizing that the vampires had every reason to want Inga dead, Levet pointed a claw in Styx's direction.

"She returned to the mermaid castle," he admitted. "But you are not allowed to hurt her."

"I have no interest in the female." Styx curled back his lips to reveal his fangs. "I want to know where Riven is hiding."

"Oh. He is at the castle as well."

Styx nodded, as if he'd already suspected where the merman was lurking. "Did you see Tarak there?"

"At the castle?" Levet studied Styx in confusion. Why would the male assume the vampire was with the mer-folk when his scent was scattered around the cavern? He sniffed the air. "He's here. Can't you smell him?"

Styx shook his head. "He moved through these caves after he escaped from his prison."

"*Non.* This is more recent."

"I think I would know…" Styx cut off his angry words as he caught the scent that was rapidly fading. His jaw tightened with annoyance. "Damn. You're right. Can you follow his trail?"

Levet flicked his tail with impatience. He didn't care about Tarak. All he wanted was to find someone who could help him find Inga. Unfortunately, he'd had enough dealings with the Anasso to know the male would use his physical superiority to force Levet to obey his commands.

Leeches were such a pain in the derrière.

Closing his eyes, Levet concentrated on the smells that threaded through the air. There were few demons who possessed his own heightened senses. It was usually a blessing. At the moment, it was a curse.

Bending low, he at last pinpointed the exact location of Tarak.

Levet opened his eyes and pointed at the ground near the altar. "He entered through a portal and left through a portal."

Styx growled with frustration. "A portal to where?" he demanded. "To the castle?"

"It is impossible to know." With a shrug Levet turned away. He had more important matters to attend to.

But before he could take a step to head out of the cavern, the stupid leech grabbed him by the horn and lifted him off his feet.

Why were demons forever doing that? It was rude.

"Not impossible," Styx informed him.

Levet flapped his wings. "Release me."

Styx hauled him up high enough that they were eye to eye. "Go back to the fighting pits your ogress destroyed," he commanded.

A pang of betrayal stabbed Levet's heart. "She's not my ogress," he protested. "At least not anymore."

"Shut up and listen," Styx snapped.

Levet wrinkled his snout, refusing to be intimidated. "You are not the bossy pants of me."

Styx muttered something about an ugly gargoyle head being mounted on his wall. Levet dismissed his words. The vampire couldn't be talking about him. His face was exquisite.

"I need you to get Troy and bring him here," Styx finally commanded.

About to inform the vampire that he had his own problems to solve, Levet swallowed the words.

"Troy?" he instead demanded. He'd met the flamboyant imp in Chicago. They weren't besties, but they'd formed a bond of mutual dislike for the vampires. Troy would no doubt be willing to open the portal he needed. "Why is he at the pits?" Levet demanded. "Is he going to fight? I do not have time now to make a bet, but—"

Styx waved his big sword. "Just go."

Levet stomped toward the arched opening across the cavern.

"There is no need to snap at me," he muttered. "I am having a very bad day."

"It's going to get a lot worse if you don't move your chunky ass," Styx called after him.

Outrage jolted through Levet as he continued out of the caves. "Chunky?" *Stomp, stomp, stomp.* He headed up the nearby staircase. "It is a fine derrière. An exquisite derrière." He exited the caves and stepped into a lush garden bathed in silver moonlight. "Stupid leech."

* * * *

Riven stood on the dais, glancing around at the sea of mer-folk that filled the throne room. Unlike earlier, the faces turned in his direction weren't filled with curiosity. Instead he could sense a rising irritation. As if they were annoyed to be commanded to attend the gathering.

Thankless creatures.

The previous king had been far too casual. He'd allowed his people to treat him with an intimacy that Riven detested. He didn't want the mer-folk to like him. He wanted them to obey. Immediately and without question.

Pursing his lips, he turned his head to regard the male standing at his side. "Is everyone here?" he demanded.

Rimm's nod was stiff, as if he was having a difficult time bending his neck.

"I believe so, sire. Except those who are on duty."

"What duty could be more important than hearing my announcement?" Riven snapped.

Rimm furrowed his brow, as if baffled by the question. "The cooks who are preparing for the banquet you commanded to be served tonight and the musicians who are arranging the ballroom for the entertainment." He nodded toward the two guards standing next to the wide doors. "And of course, the guards who are at their posts."

"Fine." Riven waved his hand in a shooing motion. "Move away from the dais."

Rimm sent him a startled frown. "Are you sure?"

Riven considered zapping the male with his Tryshu. It might ensure that the captain of his guards understood exactly who was giving the orders around here.

"I wouldn't have said it if I wasn't." He pointed toward the crowd who were attired in silken gowns and carrying delicate fans. Not one of them had ever touched a weapon. "Do I look like I'm in any danger?"

"No, but—"

"Move."

Riven could hear Rimm's teeth grinding together as he offered a deep bow. "As you wish."

Waiting until the guard had stepped down, Riven moved to the edge of the dais. He wanted to make sure he was the center of attention before he made his announcement.

He held up a silencing hand, waiting for the low babble of conversation to halt. Even then he silently counted to a hundred before speaking.

A flair for drama was as important to a king as any trident. Besides, he enjoyed the sensation of controlling the room with nothing more than his silence.

That was true power.

"My people, I know you are all anxious to discover why I've gathered you together," he said in a voice that easily carried to the back.

The crowd regarded him with varying expressions from boredom to suspicion. Riven swallowed his urge to snap at them. Soon enough they would learn to regard him with the proper respect. Perhaps he would even command them to remain on their knees when he was in the room.

Yes, that would satisfy him.

He pasted a smile on his face. "You will be pleased to know that I have been dedicating my thoughts to our future," he assured the mer-folk. He allowed the smile to fade, placing his hand over his heart. "The past, I fear, has not been to our advantage."

There was a stirring through the room at his claim. Riven struggled to keep the anger from showing on his face.

"I understand that the previous king was attempting to do his best to protect us," he forced himself to concede. "But his efforts have sadly left us isolated and trapped by our fear of the future."

The crowd began to whisper softly to each other.

"Who said we're trapped?" a voice called from the back. Murmurs of agreement flowed through the crowd like a wave.

Riven rapped the butt of the Tryshu against the marble dais.

"From now on, we will no longer cower at the bottom of the ocean," he assured them. "It's time to take our place."

"What place?" another voice called out.

Riven smoothed a hand down his gown, trying to take a mental note of the mer-folk who were glaring at him with petulant expressions. They would eventually be punished for their lack of faith in his greatness.

"Ah. I'm glad you asked," he drawled. "Together we will claim a place at the top of the demon world." He spread his arms wide in a welcoming gesture. "But first I intend to establish my harem. I need the fortunate mermaids to line up in front of the throne so I can—"

"Die!" a voice bellowed from the upper balcony.

Chapter 18

Inga hadn't intended to create such a dramatic entrance. To be fair, she hadn't given any thought to her entrance, dramatic or not.

After she'd returned to the castle, she'd been consumed with a black fury.

She'd been abused her entire life. First by the ogres who had murdered her father and tried to kill her mother. And by the slavers who'd treated her like an animal to be used and traded without any concern for her feelings.

And most of all by Riven, who'd deceived her just so he could manipulate her into helping him.

For so long she'd believed that she'd been unloved and unwanted. The knowledge had been a vast, howling emptiness in the center of her soul.

And now, like the cherry on top of the very crappy sundae, she'd forever destroyed any hope that Levet would ever forgive her treachery.

Storming down the wide corridor with her muumuu billowing around her, Inga shattered the marble floor with every angry step.

If she'd been in her right mind she would have questioned the silence that filled the hallway. Even with the diminished population of the mer-folk, the castle should have been bustling with activity. Instead there was an echoing silence.

But impervious to the warning signs, it wasn't until she'd followed Riven's scent, burst through the double doors, and stepped onto a balcony that she'd realized the halls were empty because everyone was gathered in the throne room.

By then it was too late.

Gritting her teeth, she leaped over the balustrade and landed heavily in the midst of the crowd. There were gasps of horror as the beautiful mer-folk fluttered out of her path. Inga ignored them. Why should she give a shit what the pretty creatures thought of her hulking form and big, bumpy features? She wasn't here to win friends. She was here to kill the dark-haired male standing on the dais.

Frowning, as if confused about what was happening, Riven waited for the mass of mer-folk to part. Then his eyes widened with shock.

"You," he breathed.

Reaching the edge of the crowd, Inga spread her legs and planted her hands on her hips. At moments like this she appreciated her large, impressive size. No one was pushing her around.

"Surprise, surprise," she drawled. "You never expected to see me again, did you, Riven? Or do you prefer to be called by your human name, Sir Travail?"

"Rimm," Riven snapped, glancing toward the uniformed male standing a few feet away. "Kill her."

Inga sensed the guard slowly inch forward, no doubt worried she wasn't alone. After all, only a lunatic would think they could battle Riven along with the entire population of mer-folk.

She tilted her chin to an aggressive angle. "I haven't told you why I'm here. Although you probably can guess."

Riven continued to glare at the soldier. "What are you waiting for?"

The guard held up his trident, moving to stand between her and Riven as the sound of running footsteps echoed through the room. It had to be additional soldiers. *Shit.* She wasn't even going to get a chance to try and kill Riven.

She might be able to battle her way through the guards, but the mob behind her would eventually leap in to protect their king. Unless…

Unless she could use the crowd to help her. But how?

There was no way to make them care about her, or how she'd been betrayed. She was a big, scary intruder who they were obviously eager to kill. But they might care about their princess.

"Do your precious mer-folk know that you have Princess Sabrina locked away?" she asked, allowing her voice to boom through the room.

The guard who Riven had called Rimm came to a sudden halt. "What did you say?"

"Lies," Riven rasped.

Hoping that Rimm wasn't going to stab the trident in her back, Inga forced herself to turn and confront the crowd. Her heart thundered, the taste of fear in her mouth. This was worse than facing a firing squad, she silently decided as she watched the fear and loathing spread over the faces of mer-folk when they caught sight of her.

Determinedly, she squared her shoulders and forced herself to meet their alarmed gazes.

"Have any of you bothered to check the nursery?" she demanded, continuing to speak in a loud, thunderous voice. "Her magic is failing."

There was a shocked silence followed by a low buzz of conversation. That was a good sign, right? They hadn't immediately tried to tear her head off.

Behind her she heard Riven muttering a string of curses. "Damn you, Rimm. Do your job."

A spot between Inga's shoulders itched, as if she was preparing to feel the sharp blades of the guard's trident slice into her flesh. When there was nothing, she continued.

"Do you want to know why her magic is fading?" Her gaze skimmed over the pale, perfect faces that were all turned in her direction. "Because your king locked her away in a prison and now she's dying."

"Shut up!" a voice raged behind her.

Inga turned, flashing her pointed teeth at the male who was flushed with fury. "Afraid, Riven?"

"I fear nothing," he rasped.

"You fear the truth," she said with absolute confidence.

Riven pointed his massive trident in her direction. "The only truth is that you've invaded our castle, ogress."

There was a hint of stirring among the crowd at the reminder she was an interloper. Could she convince them she was one of them?

"Not just an ogress. The daughter of Poyson," she announced in proud tones. "And my father was the tribal leader of the ogres."

Rimm made a strange noise as he ran a searching gaze over her. "Poyson's daughter?"

"Another lie!" Riven shouted. "This creature was sent here by the ogres to try and deceive us."

"Ha. Who would believe the ogres would send a lone female? If they decide to attack they will send the whole tribe along with hundreds of slaves. There's nothing sneaky about ogres. Besides, only a fey creature could open a portal to enter the castle." She glanced back at the crowd. "How did I get here if I'm not a mermaid?"

Ripples of low conversations spread through the room. Were the mer-folk beginning to question whether or not their king had been deceiving them?

Riven obviously feared they were. "Perhaps she has fey blood," he conceded in a harsh voice. "Or more likely, we have a traitor in our midst."

"Who?" Rimm demanded.

Riven's eyes darted around as he sought a reasonable lie. "Princess Sabrina," he at last announced. "She must have brought the ogress here." The guard appeared shocked by the suggestion. "Princess Sabrina?" Riven waved his hand in a dismissive motion. "Everyone knows she's been strangely secretive. I don't think she's recovered from her father's death. Maybe she's even gone insane with grief."

There was a mounting tension in the air. Like the static energy before a storm. All they needed was a lightning strike to release the tempest.

Inga smiled. "Let's go ask her."

Her words sizzled through the air, sending off the bolts of electricity she'd hoped to achieve.

Riven stiffened. "No."

"Why not?" Inga pressed. "Because she isn't in the castle?"

"How did you—" Riven bit off his revealing words, glancing toward his guard. "If you won't do your job, I will."

Taking a step forward, Riven pointed the Tryshu directly at Inga's heart. Refusing to cower, Inga stood her ground. If she was going to die, at least she would be on her feet.

"I don't fear you," she lied in a thankfully steady voice.

"I knew you were a fool," Riven sneered.

Barely knowing what she was doing, Inga lifted her hand. Not in a plea, but more of a gesture of defiance. The last thing she expected was for Riven to release a cry of alarm. With a frown, Inga glanced toward her hand. Had she released a spell without knowing what she was doing? Adrenaline could do crazy things.

But there was nothing.

Continuing to stare at her hand in confusion, she failed to notice the massive trident flying through the air. Not until the handle hit her palm with enough force to send her reeling back.

Instinctively her fingers curled around the smooth wood, belatedly realizing she was holding Riven's weapon.

The king glared at her in dismay. "What have you done?"

Inga blinked. Why was he asking her? She didn't have a clue what was going on.

* * * *

Waverly sighed, snuggling against Tarak's naked body. She should have been worried. Hell, she should have been out of her mind with fear.

Not only was she trapped in a prison she had no idea how to get out of, but Riven was leading her people into disaster. Plus her sister was as stuck as she was, endangering the mer-babies.

At the moment, however, she didn't want to dwell on the awful things in her life. She'd been doing that for far too long.

Instead she just wanted a few hours to appreciate being newly mated.

Tracing the dragon shimmering on Tarak's chest with the tips of her fingers, she relished the feel of him trembling beneath her touch.

"Tell me about the future," she commanded.

He studied her with his dark, sexy eyes. "You mean our future together?"

"Yes."

He turned his head to brush his lips over her forehead. "Once we escape this prison we will find a secluded island where you can swim in the ocean and…" He gave a lift of his brows as she burst out in laughter. "What's so funny?"

"I'm trying to imagine you enjoying a sun-drenched, exotic island. Surf and turf and vampires just don't go together."

His lips stroked down the length of nose. "As long as you're there it will be paradise."

Waverly heaved a sigh of sheer contentment. "You say such pretty things."

"It's the truth," he assured her, his hands exploring the curve of her back. "I have devoted my life to protecting my clan and then to creating peace for the vampires."

"Worthy goals."

He shrugged. "Perhaps, but none of them could match the sheer pleasure of watching you smile."

A warm, gooey heat slid through her. How had she ever been so lucky as to capture this magnificent male?

"A private island sounds lovely," she murmured. "A shame we couldn't stay there forever."

"Why couldn't we?"

"You'd get bored."

He lowered his hands to cup her butt in a firm grip. "Never."

She shivered as desire shuddered through her. How was it even possible? She should be exhausted.

Maybe her perpetual lust had something to do with the fact they were so recently mated? No. It was a predictable female response to a gorgeous, wickedly charming male who was pressing her tight against his hard body.

"Plus we both have an obligation to our people," she said, having difficulty forming the words.

He scraped the tip of his fang along her jaw. "I have done my duty to the vampires, but if you feel the need to help the mer-folk until a new king is chosen, I will stand at your side."

Waverly wrapped her arms around his neck, not doubting for a second that he would be her steadfast partner no matter where she decided to go. Or what she decided to do.

The knowledge was nestled in her heart like a precious treasure.

"You are an amazing demon," she whispered.

He chuckled, nuzzling kisses over her face. "I can show you just how amazing I truly am."

"I think you've shown me," she teased even as she looped her leg over his hip in silent invitation. "More than once."

"Well you know what they say."

"What's that?"

"Practice makes perfect."

"Do they?" She tangled her fingers in his hair, lost in the sensations swirling and eddying through her. They were intense enough that it took her a few seconds to realize that the tremors shaking through her were coming from the stone floor. "Tarak, what's happening?"

He pulled back, his expression wary. "I think the prison is collapsing."

"It has to be Riven," she breathed.

Together they surged to their feet, both scrambling to pull on their clothes as the quaking intensified.

Once they were dressed, Tarak wrapped her in his arms, his fangs bared as they struggled to remain upright.

"He's either trying to kill us, or something's happening to disrupt his magic."

Waverly frowned. "Why would Riven want us dead after he went to such trouble to imprison us? After all, he still needs your power to..." Her words trailed away as she was struck by a sudden thought. "The Tryshu."

He gazed down at her. "What about it?"

"It's trying to reject him," she rasped. "He's so busy trying to maintain his grip on the ancient weapon that his other magic is faltering."

A cold, lethal smile curved Tarak's lips. The sight of it sent a chill of unease down her spine.

"If the prison collapses, I need you to help me," he said.

She eyed him warily. "What do you want?"

"I want you to create a portal to the castle."

Oh. She studied him in confusion. Did he think she intended to take them to the deserted island before she'd ensured that Riven was dead?

"That's what I intended to do," she assured him.

"But I want you to wait for me in the cavern—"

"No," she interrupted.

Tarak scowled in frustration. "Waverly, we don't know what's happening."

That was his argument? She rolled her eyes. "Which is why you're not going there alone."

"I'll be fine," he insisted. "I'll track down Riven, kill him, and return before you even know I'm gone."

She pulled away, eying him with a narrowed gaze. "It's not happening."

There was a violent shake of the prison. The stone around them didn't crack or shatter, but a strange warping effect rippled over the walls. Proof that the prison was made of magic, not granite.

"Waverly, please," he growled.

"No." She adamantly shook her head. "I have suffered just as much as you have."

His eyes darkened with regret at the raw edge in her voice. "I know that."

"I've earned my right to be there when Riven dies."

His jaw clenched. He couldn't argue with her logic. Still, his hand lifted to gently cup her cheek in his palm.

"If I fail and Riven survives, he'll make sure you're punished."

She held his gaze. "Then don't fail."

Before he could respond, the floor shuddered and lurched. Then, with the sound of a crashing wave, a darkness swept over them. It was like being pulled through a portal, only with a speed that made Waverly's head spin.

"Hold on." Tarak grabbed her hand as they tumbled through a vast emptiness.

Waverly clung tightly to Tarak's fingers, gritting her teeth as they plummeted at an increasing speed. Eventually they were going to hit, and it wasn't going to be fun.

She was right.

Thud. They crashed onto a stone floor with a jarring impact. Waverly grunted in pain as the air was knocked from her lungs. Lying flat on her back, it took her a minute to realize they'd returned to the cavern near the witch's hotel.

Not surprising. It was no doubt the spot where the original spell had been cast for the prison.

"Ow," she muttered, grimly picking herself up off the ground.

Naturally, Tarak was standing at her side with one fluid motion. Not even a hair was out of place. She shook her head. She used to think she was graceful, but next to Tarak she was as clumsy as a baby kraken.

"Are you alright?" he asked, eyeing her with a worried expression.

She grimaced. Everything hurt, but she wasn't going to tell Tarak. He was just looking for some excuse to keep her away from Riven.

"A couple of bruises," she said with a dismissive wave of her hand.

He thinned his lips, reminding her that she couldn't lie to him. Not anymore. But before he could try to browbeat her into remaining in the cavern, Tarak was tugging her behind him.

"Stay back," he called out, his icy power swirling through the air.

A matching power blasted around them, forming a layer of frost on the walls. There was a crunch of heavy footsteps and then a gigantic male dressed in black leather stepped out of a side tunnel.

Waverly widened her eyes. *Wow.* The male was massive, with dark hair and stark features. But it was his eyes that made Waverly shiver. They sizzled with a power that was almost tangible.

"Easy, Tarak," the vampire murmured, lifting his hands in a gesture of peace.

Waverly felt Tarak stiffen in shock. "Styx?"

Chapter 19

Tarak studied the male he hadn't seen in five centuries. Long ago they'd been like brothers. Styx had been as devoted to the previous Anasso as Tarak had been. And just as unwilling to believe that their master could be deceiving them.

At some point he intended to sit down with Styx and demand to know how the previous Anasso had died and how Styx had claimed his title as King of the Vampires.

But not now.

"Thank the gods," Styx muttered.

Tarak held tight to Waverly's arm, baring his fangs at the intruder. It had nothing to do with the past. This was a primal need to keep the male from his mate. "What are you doing here?" he demanded.

Styx was careful not to glance toward Waverly who was peeking over Tarak's shoulder. "Looking for you."

Tarak arched a brow. How could Styx know where he would be? Unless...

No, he didn't believe the male would be working with Riven. Styx was many things. Stubborn. Grim. And lethal. But he possessed a fierce sense of honor.

"Did Chiron ask for your help?" he finally demanded.

Styx nodded. "He contacted me after he'd released you from your prison. Welcome home, my brother."

Styx moved forward, as if he was going to clasp Tarak's hand, but Tarak flashed his fangs in warning. "Stay back."

Waverly made a sound of shock. "Tarak."

"It's okay," Styx said, taking a deliberate step backward. "I recognize a newly mated male." He paused, studying Tarak with a wary gaze. "Can we talk?"

"Not now." He glanced over his shoulder. "Waverly, we need a portal."

"I need to speak with you," Styx insisted.

Tarak didn't answer. He was concentrating on Waverly as she lifted her arm. He couldn't see the portal, but he assumed it was forming.

Waverly's hand was still moving in a circle when there was the pitter-patter of tiny feet echoing from the same tunnel where Styx had recently appeared.

Tarak scowled. This place was as busy as Grand Central Station. Turning his head, he watched the miniature gargoyle with fairy wings and the tall, crimson-haired imp wearing some sort of stretchy orange pants and a shirt made of fishnet stroll into the cavern.

His brows lifted. Well. That was something you didn't see every day.

"*Voila!*" the gargoyle announced in a voice that was lightly accented. "I have returned along with Troy."

Tarak had seen the gargoyle before. He'd been traveling with the ogress. But the imp was new.

"Prince of Imps," Troy corrected, glancing toward Styx. "He promised me a reward. I trust you will make this worth my time?"

Styx released a low growl. "I'll let you live. How about that as a reward?"

Tarak snorted. Styx hadn't changed.

The imp gave a toss of his long hair that shimmered like fire. "I hate vampires," he muttered.

"Right? They are the worst," the gargoyle agreed, his wings fluttering. "Well, perhaps dragons are worse." There was a short pause. "And sardines."

"Sardines?" the imp demanded in confusion.

The gargoyle wrinkled his snout. "They give me a rash."

Tarak sent Styx a quizzical glance. "You have picked up some strange friends."

Styx grimaced. "They're not my friends."

Tarak felt Waverly lightly touch his arm. "The portal is open," she told him.

Tarak turned toward her. "Let's go."

"Wait!" the gargoyle called out. "Does it lead to the castle?"

"Tarak," Styx said, his tone commanding.

Tarak waved them all away. "Later."

"I am coming with you," the gargoyle said, his claws scraping against the stone floor as he hurried toward them.

"Dammit. So am I," Styx growled, pointing a finger toward Troy. "Stay here in case we need you to open a portal," he ordered the imp.

"How will I know?" Troy demanded, his expression annoyed as Styx moved toward Tarak. "How will I know?"

No one answered as Waverly led them through the invisible opening. Darkness swirled around Tarak as he stepped forward.

"Christ, we didn't need a parade," he muttered, although he hadn't made any effort to keep the gargoyle and Styx from following them.

Since Waverly was too stubborn to stay away from Riven, he was happy to have an extra sword to protect her. And there was no greater sword than the one strapped across Styx's back. Tarak had once seen the male chop a troll in half with one swing of the massive blade.

They moved quickly through the portal, stepping into a wide, marble hallway lined with fluted columns.

Styx reached over his back to pull free his sword. "This is the mer-folk lair?" he demanded.

"Yes," Tarak said in absent tones. He'd just caught a familiar scent. "I smell Riven."

"Where?" Waverly demanded.

Tarak nodded toward an arched opening. "That way."

"The throne room," Waverly said, her face pale but resolute.

"Inga is there as well," the tiny gargoyle announced, scuttling down the hall with his tail wiggling behind him.

Damn. The stupid creature was going to attract the attention of the guards.

"Stop," he growled.

Styx reached out to grasp Tarak's shoulder before he could take off after the gargoyle. "No, let him go," the ancient vampire said. "I've learned it's best to be far away from whatever disaster Levet is certain to cause."

Tarak sent his onetime clansman an annoyed glare. "I thought you said he wasn't your friend?"

"My mate is fond of him," Styx muttered, his gaze on the gargoyle who was disappearing through the opening.

"Mate?" Tarak asked in surprise. He couldn't imagine any female being able to reach the aloof male.

"Darcy." Styx's features softened, revealing a side of the vampire that Tarak would have sworn didn't exist. "She's a pureblood Were."

Tarak's eyes widened. He hadn't spent much time with Weres, but he'd heard they were nasty, feral creatures who would bite first and ask questions later. "That must be...interesting."

Styx gave a sharp laugh. "You have no idea."

Tarak paused, his gaze taking in the male who'd stood at his side during endless battles. "How long have you known?" he abruptly demanded.

Styx knew immediately what Tarak was asking. "I discovered the scroll that revealed you had been imprisoned two weeks ago. I had no idea, I swear," he said in harsh tones.

Tarak gave a slow nod. He wasn't completely willing to forgive and forget the past. But for now it was enough to know that Styx hadn't known he'd been betrayed by the old Anasso.

"Okay."

A smile of relief curved Styx's lips. "Are we here to kill something?"

"Yes, but first I need to destroy the amulet that Riven is using to tap into my powers," Tarak told him.

Styx nodded. "Where is it?"

It was Waverly who answered. "This way."

She turned and hurried down the hallway, Tarak quickly moving to take the lead. It wasn't that he doubted her ability to kick ass when she wanted, but she felt an overwhelming duty toward her people. She would hesitate to strike a killing blow, even if she was in danger.

They sped down the long hallway, their footsteps echoing eerily.

"Is the castle always so empty?" Styx finally demanded.

"I can sense Riven in the throne room," Waverly said. "I'm guessing he's called another gathering. He loves to be the center of attention."

"Nice of him to keep them distracted," Styx muttered.

"There's nothing nice about Riven," Tarak growled. "And there will probably be at least one guard waiting in front of Riven's rooms," he warned.

"Good," Styx said. "Darcy never lets me kill things anymore."

Waverly glanced toward the Anasso who was jogging next to her. "Please try not to kill them."

He sent her a frown. "What?"

"She's serious," Tarak warned the vampire.

Styx shook his head in disappointment. "Damn."

Reaching an intersection, Waverly led them around a corner. Ahead Tarak could see the double doors of the royal chambers. He could also see the two guards, who looked dumbfounded by their sudden appearance.

"I'll take that one," Styx said, pointing his sword at the guard on the left.

"Careful, they can shoot a silver net out of their tridents," Tarak told him, preparing to charge forward.

Waverly lightly touched his arm. "Remember, these are my people."

He nodded as he flowed forward, leaping high in the air at the precise second that the guard released the magic from his trident. The silvery net flew harmlessly beneath him before Tarak was landing in front of him. The male cursed, trying to back away so he could stab Tarak through the heart with the tips of his trident.

Tarak smiled, revealing his very large, very sharp fangs. The male dropped his trident and turned to flee.

That was the problem of trying to compel warriors to provide protection instead of earning their loyalty. A soldier would only fight to the death for someone he believed to be his true leader.

Whirling on his heel, Tarak intended to help Styx with his guard, but the merman had already joined his companion in running away. He shook his head. After he killed Riven, the mer-folk were going to need a king who could give them back their pride.

First, however, he needed to extinguish Riven's ability to tap into his power. It was becoming worse with every passing second. As if the male was trying to drain as much energy from Tarak as possible.

Yet another indication that something was happening.

Maybe Waverly was right. Maybe Riven had lost control of the Tryshu.

"In here," Waverly said, pushing open the doors.

They rushed inside. Without speaking, Tarak and Styx did a quick sweep to ensure there were no hidden guards. Tarak grimaced, acutely aware of how easy it was to regain the comfortable rapport that he'd once had with the ancient vampire. Just two brothers who always had each other's back.

As if sharing his sense of comfort, Styx came to a halt in the middle of the vast room and turned a slow circle.

"Impressive," he at last said.

Tarak snorted. "You used to hate fancy shit. Does becoming king rot a male's brain?"

Surprisingly, a visible shudder raced through Styx. "Trust me, I've had enough marble and gilt to last my lifetime." He pointed his sword toward the shelves lining the walls. "I was referring to the weapons."

Shaking off his sense of camaraderie, Tarak crossed the floor. "This is the amulet."

Styx quickly joined him, his nose wrinkling in disgust as he studied the metal object. "Necromancer."

Tarak sent him a startled glance. "That was quick. Do you recognize it?"

"We had to deal with the nasty creatures a few years ago."

The lights overhead flickered, a sure sign that Styx was pissed. The necromancers must have been more than a little problem if Styx was still nursing his anger.

Reaching toward the amulet, Tarak suddenly felt a sharp pain as if he was being gutted. He swayed, grabbing the edge of the shelf to remain upright.

"Tarak, what's wrong?" Waverly hurriedly wrapped her arm around his waist.

"Riven is draining me of my powers," he said between clenched teeth.

Waverly glanced toward Styx. "How do we destroy it?"

"The amulet can't be destroyed by physical means. It's the work of the Dark Lord," Styx told her, lifting his hand when her lips parted in dismay. "It will take magic."

Tarak grimly forced his knees to hold his weight. He had to stay upright. He was so close to getting his fangs in Riven.

Failure wasn't an option.

"Do we need a witch?" he asked Styx.

"No. Unfortunately."

Waverly scowled. "Why unfortunately?"

Styx grunted in resignation. "Because what we need is a gargoyle."

* * * *

Riven's initial stupefaction at having the Tryshu ripped from his hand was quickly replaced by stark fear.

What the hell?

This wasn't part of the plan. He wasn't one of those stupid kings who let the ancient weapon choose who was going to be the leader. He'd ended that tradition when he'd found the amulet. Now his grip on the Tryshu should be unbreakable.

Obviously, the ogress had to have some sort of magical artifact that was disrupting his powers. That was the only explanation that made sense.

Which meant that he had to get it away from her before the mer-folk could start to speculate whether or not she was telling the truth. They were already muttering and exchanging confused glances. Even the guards were staring around as if unsure what to do.

Dammit. How had this female managed to enter the castle without him sensing her presence? And worse, how had she managed to contact Sabrina? The princess was safely locked in her prison. No one should be able to speak with her.

Riven savagely battled against the urge to flee. He might be a coward, but this wasn't over. Not by a long shot.

He'd sacrificed too much to throw it all away.

All he had to do was inflame the mer-folks' instinctive fear of ogres, he abruptly realized. Once Inga was dead, the Tryshu would once again return to his grasp and he could continue with his determination to rule the demon world.

"You see?" he called out in loud tones, pointing an accusing finger toward the silent Inga. "I warned you that the ogres sent her to deceive us."

"She holds the Tryshu."

The voice came from behind Riven, but he didn't bother to turn around and discover who it was. Soon enough the people would be crawling on their knees to please him.

"A trick," he proclaimed.

The ogress scowled, looking at the Tryshu as if she didn't know how it'd gotten in her hand.

Wretched creature.

"How could I trick a magical weapon?" she demanded.

"Everyone knows that ogres are cunning, savage animals," Riven said without hesitation. He wanted to emphasize that this female was a crude, nasty creature. Nothing at all like the lovely mer-folk. "Who knows what foul magic you are using." He gave an imperious lift of his hand. "Rimm."

The guard moved to stand at his side, his expression troubled. "What about Princess Sabrina? I want to hear from her."

Riven bit back his furious words. Very, very soon he was going to deal with his treacherous captain of the guards. But right now he was acutely aware of the crowd muttering behind him.

"No, this might be a trap," he abruptly warned.

Rimm scowled. "What sort of a trap?"

Riven rummaged through his brain, seeking some reason to avoid an all-out search for Sabrina. Then he smiled with smug satisfaction.

He had a rare talent for turning any situation to his advantage. Even this shitshow.

He faced the crowd. "It's possible the ogress is hoping to lure Sabrina out of the safety of her private rooms to murder her."

Rimm took a second to consider the explanation. "Why would she kill the princess?" he at last asked.

"Without Sabrina's magic our children would die," Riven smoothly pointed out.

There was a rustle of silk as the crowd leaned to whisper to each other. Riven's smile widened. He was turning the tide.

"She isn't here," the ogress argued. "Riven put her in a prison."

Riven pasted an expression of shock on his face. "If that was true, the children would already be dying," he insisted.

"Go and see for yourselves," Inga called out.

Riven lifted his hands. "Don't leave the throne room," he warned. "The ogres might be hidden near the nursery."

Rimm glanced toward the ogress, his expression troubled. "How can she hold the Tryshu?"

Riven smiled even as the violent urge to destroy the guard blasted through him.

Soon, soon, soon.

"As I said, she has cast some sort of evil spell on our most precious symbol of authority." He gestured toward the crowd, urging them to move forward. "We have to destroy her before she can use the Tryshu against us."

Rimm made a choked sound of disbelief. "Surely you don't intend to put your people in danger?" he demanded. "She could kill all of them if she gains command of the weapon."

Riven pressed his lips together. Damn the male. Did he think Riven was going to put his own life in danger? "I'm beginning to suspect that you are the traitor, Rimm," Riven suggested in a low voice.

The male stiffened. "I am loyal to the throne."

"Then prove it," Riven snapped, waiting for Rimm to take a step toward Inga before he sucked as much power as possible from the vampire. He didn't believe his people could actually kill the ogress while she held the Tryshu, but they could possibly distract her long enough for him to grab the weapon. "Attack," he commanded.

The people inched forward, none of them in a hurry to confront the large female. Pathetic weaklings. But even as Riven waited for his chance to regain the trident, he caught sight of a tiny gargoyle pushing his way toward the ogress.

"*Non!*" he shouted. "You will not hurt her."

Riven clenched his hands into tight fists. "Now what?"

Chapter 20

Standing in front of the open doors leading to the throne room, Waverly ensured that no one had noticed their arrival before swiveling back to the vampire at her side.

A sizzle of panic snaked down her spine as she eyed her mate. Despite his grim effort to pretend that he wasn't on the point of collapse, she knew that Riven must be draining the last of his power.

Tarak's pale face was turning a worrisome shade of ash and he swayed side to side, as if trying to find his center of gravity.

"Tarak." She laid a gentle hand on her arm. "Let me get the gargoyle and bring him to you."

"I'm fine," he told her.

She shook her head. Stubborn vampire.

"You can't lie to me, remember?" she said.

He eyed her with a fierce expression. "I have to do this."

Styx moved to stand next to Tarak. "You're sure?" he demanded. Tarak nodded and the Anasso pulled free his massive sword. "I've got your back."

Waverly swallowed her protest. She understood. Tarak had suffered for centuries. He wasn't going to let the fact he could barely stand upright keep him from his revenge.

Swallowing a sigh, Waverly turned her attention to the swarm of her people on the other side of the doors.

At the moment, Riven was standing on the dais, waving his arms as the gathered mer-folk were inching toward the ogress who was backing away.

"I was right," Riven proclaimed in a loud voice, pointing his finger toward Levet, who had halted directly in front of the massive female. "She has a demon straight out of the netherworld as her companion."

"He's not wrong," Styx muttered.

Riven continued to give dramatic waves of his arms. As if he was herding the crowd forward. Idiot.

"We have to destroy them before she can call for her filthy tribe to overrun us," he warned.

The mer-folk became bolder, their angry mutterings growing louder. Riven had once again managed to deceive them, and even worse, he was ensuring they were the ones in danger, not himself.

Spineless coward.

With a shake of her head, she turned her attention to the ogress who'd backed away from the crowd until she was pressed against the far wall.

"How did she get the Tryshu away from Riven?" she muttered in confusion.

"A worry for later," Tarak said, his voice harsh with strain.

"Yes," she agreed, sending him a worried glance.

Styx looked equally concerned. "We have to get the amulet to the gargoyle." He lifted his sword. "I'll create a distraction."

"No." Tarak sent his companion a fierce glare. "I'll do it."

Styx arched a brow. "Forgive me, brother, but you're not looking so good."

"I can do it," Tarak insisted, then he grimaced as he swayed heavily to the side. "Just make sure I don't fall on my face."

"I got you." Styx wrapped an arm around Tarak's shoulders and braced him with his large body.

Waverly felt a strange warmth flow through her at the sight. For so long Tarak had been separated from his people, not only by his prison, but by his sense of betrayal. He'd even managed to convince himself that he had no need of them. Now, seeing him lean against Styx, she knew he would eventually return to his clan.

He was a male who'd devoted his life to others. He needed to be a part of a family.

Of course, she intended to have a few decades alone with him on that deserted island he'd promised her. After that...

She was jerked out of her inane thoughts when she heard a startled shriek. Glancing into the room, she watched as Riven was lifted high in the air. Tarak. His powers might be diminished but they were still impressive.

The gathering of mer-folk gasped, their gazes locked on Riven who was frantically twisting his head from one side to the other, no doubt searching for Tarak.

Waverly touched Tarak's hand, careful not to distract him. "Give me the amulet."

He dropped it into her palm, the muscles of his neck visible as he strained to hold Riven off the ground. "Be careful," he rasped.

She exchanged a glance with Styx. He nodded. It was a silent promise to protect Tarak with his life.

Waverly believed him. She sensed the ancient vampire's seething regret. He understood the wounds Tarak carried inside, and accepted that he was responsible for at least a few of them.

Clutching the amulet in her hand, Waverly nearly gagged at the smell of the thing. Worse, it made her feel as if she was holding a putrid piece of rotting fish.

With a shudder, Waverly squared her shoulders and headed into the room. It was time to end Riven's reign of terror.

"My people," she called out, using the voice her father had perfected when he wanted to gain the full attention of a crowd. "We have been betrayed by the supposed King of the Mer-folk."

There was a ripple of silk as the mer-folk turned to watch her march forward. Their expressions were bewildered, as if they were hoping this was all a terrible joke they wanted to end.

Above her, Riven began to flail around, trying to break free of the invisible bonds that held him.

"Traitor," he screeched. "She's working with the ogress."

"No." Waverly kept her pace steady, her head held high. She was in full princess-mode. "I have escaped from the prison where Riven trapped me along with a vampire he used to maintain his hold on the Tryshu."

A uniformed male abruptly appeared in front of her. Rimm. Waverly halted, thoroughly prepared for a fight. Nothing was going to stop her from exposing Riven.

But even as she braced for his attack, he instead offered a deep bow. "Princess Waverly." He straightened, his expression tight with regret. "I was told that you were a traitor, but I am beginning to suspect I was misled."

"You were," she told him. She glanced toward the mer-folk who were gathering around her. "Riven is a fraud. He was never our rightful king."

"Don't listen to her," Riven screeched. "I claimed the Tryshu. I am your king."

The mer-folk glanced between Waverly and Riven, looking like spectators at a human tennis match. She needed more to convince them that they'd been duped.

"He used this." She held up her hand. "An amulet from a necromancer."

As one, the crowd took a step backward, their noses wrinkling at the stench.

"I've never seen that before." Riven's voice was edged with an increasing desperation. "She's trying to confuse you."

"I've seen it," Rimm abruptly admitted, his face bleak. It wouldn't be easy for the mer-folk to accept how badly they'd been deceived. Waverly could only hope the future king could find a way to heal the betrayal left behind by Riven. "It was in the royal chambers."

"I have seen it as well." Levet intruded into the conversation, waddling forward. His delicate wings shimmered in the light of the chandeliers, but they brushed the floor as if they were drooping. "Or one similar." A visible shudder shook his tiny body. "It was used to worship the Dark Lord."

There was an audible gasp from the mer-folk as they took several more steps away from the amulet. Although they were isolated from the rest of the world, they'd heard about the evil demon lord.

Waverly's stomach clenched with disgust. It was revolting to have the nasty thing touching her skin. "Can you destroy it?" she demanded.

"No!" Riven cried.

The crowd didn't bother to glance at him. The gargoyle was far more fascinating as he lifted his hands in a dramatic motion.

"*Oui*, I can exterminate the amulet. My magic is *très magnifique*," he boasted, his tail twitching. "Place it on the floor."

"Stop the demon-spawn," Riven roared.

Levet tilted back his head to glare at the male who was thrashing and flailing in an effort to halt the inevitable. Thankfully Tarak maintained enough power to keep him trapped.

"I am a gargoyle, not a demon-spawn," Levet protested, then he paused, as if actually considering the insult. "Hmm. I suppose I am spawned by a demon. After all, my mother—"

"Please hurry," Waverly interrupted, leaning down to place the amulet on the floor.

She was still bent over when the gargoyle moved to sniff her hair.

"You smell like Inga," he said.

She froze, distracted by his words. "The ogress?" she demanded.

"*Oui.*" A wistful smile touched his tiny gray face. "And the Princess Sabrina."

Waverly sucked in a sharp breath. "My sister? She's free?"

Levet shook his head, his smile disappearing. "She's still locked away. And worse, she is fading. That is why Inga insisted on battling the King of Mer-folk even though I warned her it was a suicide missile."

Missile? Waverly shook her head. That was at the bottom of her list of questions. Along with why Inga would feel compelled to help Sabrina. Oh, and why they all smelled the same.

The top of the list was why the ogress was holding the powerful trident. "How did she get the Tryshu away from Riven?" she asked.

Levet glanced over his shoulder at the ogress who was pressed against the wall. "How did you get the pointy stick?"

"I just held up my hand and it came flying at me," Inga said, her eyes darting from side to side, as if expecting an ambush. "I swear."

Was the female lying? Waverly had assumed the ogress possessed the same sort of magical object as Riven. If she was being honest that she wasn't using a hidden power, then the Tryshu had deliberately chosen her.

"Why?" she muttered, more to herself than Inga.

It was Levet who answered. "She is the daughter of Poyson."

Waverly's lips parted to deny the claim. Even knowing that Poyson had mated with an ogre didn't prepare her for the sight of such an...an ogress-looking daughter. Surely she should have some mermaid features?

Then she caught something in Inga's eyes. A guarded vulnerability that reminded Waverly of her aunt.

"Oh," she breathed, not sure whether to laugh or cry. "All the times I would catch sight of you in the cavern, and I never once suspected we could be related."

They shared a glance of regret that was interrupted by Riven, who refused to accept defeat.

"She's an ogre whore," he snarled. "Kill her before she ruins everything."

Levet's wings snapped, as if he was personally angered by Riven's insult. "It might be best if you move," he suggested to Waverly. "My magic can be a teensy bit unpredictable."

Waverly hadn't forgotten Styx's warning about the gargoyle. Without arguing she backed away, giving the creature plenty of room. Then, barely daring to breathe, she watched as the gargoyle held his hand over the amulet.

Seconds ticked past. And past. And past. Had the gargoyle been mistaken? Waverly clenched her teeth. The thought was unbearable. Everything depended on the tiny demon.

If he couldn't destroy the amulet, then—

Any fear that Levet was too tiny to do the job was abruptly seared away as a ball of fire surrounded the amulet. It pulsed with a brilliant light, expanding until it filled the center of the marble floor. Waverly lifted her hand, narrowing her eyes as the blinding glow washed over her.

What was the gargoyle doing? She couldn't see the amulet through the magic, but she sensed the tingle of power in the air. Something was happening.

Something big.

She tried to prepare herself, but it wasn't enough as the magical sphere burst with the force of an erupting volcano. She tumbled to her knees, her hair singed by the explosion.

She felt bruised from head to toe, but she was pretty sure the amulet was destroyed.

Along with half the throne room.

* * * *

Tarak's knees had given out only seconds after Waverly began to weave her way through the gathered crowd, holding the amulet. Styx had silently wrapped his arm around Tarak's shoulders to keep him upright. At the same time he held out his sword in a blatant warning to any mer-folk who might be foolish enough to attack them.

Leaning against the male, Tarak focused on maintaining his grip on Riven. A task that was increasingly difficult as the bastard drained his power at an alarming rate.

His vision narrowed as a frigid weakness swept through his body. He needed the gargoyle to destroy the amulet. Quickly.

As if on cue, a blinding light filled the room followed by an explosion that sent mer-folk scattering in alarm.

"Holy crap," Tarak muttered. He'd thought he might feel a tingle or tug when the spell on the amulet was broken. He hadn't expected a full-out eruption.

"I warned you that Levet is a menace," Styx muttered. "It's a miracle he didn't bring the roof down on our heads."

Tarak blocked out the shrieks of fear from the crowd. He was busy looking for Waverly. Once he spotted her standing near the large ogress he waited for her to give him a nod, revealing that she was okay. Then he smiled with anticipation.

The gargoyle's dramatic explosion of magic had broken Riven's ability to draw on Tarak's powers. Of course, it'd also interrupted Tarak's hold on the merman, but Tarak wasn't worried.

He liked chasing his prey.

Pulling away from Styx, Tarak headed toward the edge of the room. He wanted to avoid the ruckus as the crowd fled for the exits. Plus he didn't want to attract the attention of the guards. He doubted any of them possessed any loyalty toward the former king, especially now that Riven had been exposed as a fraud. But there was no point in taking unnecessary risks. Not when he was so close to getting his fangs into Riven.

Circling the room, he caught the movement of the wall directly behind the throne.

A hidden panel.

No doubt it'd been created by Waverly's father, who was obsessed with protecting his family. Now, however, it was being used by a spineless coward who thought he could escape justice.

Tarak was about to prove him wrong.

Leaping over the dais, Tarak ran his fingers over the wall until he sensed the tunnel on the other side. He didn't bother to try and find a latch that would open the door. Instead he lifted his foot and kicked a hole through the brilliant fresco. He grimaced. Waverly would no doubt nag him about ruining the priceless work of art, but she'd be a lot more upset if he allowed Riven to escape.

He continued to kick through the wall, creating a hole large enough to crawl through. As he'd expected, he found a narrow tunnel that was lit by the strange glowing orbs he'd seen throughout the castle.

Tarak rushed forward, not bothering to worry about whether or not he might be running into a trap. As soon as Riven realized he was being followed, the bastard would create a portal and disappear.

He followed Riven's scent, rounding a corner to discover an opening in the tunnel. Stepping through the narrow doorway, he blinked in surprise. He was back in the royal chambers.

His fangs lengthened as his gaze caught sight of Riven cramming large gems into the pockets of his robe. Clearly the merman wasn't going to flee without pillaging at least a few of the mer-folk treasures.

Moving with the silence only a vampire could achieve, Tarak crossed the marble floor. He'd nearly reached the merman when the male belatedly sensed he was no longer alone. Turning his head, Riven squawked in terror, his hand lifting to create a portal.

Tarak swiftly wrapped his fingers around the male's throat and lifted him off the ground.

"I suspected you would try to scuttle away. Like the worthless cockroach you are," he drawled.

Riven made a strangled sound, grabbing at Tarak's hand in a futile effort to pry away his fingers. "Release me."

Tarak tightened his grip. "Don't worry. This won't take long."

The merman's eyes widened. Could he see his death written on Tarak's face?

He hoped so.

"Wait," the merman gasped.

Tarak smiled, revealing his fully extended fangs. Just a fun reminder of how he was about to die.

"Ah. Is this the pleading-for-your-life portion of our encounter?" Tarak mocked.

Riven licked his lips, sweat dripping down his face. "I can get you anything you want," he assured Tarak. "Treasure. Power. Females."

Tarak laughed. "You aren't stupid enough to think you can bargain with me?"

Riven struggled to speak as his face turned an interesting shade of magenta. "Just name your price."

Tarak shook his head. "You truly are a pathetic creature."

"Tell me what you want," Riven pleaded.

"Simple." Tarak lowered the male. "I want you dead."

The male's lips parted to continue his begging, but Tarak was done. He'd waited so long for this moment. He'd even fantasized the thousands of ways he could kill the merman. Slowly, brutally, and as painfully as possible. But now that he held him in his hands, he just wanted to be done with him.

Yanking him close, Tarak widened his mouth and struck. Riven screamed, his body jerking as Tarak's fangs bit deep into his flesh.

Tarak drank deeply, his strength returning as the male's blood filled his body. He might hate Riven with every fiber of his being, but he possessed a potent fey essence. It was like high-octane fuel.

The smell of salt and pure terror swirled through the air as Riven's struggles started to fade.

In the end it took less than five minutes to drain the male completely. Then, tossing him on the floor, Tarak moved toward the powerful weapons that lined the walls. He dismissed the magical artifacts. He couldn't wield them even if he knew what they did. At last he grabbed one of the spears Riven had stolen from the Jumbee demons.

He returned to stand over Riven's body, surprised to discover his lack of joy at the sight of his pale, lifeless face. He'd already shut the door on the past. Now all that mattered was Waverly and their future together.

Still, he couldn't leave without ensuring that Riven was dead. If the male escaped he would spend the rest of eternity plotting to regain control over the mer-folk. Not to mention being a threat to Waverly.

Lifting the weapon high over his head, Tarak thrust it down with enough force to impale Riven on the marble floor. The spearhead pierced the merman's heart, releasing its dark magic.

Tarak grimaced, yanking his hands off the shaft as a shadow spread over Riven. The black fog wasn't just crawling over the merman, it was turning his flesh to dust.

Assured that Riven was well and truly dead, Tarak headed out of the royal chamber.

He had a mate and a deserted island waiting for him.

Chapter 21

Inga watched in horror as the crowd that had been fleeing from Levet's massive explosion now turned to regard her with a wary suspicion.

She wasn't sure where Riven had gone after the amulet had been destroyed, but she'd caught a blur of motion out of the corner of her eye. She assumed the vampire was busy dealing with the former King of the Mer-folk. That was fine with her. She didn't care who struck the killing blow as long as Riven ended up dead.

Now she just wanted to get out of the castle before the mer-folk decided she should be in the dungeons.

Or worse.

With a jerky motion she threw away the trident. The last thing she wanted was for the crowd to think she was trying to threaten them. But the weapon had barely left her hand when it was flying back at her with a terrifying speed. Instinctively she grabbed the shaft before the stupid thing could skewer her.

Shock rippled through the gathering as the mer-folk pointed toward her, whispering to each other in low voices. Inga desperately glanced around, discovering the pretty mermaid standing just a few feet away.

Princess Waverly. Yes, that was her name. She was some sort of cousin. Plus, she didn't seem quite so eager to want Inga dead.

A bonus.

Inga held out the weapon. "Here," she said in strained tones. "You take it."

Waverly took a step back, shaking her head. "I can't."

"Why not?"

"Because it's chosen you," she said.

Inga ground her pointy teeth together. Was it Let's Be Cryptic Day in the mermaid castle? "Chosen me for what?"

Waverly raised her brows, as if baffled by the question. "To be the leader of the mer-folk."

Inga's mouth went dry. Drier than the Sahara Desert.

Leader of the mer-folk? Did she mean…

No. Inga shook her head. Obviously this was some cruel prank. She hunched her shoulders. She was used to people mocking her, but it still hurt to think her own relative would try to make her look like a fool.

"This isn't the time for jokes," she snapped.

Waverly tilted her head to the side, her golden hair spilling over her shoulder.

"It's not a joke, Inga," she said, her voice gentle. "The mer-folk have allowed the Tryshu to reveal our leader since the beginning of time."

Inga blinked. Then blinked again. She was being serious. The realization did nothing to ease the hard ball of unease in the pit of her stomach.

In fact, it only made it worse.

She glanced down at the heavy trident, giving it an experimental shake. "Obviously, it's broken."

Waverly frowned. "It appears to be undamaged."

Inga stomped her foot in frustration, indifferent to the fact her large foot was smashing the marble floor. There was already a big hole in the middle of the room. What did a few more cracks matter?

"Then how do you explain Riven?" she demanded. "This thing clearly doesn't know what it's doing if it picked that lunatic to be your leader."

Waverly was shaking her head before Inga finished. "No, he used the powers of the amulet to gain control of the weapon," she said. "The necromancer magic gave him the ability to touch the Tryshu and he tapped into Tarak's power to use the weapon's magic."

Inga didn't completely understand how Riven had cheated, but she didn't argue. The nasty merman was willing to sink to any level to get what he wanted. She'd learned that painful lesson.

Still, there had to be something wrong with the Tryshu.

"What about me?" she pressed. "I can't be the leader."

"Why not?" Waverly asked.

Inga floundered. Such a simple question, but the answer was as vast as the universe.

Unfortunately, she didn't have the words to express just how wrong it was that she would be the leader of anyone, let alone the mer-folk.

Finally, she spread her arms wide. "Look at me."

Waverly shrugged, as if she wasn't at all put off by the sight of Inga's lumpish features.

"You're Poyson's daughter."

"And the daughter of a tribal leader of the ogres," a small voice said from beside her. She turned her head to discover Levet standing there, his expression impossible to read. Her heart squeezed with a combination of joy, regret and a wistful yearning for what she would never have.

He'd followed her. Even after she'd revealed that she'd stolen his memories and manipulated him into helping her. But she wasn't stupid enough to believe it was because he cared. Levet would risk his life to try and save any female he thought was in danger.

"Royal blood from both your mother and father," Waverly murmured. "You were clearly born to sit on the throne."

The mermaid's words had Inga swiveling her head back around to meet Waverly's steady gaze. "I never asked for this," she insisted. "I can't."

"You must." Yet another voice intruded into the conversation. There was a flutter of movement among the crowd of onlookers to reveal a slender female who was approaching with determined steps.

Inga easily recognized the deep blue eyes and golden hair with hints of blue, although she was looking far healthier than the last time she'd seen her.

"Sabrina!" Waverly exclaimed, rushing to wrap her arms around the female.

"Sister," Princess Sabrina choked out, both of them laughing and crying at the same time.

"Blessed goddess," Waverly finally managed to say, pulling back to regard her sister with tear-filled eyes. "I searched for you for five hundred years. I swear I never gave up hope."

Sabrina lifted a hand to touch Waverly's cheek. "I know."

Inga felt a familiar stab of envy as she watched the sisters. The love between them was tangible. She would give anything to have someone care about her like that.

"Riven," Waverly started to say, only to be halted when Sabrina pressed her fingers to her sister's lips.

"Shh. We will have time later to discuss the previous king," she said, a strange smile touching her lips as she moved her fingers to touch the crimson tattoo that ran along the inside of Waverly's arm. "As well as this." Waverly blushed, but before she could speak, Sabrina was nodding toward the mer-folk who were gathering closer and closer, as if seeking the comfort of the two princesses. "For now we must concentrate on calming our people," Sabrina said.

Waverly nodded. "Yes."

Inga found herself as susceptible to Sabrina's serene presence as the others. This was a female who was clearly destined to be a queen.

"Here," Inga said, holding out the Tryshu.

Sabrina offered Inga a sad smile, as if sensing Inga's horror at being thrust into her current position. "It doesn't work like that, I'm afraid."

"I don't want it," Inga insisted.

Unexpectedly, it was Levet who answered. "You wanted a home, *ma belle*. And a family," he reminded her. "Now you have both."

Inga paused. He was right. She'd gone from being a blight on her family to being warmly welcomed by her cousins, and presumably her mother who was supposedly searching for her. Even the gathered mer-folk were beginning to eye her with more curiosity and less fear.

"But…" She wasn't sure what she was going to say. Thankfully the room was distracted as the tall, gorgeous-as-sin vampire strolled out of a hidden door and crossed the floor to wrap a possessive arm around Waverly's shoulders.

"Is he dead?" the mermaid demanded before she was wrinkling her nose. "Sorry, that was a stupid question."

Tarak smiled, his fangs flashing in the glow of the overhead chandeliers. "You never have to worry about Riven again."

There was a collective sigh of relief through the room. No one was going to mourn Riven. Which might have been sad, if he hadn't been such an ass.

Tarak glanced down at Waverly, as if he was impervious to the numerous eyes watching them with avid interest. As if they were alone in world.

Inga felt another pang of envy. If only…

"Now I believe you promised me a few centuries on a deserted island," the vampire growled.

Waverly bit her lip, glancing toward Inga before her gaze shifted to her sister. "I should stay."

Sabrina lifted her hand to make a shooing motion. "Go," she commanded. "I will be here to assist Inga. Plus, Poyson will return as soon as she discovers her daughter is home."

The young mermaid wavered, clearly torn between her duty to her people and her desire to be alone with her mate. At last she heaved a small sigh.

"You will let me know if you need me?" she asked her sister.

Sabrina smiled, giving another wave of her hand. "Go."

Snuggling close to Tarak, Waverly lifted her hand to create a portal. Then, with a wave toward Sabrina, the two were moving forward to disappear from view.

There was a brief silence before Sabrina was bustling toward Inga with a determined expression. "Come along," she said as she grabbed Inga's arm in a firm grip.

"Where are we going?" Inga demanded, alarmed to discover herself being urged toward the front of the room.

"To place you on the throne," Sabrina told her, as if it wasn't the most ridiculous thing anyone had ever said in the history of the world.

Panic thundered through Inga as she glanced around, searching for a way to halt the inevitable.

"Levet?" Her gaze skimmed the crowd, searching for the tiny demon. He was nowhere to be seen. "Damn."

Sabrina shoved her onto the dais before turning toward her people. "I give you Inga, Queen of the Mer-folk."

Without warning the crowd began bowing in her direction, their silk rustling like waves.

Inga's heart forgot how to beat. Oh…hell. Life was never, ever going to be the same again.

* * * *

In the end they didn't travel to a deserted island. Waverly had been right. Beaches and vampires really didn't mix. Instead they chose his isolated lair on the cliffs of northern Scotland.

The castle was a crumbling ruin when they arrived, but the underground tunnels were still intact and thankfully dry. Best of all, it was miles from the nearest town.

No. Tarak shook his head. That wasn't the best thing.

Waverly's joy as she played in the vast ocean that spread as far as the eye could see was the best thing.

He'd been enchanted the first time he'd seen her transform into her mermaid form. With a burst of magic her lower body had been covered in scales that shimmered like rainbows in the moonlight. Then she'd been skimming through the water and he'd gaped in sheer wonderment.

He could feel her sheer ecstasy as she'd danced among the schools of fish and surfaced to splash him with the icy water.

The only drawback to the location was that it wasn't as private as an island in the middle of nowhere.

Already Chiron had tracked him down. Not that Tarak regretted the visit from his clansman. The two had enjoyed a long overdue reunion. The younger vampire had tried to apologize for not finding Tarak sooner, but Tarak had refused to let him feel guilty. Those who were to blame for holding him captive were dead.

He was far more interested in how Chiron had gone from a vampire who had been banished by the previous Anasso, with nothing but the clothes on his back, to acquiring a chain of fancy spas and casinos that were spread around the world.

As they chatted and laughed about the time they'd spent together, Tarak had felt the bitterness inside him begin to fade. It reminded him what it meant to be a part of a clan.

Now, standing alone on the edge of the cliff, Tarak barely noticed the wind that tugged at his hair and chapped his cheeks. His concentration was consumed by the exquisite female emerging from the water.

Eventually they would leave this place, he silently acknowledged.

Waverly wanted to spend time with her sister, as well as make sure that Inga was settling into her role as the Queen of the Mer-folk. While he wanted to discover what had happened to his clansmen.

But not tonight.

Stepping off the edge of the cliff, Tarak plummeted downward, landing in front of Waverly. She sucked in a startled breath before her expression softened and a welcoming smile curved her lips.

Wrapping her in his arms, Tarak buried his face in her wet hair. Behind them the ocean crashed against the rocky shoreline, and overhead the sky was spattered with a million stars.

It might not be tropical, but they'd found their paradise.

Together.

Printed in the United States
by Baker & Taylor Publisher Services